THE CAMERONS OF TIDE'S WAY
BOOK #3

Trusting Will

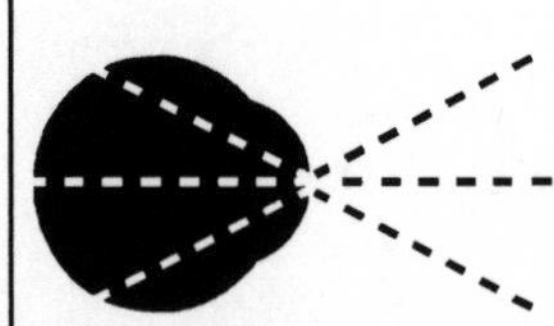

TRUSTING WILL

SKYE TAYLOR

THORNDIKE PRESS
A part of Gale, Cengage Learning

Farmington Hills, Mich • San Francisco • New York • Waterville, Maine
Meriden, Conn • Mason, Ohio • Chicago

GALE
CENGAGE Learning®

The Camerons of Tide's Way #3.
Thorndike Press, a part of Gale, Cengage Learning.

Thorndike Press® Large Print Clean Reads.
The text of this Large Print edition is unabridged.
Other aspects of the book may vary from the original edition.
Set in 16 pt. Plantin.

LIBRARY OF CONGRESS CATALOGING-IN-PUBLICATION DATA

Names: Taylor, Skye, author.
Title: Trusting Will / by Skye Taylor.
Description: Large print edition. | Waterville, Maine : Thorndike Press, 2016. | Series: The Camerons of Tide's Way series ; #3 | Series: Thorndike Press large print clean reads
Identifiers: LCCN 2016028246| ISBN 9781410493910 (hardcover) | ISBN 1410493911 (hardcover)
Subjects: LCSH: Large type books. | GSAFD: Love stories.
Classification: LCC PS3620.A974 T78 2016 | DDC 813/.6—dc23
LC record available at https://lccn.loc.gov/2016028246

Published in 2016 by arrangement with BelleBooks, Inc.

Printed in Mexico
1 2 3 4 5 6 7 20 19 18 17 16

In memory of my Grandson,
Samuel John Taylor
Sammy's life was brief, but he left his
footprints on our hearts forever.

TO MY READERS

The Camerons are a big, close-knit, loving family, descendants of hardworking folk who came from Scotland with little more than the clothes on their back and a steadfast faith in God. They are a patriotic, enterprising clan more apt to spend their spare time volunteering in the service of others than playing golf or checking their investment accounts. They've settled in Tide's Way, a little town that grew up around the old Jolee Plantation in Coastal North Carolina, and planted their roots deep.

Sandy Marshall Cameron always dreamed of having a big family and when she married Cam, her dream came true. She loves every moment of it, especially worrying about her grown children when they let her and fussing over a growing brood of grandchildren. Will is her third son, younger than his twin Ben by just minutes. He has always been the most outgoing of her boys, but in spite of being a daredevil and the ringleader in the most daring of escapades, he also loved helping in the kitchen where he learned how to make all his favorites from her box of recipes. He's not married yet and she's hopeful he will find a woman he can give his heart to and be loved in return. I hope you will enjoy *Trusting Will* as much as I enjoyed writing it.

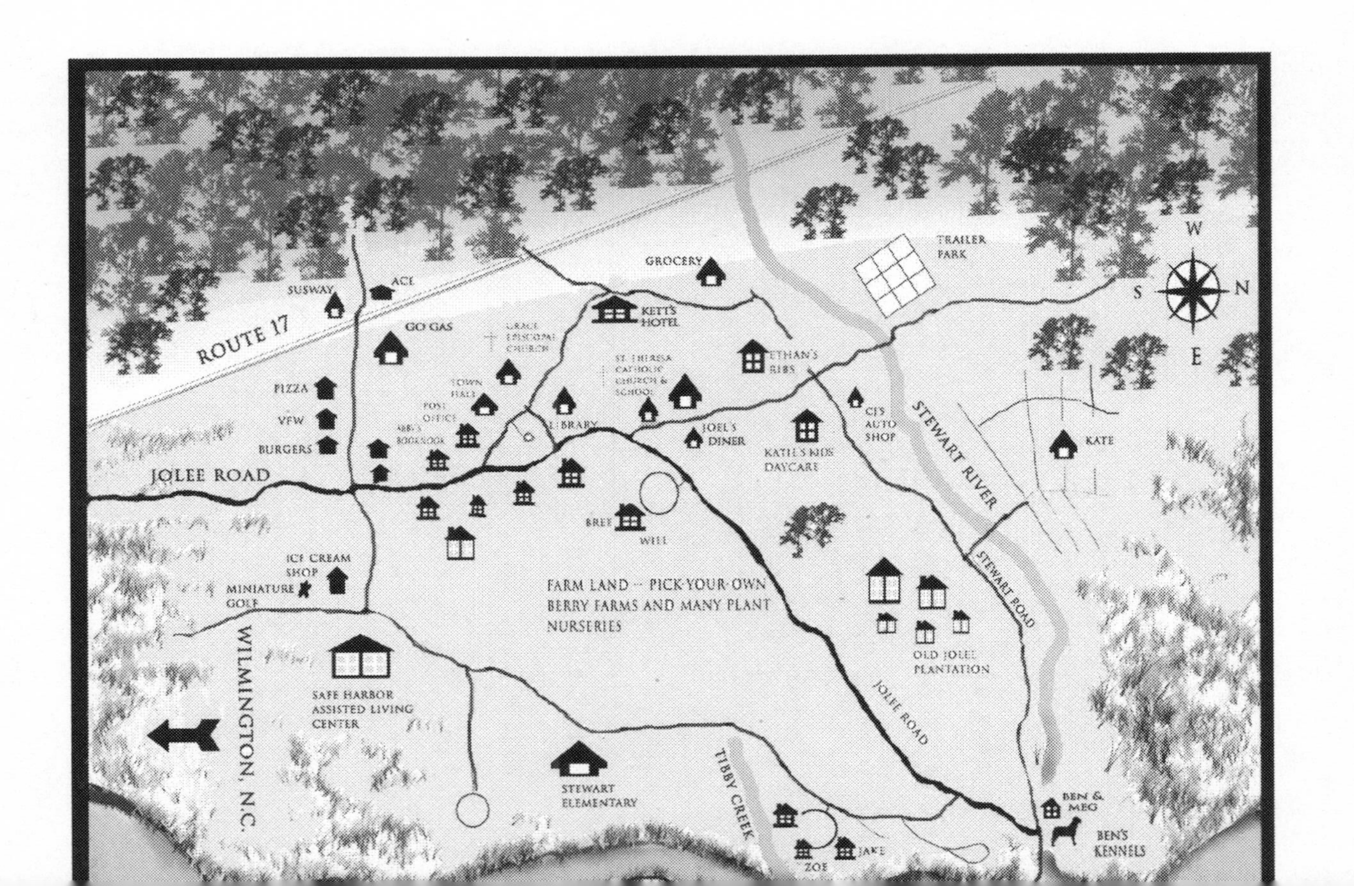
W
N
E
S
TRAILER PARK
GROCERY
KETT'S HOTEL
SUSWAY
ACE
GO GAS
ROUTE 17
GRACE EPISCOPAL CHURCH
ST. THERESA CATHOLIC CHURCH & SCHOOL
ETHAN'S RIBS
CJ'S AUTO SHOP
STEWART RIVER
KATE
PIZZA
VFW
BURGERS
TOWN HALL
POST OFFICE
ABBY'S BOOKNOOK
LIBRARY
JOEL'S DINER
KATIE'S KIDS DAYCARE
JOLEE ROAD
BREE
WILL
ICE CREAM SHOP
MINIATURE GOLF
FARM LAND — PICK-YOUR-OWN BERRY FARMS AND MANY PLANT NURSERIES
STEWART ROAD
OLD JOLEE PLANTATION
WILMINGTON, N.C.
SAFE HARBOR ASSISTED LIVING CENTER
JOLEE ROAD
STEWART ELEMENTARY
TIBBY CREEK
ZOE
JAKE
BEN & MEG
BEN'S KENNELS

ATLANTIC OCEAN

TIDE'S WAY NORTH CAROLINA

Prologue

Fort Benning, Georgia, three years earlier

Brianna Reagan woke with a start. Her heart raced as she sat up, her chest tight with apprehension. She listened for something unusual. Something unexpected. But there was nothing.

Nothing but the sound of her heart thrumming in her ears and her son playing in the next room. And morning sunlight slanting in across her bedroom floor.

Sam's piping five-year-old voice issued orders to his army of tiny soldiers. He had always loved the little figures his father had given him, but since the day they'd taken Ed to the airport at the start of his most recent deployment, the little green men had become an obsession.

"Guess what, Daddy? I'm going to be a general when I grow up," Sam announced, nodding his head in determination. "And you're going to be really proud of me."

"I'm real proud of you already," Ed replied with a sheen in his bright blue eyes. He stiffened into a formal salute, then, unable to maintain the distance, scooped Sam into his arms and hugged him hard before putting him back on his feet and turning to Bree.

Bree dismissed the vivid memory and swung her feet over the side of the bed. As she reached to shut off the alarm she hadn't needed, she stopped a moment to gaze at Ed's photo next to the clock. It was his formal military portrait, but even in that solemn pose, Ed hadn't been able to keep the merry twinkle out of his eyes. Sam was a miniature of his dad. Same dark hair, same blue eyes. Same mischievous sparkle. Bree blew the portrait a kiss and slid to her feet. It was time to get Sam moving, get some breakfast into him and head off to work.

At her dresser, Bree dragged a brush through her tangled blond hair and considered the possibility of cutting it. Except that Ed loved it long. She pulled it into a ponytail, worked an elastic band around its thick bulk, and leaned forward to check for new wrinkles. Twenty-seven wasn't old, but already little lines fanned out from the corners of her dark eyes. *Too much worry and stress,* she thought as she reached for her robe and headed for the hall.

The solid *thunk* of a car door shutting out in front of their base-housing duplex made her pause. *Who would be coming here this early?* She hesitated a moment longer before moving toward the glitter of sunlight streaming in the window.

She squinted against the glare, and her heart froze in horrified denial.

Bree's world telescoped into a narrow tunnel focused on the flat gray-blue tops of the dress uniform caps moving purposefully up her front walk. Desperately, she tried to think of any other reason two officers in dress uniforms would be coming to her door so early on a Monday morning.

But her heart already knew. There could be only one reason these men had come.

Her chest constricted in pain. Her eyes ached, but there were no tears. Not now. Not yet. She raised a clenched fist to her mouth, knuckles white with strain as her heart plunged into the unavoidable knowledge that her life would never be the same again.

Chapter 1

Tide's Way, North Carolina, today

Will Cameron turned onto Carlisle Place, a big looping drive lined with townhouses and condos built with the southern charm of Tide's Way and coastal North Carolina in mind. Even at this time of year, the tunnel of live oaks dripping with moss created a shady retreat from the glare of the Carolina sun as Will slowed to go over the speed bump and continue on around the drive.

A couple months back when he'd followed a suspected stolen car into the development, it had occurred to him that if you couldn't afford to live on the beach in Tide's Way, this would be a pretty sweet second choice. In the center of the loop, beyond the tennis and basketball courts and half-hidden behind a thick stand of pampas grass, were two pools, one built for toddlers, the other with diving boards and slides. At the moment, both were covered with canvas tarps, but that would change soon, and the sounds of splashing and giggling would be added to the dribbling *thunk* of basketballs and the sharp pop of yellow tennis balls. Kids at play always made Will smile. Probably because his mother was right, and he was just a big kid himself.

"There's where Sam lives," Will's eight-year-old nephew Rick spoke up, pointing to a shallow set of stairs leading up to a small porch at the far end of the condo complex.

Will pulled into a slot and turned off the engine in his rugged all-terrain four-by-four. He rode a motorcycle for work, but with two small boys to drive to their Cub Scout meeting, he'd taken his Jeep instead.

"Will Sam be watching for us and come on out?" Will hooked an arm over the back of the seat to speak to his nephew.

Rick made a face.

"What's that for?" Will chuckled at the look of disgust.

"We gotta go in and get him. Sam's mother worries a lot. Like she says she's gotta be sure who he's going off with. Even my dad has to go in, and he's been here a bunch of times."

Poor Sam, Will thought. "Even though she knows we're picking him up?"

"Yup." Rick unbuckled his seatbelt and

opened his door.

Will hurried to join Rick as he dashed up the short flight of stairs and into the entryway of the building. It was a double-door entry. The kind you have to call up and wait for someone to buzz you in if you don't have a key to the inside door. *Another nice feature,* the cop in him noted, even in a place like Tide's Way where crime was pretty rare.

Rick pressed the bell and hopped impatiently from foot to foot. While they waited, Will surveyed the patchwork of notices posted on a corkboard next to the bank of mailboxes. One, he noted, advertised one of the units in the building was available for short-term lease.

Maybe he should grab one of the tear-off tabs. His current and very ideal dwelling was being sold out from under him, and he was going to have to find at least temporary digs until he figured out where he was going next. At the age of thirty-four, maybe he should have been thinking about buying instead of just renting. But if he landed a spot on the new Rapid Response Team that the North Carolina State Highway Patrol was putting together, it might require a move away from his hometown. He hoped it wouldn't come to that, but the details weren't set yet, and he couldn't be sure.

One advantage of renting in this building would be that he could walk across the street to the best little diner in Tide's Way when he got sick of his own cooking or hop on his bike and be at the beach in less than ten minutes.

"Yes?" a delightfully musical voice came over the speaker. How could anyone make a single word sound like an invitation to something fun or maybe even naughty?

"It's Will Cameron. Here to pick up Sam?" Will's heart pattered a little faster than it should have.

"Will Cameron?" The voice sounded confused.

"That's me," he confirmed. Why should his name invoke confusion? "Rick told me he told Sam we'd pick him up on our way to the Cub Scout meeting."

The door buzzed, and Will pushed it open. Rick ducked under his arm and moved toward the elevator, one finger poised to punch the up arrow.

"Elevators are for ladies and old men," Will told him, heading through the door to the stairwell. "They're only on the second floor, right?"

Rick grinned. "Bet I can beat ya." Then he scooted past and started up the stairs.

Will let Rick get a head start before taking

the stairs two at a time and almost catching up. Rick beat him to the top by a hair and turned to grin triumphantly.

"So, what — do I — win?" Rick gasped.

"We didn't put any money on it. You don't win anything. But you did get some great exercise."

"Dad says I get exercise throwing sticks for Kip."

"Kip is getting most of that exercise. You're just building up your throwing arm."

Rick stopped at a door on the left at the end of the hall, but before he could knock, the door opened, and Rick's friend Sam Reagan stuck his head out.

Sam opened the door wider and gestured them inside.

The woman, who had to be Sam's mother, was gorgeous. Stunningly gorgeous. If Will had been wearing his hat, he'd have been inclined to sweep it off his head and offer a totally uncharacteristic bow. As it was, he struggled not to gawk. The long, wavy blond mane and striking whiskey-colored eyes looked vaguely familiar, but he couldn't believe he'd have forgotten her if he'd ever met her before. Not a woman this heart-stoppingly beautiful.

"Will Cameron," he introduced himself and held out his hand.

"Brianna Reagan," the head-turning stunner reciprocated and placed her hand in his. "But please, call me Bree."

Her hand was slight and soft. Will felt as if he might crush it if he weren't careful. When Bree looked down at their clasped hands he realized he'd been holding hers too long for mere politeness. He let go. Mr. Reagan was one lucky son of a gun. A terrific kid like Sam and a wife that must turn heads everywhere she went.

In the few months Will had been den father to a pack of energetic eight-year-old Cub Scouts, he'd tried hard not to let Sam become a favorite. But it wasn't easy. Sam was bright, eager to learn, full of questions, and always cheerful. He was also quick to notice when other boys less talented than himself were having trouble, and he'd drop his own stuff to help out. Will had never met Sam's dad and often wondered if the man knew what a genuinely nice son he had.

"I'm sorry for my confusion," the pretty woman interrupted Will's vaguely jealous thoughts. "You look just like Rick's father. I forgot there were two of you. I mean —" She broke off and colored slightly. "Besides, I thought it was Ben that took over the Cub Scout den when Mr. Hudson got transferred so suddenly."

"Knowing my brother, he probably would have, but with Meg out of the country, he was already pretty stretched, so I stepped up to the plate instead. It's been fun, and I've really enjoyed it. The boys are terrific. I had no idea. Now, of course, Ben's ragging on me, telling me I need to find a wife and have some kids of my own, but —" Will shut his mouth abruptly. In another minute he'd be telling this woman his life story. Something she definitely didn't need to hear.

"I must have seen you at Jake's wedding," she said, "but I never realized. Zoe said you were twins, but —"

That's where he'd seen her before! At his brother Jake's wedding to Zoe Callahan last fall. Must have been the chaos of family and kids, otherwise he'd definitely have remembered this woman.

"You were Zoe's maid of honor."

"Matron of honor," Bree corrected.

"Are we going to get going, or what?" Rick interrupted.

"Yeah, right." Will shook his head and turned his attention to Rick and Sam, both immaculately attired in their Cub Scout uniforms, standing impatiently by the door.

"It was nice to meet you, Mrs. Reagan." Will started to tip his hat and remembered he still wasn't wearing one.

Her pretty face clouded briefly. "Just Bree," she said after a moment.

"It was nice to meet you, Bree," he answered dutifully. "Will it be okay if we stop for ice cream on the way home? I promised Rick, and I assure you, I'll have Sam home by eight."

"I guess that would be okay." Bree smiled, and the corners of her eyes crinkled.

Will nodded and followed the boys out into the hall. Rick explained about the elevator being for ladies and old men, and the boys peeled off and started clattering down the stairs. Will followed, his senses still reeling from his reintroduction to Brianna Reagan.

"Mom's got a date tonight," Sam said over his shoulder as he beat Rick to the first landing. "He's such a dork."

Rick mumbled something Will couldn't hear, but Sam's comment about the date stopped Will in his tracks. If Bree was married, why was she going out on a date? Surely Sam wouldn't talk that way about his own father.

"She thinks I need a new father," said Sam, as if answering Will's unspoken question. "Like I need a dork for a father. I have a father. He just happens to live in Heaven is all." His last words ended on a hiccough.

Rick wrapped his arm about Sam's shoulders.

Bree was a widow. And Sam had lost his father. Will's heart suddenly ached for both of them — the boy he'd been working with for over two months who still grieved for his missing dad and the woman whose pretty face had clouded over when called Mrs. Reagan. *How long ago?* he wondered as he pushed open the first of the two doors to the outside.

He'd almost reached the top step outside when he remembered the notice. He turned back and snatched one of the tear-off tabs with the phone number for the apartment for rent.

How could he not have known about Sam's dad?

Bree took one last bite of her Alfredo and then followed it with a sip of wine. Bob Cahill droned on about his newest client, a bigwig with offices in Wilmington and Raleigh and a huge and complicated tax return. Bob was clearly bursting with pleasure about the deal. It was probably why he'd decided to treat her to dinner at the country club instead of the local diner.

Bree glanced about the posh interior of the restaurant with its thick, sound-swallowing carpets and snowy white table linens. This was so not her kind of place, but Bob thrived here. She was happy for his success. Happy that he was feeling on top of his little world at least, but he'd been going on about this guy for the entire meal. Maybe by the time coffee was served he'd get past it, and Bree would get an opening to bring up her big question.

Her big favor, actually.

Sam had come home from his last Cub Scout meeting with a Pinewood Derby kit, and it was still sitting on his desk untouched. Up to now, none of Sam's activities had required expertise she didn't have, but she'd taken one look at the small square block of wood and knew she was out of her league. Sam needed someone with more know-how than she possessed to help him create anything with a chance of making it to the end of the track, never mind having a chance to win. It was a guy sort of thing, and Bob was a guy.

Bob liked Sam. He made an effort to draw him out in conversation when they were together and had taken him to a baseball game once, but perhaps asking Bob to help with a model race car was pushing things. Bob was a nice guy, but he'd never been married. Never had kids. Maybe spending time helping an eight-year-old with his scouting project wasn't something Bob would enjoy all that much.

It might be pushing things in more ways than one. While Sam had not been all that enthusiastic about Bob's attempts to engage him, Bree wasn't certain where her own relationship with Bob was going.

She'd started dating him because Sam had arrived at an age where boys began to need a male influence in their lives, and perhaps it was time for her to consider letting another man into hers. Someone safe. Someone who wouldn't end up breaking her heart.

They had met at the Jolee Historical Society meeting right after she joined the group. They clearly had at least one thing in common — an interest in preserving history, specifically the history of Tide's Way and the Jolee Plantation. Reserved and easygoing, a CPA with a reputation for reliability, Bob was unlikely to get involved in the kinds of things that got people hurt or killed. He was a gentleman, maybe a little old-fashioned and chauvinistic, but in a courtly sort of way that made her feel appreciated.

The waiter came and began clearing their dishes. He asked if they would like to see the dessert menu. Bob agreed without consulting her. A sudden image of her late husband's taut six-pack abdomen flitted into her head followed just as quickly by another unexpected recall of Will's trim, flat stomach, obvious even beneath his bloused scout leader's shirt. She shook her head to dispel the images and forced herself not to dwell on the soft roll of flesh that spilled over the edge of Bob's belt. It wasn't like he was grossly overweight. Just a little soft.

Will Cameron had looked anything *but* soft, but she had no business thinking about Will Cameron's tall, sexy body. Or anything else about him beyond his role as den father to her son. She knew next to nothing about him or what kind of a man he was.

Bob ordered them both a slice of warmed peach pie with vanilla ice cream and coffee. He folded his hands and looked earnestly at her.

"You've been awfully quiet. How's the new position at Kett's going?"

Her job at Kett's was going well. Really well. She loved the challenges and the people she worked with, but she knew Bob thought women were best employed as secretaries, not program managers. Although he'd never said it in so many words, he'd given her the impression that when women worked at all, it should only be from necessity. A true lady would be far more concerned with making her husband's home his castle than making a name for herself in a man's world. Another reason she'd begun to question her relationship with Bob and where it might be going.

"It's going okay." She took a deep breath and hurried on before she could change her mind. "But I was wondering. I have a favor to ask. I . . ." She hesitated.

"A favor?" Bob urged helpfully.

"Sam needs someone to help him with his Pinewood Derby racer."

Bob frowned. "What's a Pinewood Derby racer?"

"Weren't you ever a Boy Scout?"

Bob shook his head. "I was in the math club."

Didn't seem like the two were mutually exclusive, but Bree didn't say so as she launched into an explanation of the Pinewood Derby. "It's a really big deal for the Scouts. Each boy has to make his own race car from the kit, and then they have a big race day."

"From a kit, you say?"

The waiter returned bearing pie and coffee. Bree sat back and waited for him to finish serving.

"Have you ever done anything like that?" she asked.

Bob's eyebrows rose. "No. But I'm sure I can figure it out if it's a kit like you say. I'd be glad to help Sam. I'd be especially glad to help him out for his mom's sake." He reached across the table and laid his hand over hers.

Bree wanted to pull her hand free but didn't. "Thanks. I appreciate it."

Bob patted her hand and then drew his back to attend to his pie. "Sam needs a man in his life. So does his mom."

Alone in her room, Bree stepped out of her skirt and reached for a hanger. The look in Bob's eyes when he'd walked her to her door and repeated his comment about Bree needing a man in her life made her uncomfortable. His obvious insinuation had caught her off guard, and the feeling of unease grew stronger as she reviewed the evening and tried to remember if she'd said anything to lead him on.

She liked Bob, but she didn't know if she was ready for their relationship to go where he seemed to be headed. Bob didn't light any fires in her that needed quenching. Which should be a good thing considering she didn't want her heart getting broken again. But neither was she eager to become intimate with the man. She wasn't into sex without at least some passion. Maybe all that was needed was a little more time before she felt that kind of desire, but Bob didn't appear to need more time. Tonight he had definitely been sending out signals that he'd like to share her bed and possibly a whole lot more.

What would it be like to become Mrs. Robert Cahill? To have a nice, safe husband who would come home every day at the same time and never once give her a reason to worry, either over his safety or his fidelity? Although passion had not yet been part of their relationship, if she was to become his wife, there would be intimacy and perhaps more children. She would like more children. She would enjoy the busyness of a growing family and the comfort of sharing her nights with someone again. So, maybe Bob didn't fill her with the heady desire Ed had once evoked in her, but he would be good to her, and she wouldn't be so alone. She should be happy with that, shouldn't she?

Without invitation, the lean, powerful image of Will Cameron as he'd stood in her doorway with one hand on Sam's shoulder, apologizing for being five minutes late, totally eclipsed the picture of Bob standing in the same doorway angling to kiss her good night. A kiss she let him have but hadn't been able to muster any enthusiasm for.

All she could think of now was the ice cream sundae Will had thoughtfully brought for her and the admiring look in his sky-blue eyes that had nothing to do with either apologies or ice cream. *What would Will's mouth feel like if he'd been the one doing the kissing?*

Chapter 2

Will whistled as he pulled into his brother's driveway. Not that it had been a particularly whistle-worthy day on the whole, but that morning he'd woken with the most glorious hard-on. An occurrence he was sure had everything to do with the lovely Mrs. Brianna Reagan and the way she'd looked at him when he'd presented her with an ice cream sundae the night before. It had taken a very long, cold shower to convince Little Will to stand down so Big Will could get dressed for work. But the sense of impending adventure had lingered, brightening his otherwise business-as-usual workday.

He turned the motorcycle off and swept his leg over the back. Kicking the stand down, he headed toward his brother's main kennel building, then detoured and followed a newly beaten dirt path around to the far side to check on the progress of Ben's new Paws for Heroes project.

Will's identical twin Ben, older by just minutes, was his best friend and closest to his heart of all his family. Sometimes Will felt like they were two halves that should have been one whole. Everything Will wasn't Ben was. Will admired his brother and sometimes wished he could be more like him.

Among other things, Ben had more patience than any man Will knew. He'd waited years for the woman he'd fallen in love with to grow up. Ben's sons were typical boys and often up to mischief, yet Ben never seemed ruffled. His calm good sense brought about the desired results without ever raising his voice.

That patience showed in the career Ben had chosen as his life's work, too. He raised and trained dogs for police work. Something that took endless hours of patient repetition and calm strength. Ben's new project was training dogs rescued from shelters to become service animals for veterans suffering from war-related injuries, both physical and emotional.

At the moment, their baby brother Jake's construction company was nearly finished with building the home where the veterans would live while they were being paired with their dogs and learning to rely on them.

While that had been going up, Ben had visited dog pounds in half a dozen cities and adopted eleven dogs, some of mixed heritage and some purebred, and all of them were now being groomed to become service animals.

Will loved dogs and hoped one day he'd live in a place he could have one of his own, but he'd never have the patience Ben had for such intensive and demanding training. If he ever did get a dog, Will was sure the animal would be in charge, sleeping on his master's bed and sprawling on the couch, totally unconcerned with any human companion's comfort. It would probably be some big goober of a dog with a lolling tongue and half a brain devoted to chasing a tennis ball and licking the face off anyone who got close enough.

Will looked up to admire Jake's plan. Nobody could fault either his brother's design or the setting. The six-bedroom house that would eventually accommodate up to ten veterans at a time was set far back on the property. A porch wrapped about two sides facing the marsh and the coastal waterway beyond. Sunrises here were incredible and the scent of the ocean a constant presence. A quiet, peaceful place for men struggling to forget the horror and noise of war.

Acquiring this particular tract of land was another example of Ben's patience. The property, nothing but a ruined skeleton of a house and overgrown fields, had come on the market while they were still in college, but Ben had immediately pictured his forever house located there. He'd borrowed the down payment from their father and worked two jobs to pay both tuition and a mortgage. Ben loved Tide's Way, the close-knit community, and living near the sea, and it hadn't mattered how long it took to build his own place, another seaside home like the one he'd grown up in.

Will thought about his own life and the contrast between he and his twin. Unlike Ben, when Will decided he wanted something, he was eager to have it happen as soon as possible. Like the apartment he'd just put a deposit on. And the reason he'd chosen that particular place.

His current abode, the upper half of a duplex on the outskirts of Wilmington, had been perfect: close to the station he worked out of, reasonably close to his family in Tide's Way, not too far from the closest beach, and with plenty of space. There was a shed for all his various sporting equipment, parking beside the garage to accommodate the trailer the NC Highway Patrol had issued to go along with his motorcycle, garage space for the motorcycle, and driveway space for the cruiser and his Jeep. He'd probably never have considered moving if the old man hadn't decided to live with his son and sold the property to a family who needed it all.

Ideally, Will should have sought out another accommodation that suited his unusual garaging requirements, but that would have been before he'd met Brianna Reagan, discovered she was a widow, and seen the advertisement for a short-term rental in her building.

That flicker of quickly hidden interest in her eyes last night had not only haunted his dreams, but kept returning to his thoughts during the day. For several breathless moments, he'd felt like he could stare into Bree's mysterious whiskey-colored eyes forever. Except there was so much else to admire besides the intriguing eyes. In a world where so many blonds came from a bottle, Brianna Reagan was naturally blond. He'd swear to it. Of course it would be even more fun to prove it beyond doubt. Her ash blond waves were thick and shining, the kind of hair a man ached to run his fingers through or feel tickling his bare skin. And then there was her body.

"You going to stand there gaping at a half-finished house forever?"

Jerked from his pleasant daydream, Will turned and grinned at his twin. "Jake's doing a mighty fine job."

"Did you expect anything less?"

Will shook his head and then glanced down at the half-Lab dog at his brother's side. "Is he on the job, or can I pet him?"

Ben gave the command that was permission to socialize. "Say hello, Booker."

The chocolate-colored dog raised a paw for Will. His tail wagged, sweeping an arc in the dusty path, and his butt looked like he was having a hard time keeping it planted.

Will squatted, grabbed a handful of fur on either side of the dog's face, and shoved his nose up against Booker's. "Good dog, Booker. You're going to make a fine companion."

"You didn't come over here to admire Booker or the house, I'm betting. So what's up?"

Will straightened. "I just put a deposit on a new apartment, so it looks like I'll be out by the date the old man gave me after all. Just one problem. I need a place to park my trailer and motorcycle. And some of my other gear as well. I was hoping you could make room for it."

Ben raised his eyebrows. "You don't need the bike where you'll be living?"

"I'd rather not leave it outside in a lot shared by everyone else in the development. The trailer — I'm not allowed to leave in the lot at all."

"Plenty of space here." Ben swept an arm out, taking in the entire property. "Got room in the garage for the bike, too." Ben turned to head back toward the house. "Can you stay for supper?"

"I thought you'd never ask." Will punched his brother on the shoulder.

"So why this particular apartment? Won't it be kind of a pain hustling all the way over here every day before going to work?"

"It's not all that far, actually." A totally unexpected heat crept up Will's neck. "It's just down the street, across from Joel's Diner."

Ben stopped walking and looked at Will with one blond eyebrow raised. "The same place Sam Reagan and his mother live?"

Will nodded.

Ben grinned. "And you've just met Bree."

"I met her before," Will tried to defend himself. "At Jake's wedding."

"But you're just now noticing her." Ben grinned and turned back toward the house.

"Wait 'til I tell Meg."

Bree hated it when she had to work late. It meant dashing home to meet the bus, grabbing Sam, and dragging him back to the hotel to do his homework while she finished up whatever event she was working on. But today was different. A new, potentially good client was winding up their first conference at Kett's. Her first big affair in her new position, and she was pleased that it had all gone so well.

"Hey, beautiful!"

Bree looked up, her heart jumping into her throat. It steadied quickly. The voice, which for a moment, had sounded so much like Will Cameron's, was not his after all. Maybe it was only because she'd been thinking about Will just moments before. She'd tried to banish thoughts of Sam's scout leader in the busyness of her day but hadn't succeeded.

"Sorry. Not politically correct, I know." The man standing in her doorway grinned, totally unapologetic. "I just wanted to thank you for everything. It went well. Largely thanks to you and your staff. And because you did such a great job, we're ready to book our next mini-conference here in six months. How soon can we set dates?"

Bree opened the events scheduling book and flipped forward six months. "Same number of people? Same room?"

Harold Isaacson crossed the office and peered down at Bree's book. "Only about half as many people. You have a smaller room?"

"Sure, let me show you." Bree glanced again at the book. "Several openings in August at the moment. The ballroom is available as well except for two wedding receptions. Of course, those are one day events, Saturday only." She got to her feet. "Be right back, Sam," she said to her son who was bent intently over his Kindle Fire.

"Mmmm," Sam acknowledged absently, never looking up.

"Your son?" Isaacson asked as he followed her out into the hall. "Good-looking kid. Like his mom."

Bree smiled at the man she'd been doing business with over the last few weeks while his event had been in the planning and organizing stage. "He looks like his dad, actually, but thanks for the compliment."

One thing Bree didn't get bent out of shape over was compliments about her appearance. She knew she was a strikingly pretty woman, and she knew heads turned when she passed by. It would be useless to get upset every time a man voiced his appreciation. Besides, Harold Isaacson was always respectful. Too bad he was married. He had the kind of easygoing personality and sense of humor she enjoyed. A lot like Will Cameron.

She shook her head and reached for the doorknob of the smallest of the meeting rooms. What did she really know about Will Cameron's personality? Good or bad?

"This room is great for more intimate meetings and smaller groups. Actually, the room can hold as many as eighty depending on how it's set up."

Isaacson wandered farther into the room and turned slowly, studying the room carefully. "You would still set up a coffee and water station inside the room, right?" He glanced around more quickly as if trying to determine where this would go.

"Of course." Bree handed him a laminated sheet that showed setup options. "Pretty much anything you had in the bigger room, you can have here. Just on a smaller scale."

"Works for me. Just need to discuss dollars and cents." He pulled his wallet out of his back pocket, fingered through it, and drew out two folded checks. "Here's the balance for this week." He handed her one of the two checks, already made out. "What do you need for a deposit to hold this room for a midweek conference in early August?"

This man came prepared. Although it wasn't a large company, and Isaacson wasn't the CFO or the treasurer, he'd thought to bring a blank check to nail down a deposit. Bree felt a small swell of pride in having secured an ongoing relationship with a rapidly growing company that wanted to hold regular conferences in the Wilmington area. And more specifically, at Kett's Hotel in Tide's Way. *Her* hotel.

Back in her office, Sam was still intent on whatever game he was playing and didn't look up when Bree hurried to her desk and waited for Isaacson to consult his Black-Berry. "How about the tenth through the thirteenth?"

Bree began typing, and before she even hit print, Isaacson had written out the check and pushed it across her desk. "It's a pleasure doing business with you." She handed him his copy of the signed document. "I only wish everyone was as easy to work with." She grabbed a non-laminated copy of the layout possibilities and handed him that as well. "Give me a call when you know how you want it set up and what meals you want brought in. If I'm not available, you can talk with Owen or leave a message with him, and I'll get back to you."

Isaacson folded the papers in thirds and shoved them into his shirt pocket. "Beauty and brains." He grinned. "My pleasure, ma'am."

He offered his hand, and Bree took it. A stab of breathless surprise caught her when he brought her hand to his lips and kissed her knuckles. She knew she was blushing. *He's married, and he's still a flirt!*

"My wife will be with me next trip. I look forward to introducing you. She's going to like you." With that he turned and strode out.

"Why did that man kiss your hand?"

Sam had chosen an awkward moment to start paying attention to what was going on around him.

"He's just old-fashioned."

Sam frowned. "He's not old. Not like Grampa. And Grampa never kissed anybody's hand."

"Never mind. You ready to go?"

Sam scooped up his Kindle and dropped it into his backpack. "About time."

Bree put her computer to sleep, grabbed her purse, and joined Sam, who was already headed for the door.

"I still don't get why he kissed your hand."

"Maybe he was flirting. Just a little," Bree

conceded as they made their way out to the parking lot.

Sam was clearly thinking this last comment over as he climbed into the car and buckled his seatbelt. Bree slid into the driver's seat and started the car.

"So," Sam asked just as Bree was pulling out of the lot and into traffic. "Is flirting what a guy does when he likes someone?"

"Something like that," Bree agreed, wondering just how far this conversation was going and wishing she hadn't introduced the word *flirt.*

"Do girls like it?"

There was flirting, and then there was flirting that sometimes bordered on harassment, but Sam didn't need to know about that just yet. "Yes, girls like it. Sometimes. It makes them feel — special, I guess."

"Do I have to kiss Josie's hand?"

Bree's gaze flew to the rearview mirror. "Who's Josie?"

"Just a girl," Sam answered, his attempt to sound offhand failing completely.

Bree shook her head. Her little boy was growing up way too fast. At least he still considered kissing something reserved for moms and grandmoms. "There are other ways to let a girl know you like her and make her feel special. Like holding the door

for her or paying her a compliment."
Sam nodded sagely. "Or like bringing her an ice cream sundae."

CHAPTER 3

Will carried the last of the boxes of personal papers and books through the double doors and past the stairwell to the elevator. He was trying to balance the boxes on his thigh and summon the elevator when Sam dashed in from outside.

"Hi, Mr. Cameron!" Sam tapped the bottom box in Will's stack. "Where are you taking all those boxes?"

"Up to my new apartment. Mind pushing the button for me?"

"I thought elevators were for ladies and old men." Sam pushed the *up* button.

"Normally, they are, but I've made a lot of trips today, and I'm getting kind of tired."

"Are you going to live here now?" Sam's eyes widened in speculation.

"For now," Will answered, wishing the elevator would hurry before his arms gave out.

"Mom!" Sam shouted as Brianna Reagan

came through the doors with her briefcase in one hand and a stylish jacket folded over her other arm. "Mr. Cameron's gonna *live* here." He turned back to Will. "Which floor?"

"Third."

"You hear that, Mom? Right upstairs from us. Isn't that cool?" The elevator finally arrived, and the door slid open with a soft *ding.* Will gratefully stepped inside and dropped his load in the corner. Sam and Bree filed in behind him, and the door slid shut.

This close, in the confines of the tiny elevator, her perfume surrounded him. He had no idea what the scent was, roses maybe, but he wasn't sure. He was *very* sure he liked it, and it suited her. He, on the other hand, was dressed in a torn T-shirt and jeans with holes in the knees and fraying hems. He was layered with dust and sweat and God only knew what else. Not the way to impress anyone, never mind this gorgeous fresh-smelling eyeful.

"Are you renting Mr. Leach's place?" Bree transferred her briefcase to her other hand, and burrowed in her purse, then withdrew a key ring with the logo of the Army Rangers on it.

"Just for six months or so." Hopefully long

enough to get something going between himself and the lovely Brianna Reagan. It seemed strange that in just three short days, this goal had become so important to him. He hadn't been really serious about any woman since Linda broke off their engagement three years ago, and he barely knew Brianna Reagan. He knew her son better, and he hadn't even been aware Sam had lost his dad, so that wasn't saying much. If the key ring meant anything, her husband had been an Army Ranger. How long had she been a war widow? Maybe he needed to take things a little slower. He needed a little of Ben's patience.

"It's temporary. My digs got sold out from under me, and I'm not quite ready to commit to homeownership."

"Have you got any more boxes to carry up?" Sam piped up. "I can help carry some. I'm really strong. Right, Mom?" He turned to his mother for confirmation.

"I bet you are." Will chuckled at the boy's eagerness to be helpful. "But this is the last of them for now." At Sam's crestfallen expression, he hastened to add, "But I could sure use some help lugging the empty boxes out to the dumpster once they're unpacked."

The elevator slowed to a stop and dinged

as the door swept open. Bree stepped out, gesturing for Sam to follow her.

"What time do you need me to come up?" Sam stood in the open doorway, refusing to let the door shut before he'd gotten this detail confirmed.

Will looked at Bree for permission. She shrugged her elegant linen-clad shoulders.

"How about tomorrow morning? If you haven't got any plans, that is."

"Sure thing, Mr. Cameron. I'll be up soon as I finish breakfast."

"Not too early. I like to sleep late on Saturday mornings, but if you work really hard, maybe your mom will let me take you over to Joel's for lunch." Will glanced at Bree and considered inviting her as well, but the look on Sam's face told him that time *mano-a-mano* was what the boy was hoping for.

"I don't want him becoming a pest." Bree looked cute when she frowned like that.

"Not a problem." Will ruffled Sam's hair. "See you in the morning, sport."

As the door slid closed, Will winked at Bree and grinned with satisfaction when her beautiful fair skin pinkened in response. He wondered how serious she was about the man who'd taken her out three nights earlier. The one Sam called a dork.

What kind of a man attracted this quietly elegant woman? Once upon a time it had been an Army Ranger. But what about now? Was the dork as well-dressed and quiet as Brianna? What did he do for a living? Some instinct told Will the guy was probably the exact opposite of her deceased husband. But he could be wrong. Maybe the guy loved to hunt and go hang-gliding in his spare time. But whatever he was or did, Will planned to make every effort to cut in on his action.

Sam was up earlier than usual the next morning and impatient with waiting until Bree let him head up to help his new "friend" with the unpacking. An hour or so later, Bree went upstairs to check on him. She told herself she just wanted to make sure Sam was actually being helpful and not a nuisance, and it had nothing to do with wanting to see Will herself.

His door stood wide open, so she walked in without knocking and caught Will bent at the waist slitting boxes with a dangerous-looking knife. He was naked from the waist up and clad in a pair of cut-off denim shorts and running shoes, with sweat glistening on muscles that looked like they belonged in a men's fitness magazine. Bree gulped at the spectacle while her heart rate jumped.

Will continued to work, unaware of her presence. She gawked like a groupie, more than a little turned on by all that masculine grace in action. Then Sam bounded in the door behind her, and Will looked up and noticed her.

She flushed royally. The problem with being fair-skinned meant her face surely looked as heated as it felt. She tried to cover her embarrassment with an explanation of why she'd come up in the first place.

Sam was shirtless as well, obviously in imitation of Will, but his pale boyish frame was a stark contrast to Will's out-of-season tan and toned masculine glory. Sam grinned at Bree with unabashed happiness. He'd never looked so pleased in Bob's company, even when Bob had gone out of his way to do something he thought Sam would enjoy. Will hadn't done anything special, but apparently just being allowed to help was all Sam needed to make his day.

Suddenly feeling totally out of place and awkward, she excused herself and beat a hasty retreat. Bustling around the apartment in a cleaning frenzy, she did her best to forget the alarming effect Will's bare chest and piercing blue eyes had wreaked on her carefully erected wall of self-preservation.

How could she have met this man at Zoe's

wedding and not been impressed enough to think of him again in the three months between then and now? Perhaps it was the overwhelming impression five tall, handsome blond men had on any woman's senses. All the Cameron men had enough good looks and charisma to charm the devil himself. She remembered the oldest brother Philip the most clearly and suspected half that magnetism was the Marine dress uniform. But identical twins should have been just as memorable.

She wasn't sure she wanted to be impressed with Will now. The fluttery feeling in her gut and the inability to control the flush of pleasure his wink caused bothered her. She didn't plan to ever care about another man the way she had cared about Ed. Losing Ed had crushed her heart so thoroughly, it had taken months to stop weeping every time she heard Ed's name or saw something of his lying carelessly in a place she hadn't expected to find it. She never wanted to be so vulnerable again. For Sam's sake, she couldn't let herself take that chance.

But she couldn't *stop* thinking about this bigger-than-life man who dazzled without even trying. Even Ed had not had that effect on her. Or maybe her memories were fading.

The thought appalled her. She had loved Ed since her first year in high school. He'd always seemed bigger-than-life. Hadn't he?

With a sense of sudden purpose, she went into the living room and removed the photo albums from the bottom shelf of a tall bookcase in one corner. She settled herself on the sofa and set the albums on the coffee table. But then didn't open them. She hadn't looked at them since those first agonizing days when she'd forced herself to go through them to pick out photos to display once the funeral could be arranged. She hadn't wanted to look through them then and couldn't bring herself to do so afterward.

Sam spent a lot of time with the albums when he thought she didn't know, and she'd let it go unmentioned. Ed was his father, and Sam clung desperately to his fading little-boy memories. At some point Sam had removed several photos and kept them tucked under the clock on his bedside table where he thought she wouldn't find them. She had, of course, one day when Sam was at his grandparents' house, and she was turning his room out for a thorough cleaning. That day she'd sat on Sam's bed bawling her eyes out with the fistful of stolen photos clutched in her hand. When the storm had subsided, she'd tucked the purloined photos back under the clock where she'd found them and never mentioned them to Sam.

She leaned forward and ran her fingers along the edge of the top album. Then, with a deep sigh, she opened it.

The album began before she'd met Ed, so after smiling at a few snapshots of her girlish antics, she flipped forward to the first year of high school. Ignoring her own youthful self, she focused on Ed. Ed with his horse. Ed with the motorcycle he'd fixed up in anticipation of attaining his first driver's license. Ed with her tucked against his side at their junior prom. Ed wearing his older brother's Special Forces beret.

Bree sucked in a gasp at the sudden memory. Ed had always dreamed of being a Ranger. The recruitment office had been the first place he'd gone after receiving his high school diploma. He'd even taken her with him, and she'd gone, happy to be with him and proud of what he was doing. She closed her eyes and tried to remember that feeling of naïve patriotic pride.

Opening her eyes again, she flipped to the end of the album. The last page held several worn photos that Ed had sent her from advanced infantry training. In every photo it was obvious he was totally into the whole thing. One photo showed him still wearing the harness from his first jump, the limp parachute spread out behind him, a grin as broad as the sea splitting his face. Another showed him working his way on his elbows, covered in mud through an obstacle course, sweat dripping from his chin, and a look of utter determination on his face. The last showed him on another soldier's shoulders, one fist pumping the air. God only knew what they were celebrating.

She closed that album and slowly opened the next. Her wedding day.

She had never been so happy either before or since.

Abruptly she shut the book and sat back. Ed had loved her, there was no question. But he'd loved the life of a soldier more. With the country at war, they had expected he would get deployed eventually. But rarely did a soldier, especially one with a family, get sent over to the sandbox, as Ed always referred to it, as often as Ed had. Bree hadn't wanted to accept it at the time, but in retrospect, she knew he'd volunteered for most of those deployments. After being home for a few months he'd be restless and itching to go again. When Sam was born, she thought things would change. But they hadn't.

Ed had been a decorated soldier, good at what he did. He'd earned his reputation with countless acts of sacrifice and heroism. But in the end, her bigger-than-life husband had taken one risk too many.

Bree grabbed the albums and moved to put them away. A little stack of photos that had never been mounted slid out and spilled across the coffee table. The photo on top was of a flag-draped coffin with a solemn five-year-old boy saluting it.

Almost angrily, Bree shoved the photos back into the album without looking at the rest. She squared her shoulders and headed for the kitchen. Time to think about supper and stop thinking about men. Any man. The last thing she needed in her life was another bigger-than-life hero.

CHAPTER 4

Will hummed along to a new Cody Joe Hodges CD he'd recently purchased as he mashed several lumps of butter into the mixture of flour, sugar, and baking power in his favorite blue bowl with the handle on the side that made mixing and pouring easier. Then he added milk and began stirring. He'd gotten up a little earlier than usual for a Sunday morning, which meant he'd have time for a shower and a leisurely perusal of the paper before church. What better way to celebrate his first Sunday in his new apartment than with a batch of his favorite scones? The kind his mother used to make for him when he was growing up.

Yesterday, after dropping Sam back at his apartment, Will got a call that sent him out to spend the rest of what should have been his free Saturday afternoon following up on a report of a meth lab. A gentleman out walking his dog said he'd seen suspicious activity in the tumbledown ruins that were once the slave quarters at the old Jolee Plantation. There was debris that looked like leftovers from a meth cook, but no lab and no perps anywhere on the premises. He didn't have the proper protective gear, so he'd had to call in the team that specialized in meth cleanup. Then he'd had to wait for them to show up. All in all, it had been a tiring day. Will looked forward to his Sunday off. And it didn't get much better than enjoying fresh baked scones on his new deck.

At a knock on his door, Will jerked his head up in surprise. Except for Ben, he hadn't had a chance to let anyone know where his new digs were. Besides, whoever it was should have had to buzz him to get into the building. It couldn't be his new landlord. That guy was four states away and getting ready to deploy to the Middle East.

"Coming," he called as he wiped his hands on a soggy towel.

The knock came again, a little softer this time.

"What can I do for —" Will adjusted his gaze downward to where Sam Reagan stood, barefoot and clad in pajamas decorated with cheery yellow Minions. "What's up?"

"Mom's sick."

Will's heart rate clicked up a notch. "Sick? Like really sick? Or just not feeling too good?"

"Just not feeling too good." Sam frowned.

Okay. Not an emergency. "Well, that's no fun. Is — there — something I can help with?"

"I need you to take me to church. It's Boy Scout Sunday."

"And your mom's not feeling up to going, I guess."

Sam shook his head. "She didn't even feel like ironing my uniform."

Concern rebooted itself in Will's head. Just how sick was Bree? He didn't know her well enough yet to just go downstairs and check on her. If she was still in bed, she'd be embarrassed. So would he, actually. But perhaps he should call down.

"Come on in. I was just putting some scones in the oven for breakfast." Will stepped back and gestured for Sam to come in, then led the way out to the kitchen.

"So, what's got your mom feeling not so hot?" Will asked as he scooped globs of scone batter onto a baking sheet.

"She says her cold is making her head hurt, and her voice sounds kind of squeaky," Sam explained as he watched Will. "What are scones? What's the blue stuff in 'em?"

"Scones are like biscuits. Scottish biscuits. And the blue stuff is blueberries. They're my favorite kind. I'll let you try one when they're ready."

Sam hiked himself up onto a stool at Will's kitchen table. "I didn't know guys could cook."

"I'd get pretty hungry if I didn't know how to cook."

Sam glanced around the kitchen, then back at Will. "You need a wife."

"That's what my brother says." Will chuckled.

"Did you ever have one?" Sam propped his chin in his palms. His eyes were suddenly serious.

"Almost," Will admitted. "But —" This was definitely not the kind of conversation one should be having with an eight-year-old boy. The breakup of his engagement to Linda had stopped hurting a long time ago. It was old business.

"Mom had a husband once," Sam offered, his blue eyes clouding. "But he got killed."

"I'm sorry to hear that." The urge to pull the little boy into his arms and hug him slammed into Will's gut with unexpected force.

"He was a soldier," Sam confirmed Will's

earlier guess. "He was a hero. I wanna be a soldier when I grow up, but Mom says I should go to college instead."

Losing a husband was hard enough. The pain of losing a son, too, would do in just about any woman. No wonder Bree was intent on sending Sam to college instead of into military service.

"Well, you've got a lot of years left before you have to decide." Will slipped the baking sheet into the oven and set the timer.

"I guess." Sam perked up. "Can I have breakfast with you?"

"You haven't eaten yet?"

"I had cereal. But there's still more room left." Sam formed a circle with his thumbs and forefingers and pressed it against his stomach. "See?"

What Will saw were two Minion eyes peering out between Sam's fingers, but if Sam was anything like Will had been at that age, he could always find room for more. Especially blueberry and white chocolate scones.

He grabbed his phone off the counter. It rang several times before Bree picked up. "Hello?" Sam was right about the squeaky voice.

"Sam says you're not feeling so hot."

What started out sounding like a chuckle turned into a cough. "A little too hot, actually. I'm sorry he bothered you. I told him not to call you."

"He didn't call. He came up." Will laughed at Sam's solution to being told not to call. He hadn't exactly disobeyed. "I was up anyway. Is there anything I can do besides take him to church? Missing Scout Sunday seems to be his main concern at the moment, and I really don't mind. I'm going anyway."

"His uniform isn't even pressed. If you're sure you don't mind, I'll see to —" she broke off in another coughing fit.

"Honestly, I don't mind at all. I'll send him down for his shirt. I haven't ironed mine either, so I'll do them both. You stay in bed and get some rest. Is there anything *you* need that I could bring down?"

"Nothing, thanks. I'm — I — thanks, Will. I appreciate it."

"My pleasure." He'd be more pleased if he could think of something he could do for her personally. Something to make her feel a little better than she sounded.

The timer on the stove buzzed. Will hit *end* and set his phone back on the counter. "These will be too hot to eat right off," he told Sam as he grabbed a potholder and removed the baking sheet from the oven. "So you run back downstairs and get dressed. Bring your Cub Scout shirt back with you, and I'll iron it for you."

Sam bolted for the door. All was right with his world. Or almost all was right.

"Don't disturb your mom, either. Got that, sport?"

"Roger that, Mr. Cameron," Sam called back as he dashed out the door. His bare footsteps faded as he ran down the hall and then disappeared abruptly as he ducked into the stairwell.

Will set up the ironing board and plugged in the iron. When he'd first joined the Highway Patrol, he'd had to learn how to iron. Not just passably but with creased perfection. One thing the North Carolina troopers were known for was their smart, impeccably pressed uniforms. He'd been living at home at the time but had never expected his mother to take on the chore, so he'd gotten her to teach him. His current salary allowed him to have his uniforms professionally pressed, but he still knew how, and there were times like this when that skill came in handy.

He'd just finished his own scouting shirt when Sam dashed back into the apartment.

"Here ya go." Sam thrust his blue uniform top into Will's hand. "Be careful of the beads," he warned. "Mom usually takes them off when she irons it."

"Yes, sir." Will suppressed a smile and carefully removed the "Progress Toward Ranks" badge with its dangling cord of beads from the pocket flap button and laid the shirt across the ironing board.

"You know how to do everything. Even iron," Sam observed in awed tones as he watched Will move the hot iron over the collar of the shirt.

"My mom taught me," Will answered.

"Can you teach me?" Sam looked up eagerly.

Will hesitated. The iron wasn't all that hot. It was probably okay for an eight-year-old to learn how to iron. "I'll do half, and you watch, then you can come around this side, and I'll help you do the other half. Sound good?"

"Okay."

Sam watched intently as Will ironed creases out of the little sleeve, then began on the front of the shirt.

"Your turn, sport." Will stepped back to allow Sam to squeeze himself between Will and the ironing board. Sam grabbed the iron, but Will caught his hand and stopped him. "First you have to smooth the shirt out a little so you don't end up ironing more creases into it."

Will demonstrated.

Sam copied Will's actions. "Now?" He glanced up at Will with a furrow of concentration on his brow.

Not for the first time, Will took notice of how very blue Sam's eyes were, almost as blue as his own; Bree's were brown. What other traits had Sam inherited from his dad? What had Sam's father been like? Had Bree fallen in love with the uniform, or had they been in love before he became a soldier?

"Now?" Sam asked again, bringing Will's thoughts back to the present.

"That's good," Will agreed, then closed his hand over Sam's and helped him finish the task of ironing his uniform.

"I did good? Right?" Sam grinned in triumph as he removed the shirt from the ironing board and held it up.

"You did especially good," Will told him. "Now get it on, and I'll serve us up some scones."

When Bree woke again, she was relieved to find her headache gone. Her throat still hurt but not as bad as before. She sat up, and swung her feet over the side of the bed, then let out a murmur of surprise.

A small tray with a beer logo on it sat on her bedside table. It held a glass of orange juice and a plate with two scones carefully covered with plastic wrap. The plastic had hints of moisture on the inside, and when she placed her fingers on the scones, they were still warm. An index card had been folded in half and set beside the plate with the words, *Get Well Quick* scrawled across it and what looked like a sketch of a rosebud.

Except for Sam, Will was the only person who knew she'd been feeling lousy this morning, and that wasn't Sam's handwriting. Nor was her son capable of drawing a rose that was recognizable. Or baking scones.

She touched the little sketch. What a thoughtful thing to do. Perhaps Will's mother had dropped the scones off on her way to church, and he'd decided to share. Bree lifted the plastic and broke off a small piece. It crumbled, so she popped it into her mouth quickly.

She closed her eyes as the sweet berry flavor hit her taste buds. Was that a hint of chocolate? Her eyes snapped open, and she inspected the scone more closely. It was indeed chocolate. White chocolate. And blueberries. She was definitely going to worm this recipe out of whoever had baked them.

In the bathroom, she soaked a facecloth

with cold water and held it to her eyes. After a few moments she checked again. They still looked a little pink, but they felt better. She washed her face, then brushed her teeth.

Returning to the bedroom, she decided perhaps she should get dressed in case Will came in when he brought Sam home from church. It suddenly occurred to her that either Will had entrusted Sam with the delivery of her breakfast treat, or he'd been in her bedroom himself. Please God, let it be the former, because she was definitely looking her worst today. The thought of Will watching her sleep with swollen eyes and tangled hair made heat rush into her cheeks. She'd probably been snoring, too.

With a groan, she pulled on a new pair of lounge pants her sister had given her for her birthday last August. She'd never worn them before now, but she still felt shivery, and they were warm. She dug out a clean sweatshirt and tugged it over her head. Shoving her feet into comfy slippers, she fetched the tray from beside the bed and carried it to the living room.

Armed with a fresh box of tissues and a hot cup of tea to augment the juice and scones, she settled into her favorite chair and put her feet up on the ottoman. The Sunday paper was still down in the foyer, so she settled for a book Zoe had loaned her. Then, finally, she allowed herself to take another bite of the heavenly scones.

They were gone way too soon. She felt like a pig for having devoured them so quickly but then decided it must be the hour. It was nearly noon, and she hadn't eaten since supper last night. Hunger will do that.

In fact, she was still hungry. But hungry enough to get up and find something else? She was still debating when the door flew open, and Sam rushed in, beaming. Clearly he'd had a great morning in spite of her absence. A momentary pang of loss hit her, but she shoved it aside when Will followed Sam in and closed the door behind him.

"You're up," Will said. "Feeling better?" He crossed to the couch and lowered himself to sit on the edge.

"I am. Thank you for the scones and the get well note. And thanks for taking Sam to church."

"He can attend church with me any time. You've got a really great boy, and I enjoy his company."

"Look, Mom!" Sam peeled off his jacket and turned slowly about in front of her. "Did I do good or what?"

Bree looked at Will in puzzlement, but Will

just looked at Sam.

"I ironed my own shirt. Didn't I, Mr. Cameron? I did really good, right?"

Bree felt another pang of alarm. What was Sam doing with a hot iron all by himself? "It looks very nice."

"And I'll get better with practice. Mr. Cameron said so."

"Better hang it up before it gets wrinkled, sport."

"Roger that." Sam whirled and headed to his bedroom.

"He didn't actually do it all by himself, if that's what you're frowning about," Will said as soon as Sam was out of earshot.

"N-no. I just — what if he burned himself?"

"It's polyester. The iron wasn't all that hot, and I had one hand on it all the time. Not to worry."

Worry came second nature to Bree these days. She hadn't always been this way. Not before Ed died anyway. Will was frowning now, too. He still perched on the edge of the couch as if uncertain of his welcome, his big hands dangling between his knees. His blue eyes searched hers with a question in them.

"I'm sorry. I try not to worry so much, but — he's — he's all I have."

Will tucked his cheek between his teeth, sharpening the dimple that already creased the tanned surface of his face. Bree had the strongest desire to reach out and touch the depression. She shook away the temptation and looked for something else to focus on.

"Thank you for the scones and the juice. Did your mom make them? They were delicious."

He winked, and the puzzled look left his face. "Mom's recipe, but I made them. I'm glad you liked them."

"Y-you made them?"

"Why? You think guys can't bake?"

"Ed never did," Bree blurted out, then wished she hadn't. Will wasn't Ed, and Ed was gone. Why was she comparing them?

"My mom's a great cook, and I learned from her." Will got to his feet. "I guess I should be going. Unless there's anything I can do. Anything I can get that maybe you need and don't have on hand."

Bree started to scramble to her feet, but Will put his hands on her shoulders and gently pressed her back into the chair.

"I can see myself out."

Sam reappeared in a T-shirt and jeans. "You're leaving? Already?"

"Sorry, sport. I've got to go grab my fishing gear and make sure I didn't leave anything else behind at my old place."

"Can I go too?" Sam glanced from Will to his mother. "Can I go help Mr. Cameron?"

"Maybe your mom would like you here to help out if she needs anything," Will began at the same time Bree spoke up.

"Mr. Cameron doesn't need you tagging along bothering him."

"I'm not a bother. Am I, Mr. Cameron?" Then, before Will could answer, Sam turned to his mother again. "Do you really need me to stay? I will if you really, really need me to."

Bree looked at Will over Sam's head and bit her lip. What she really wanted was another nap. She would have a busy day tomorrow, and if an afternoon nap brought about as much healing as the morning one had, she sorely needed it.

"I don't want him to be a bother." Her protest wasn't as strong as it had been the first time.

"He's not a bother at all." Will winked at her again, and her heart jerked in reaction.

Sam gave her a quick hug and followed Will to the door, almost bumping into him when he stopped and turned back. "I'll send Sam back with a couple more scones and the recipe." Then he opened the door and stepped out of sight.

Just before the door shut again, Bree heard Sam say, “You like my mom a lot. Right?”

Then the door closed, and Bree didn’t hear Will’s response.

Chapter 5

With Sam chattering away in the back seat, Will pulled out of Carlisle Place and headed for his old apartment on the outskirts of Wilmington. He only half-listened to Sam as he delved into why exactly he was so attracted to the kid's mother. Beyond her looks, anyway. A man would have to be blind not to appreciate the delectable package that was Brianna Reagan. But gut deep, it was more than just her looks, and yet he couldn't explain it even to himself.

He'd spoken to her no more than half a dozen times and knew almost nothing about her. Well, maybe not nothing. She was his new sister-in-law's best friend. She was Sam's mother. She worked at Kett's Hotel, but he wasn't sure what her job there was. She was a war widow, but the only thing he knew about Sam's father was a guess. An Army Ranger and hero would be a hard act to follow. And she looked cute with a pink nose in an oversized sweatshirt and dorm pants.

He'd known all the women he'd had relationships with since high school a whole lot better than Brianna Reagan. He'd even proposed to one of them and only realized how lucky his escape had been months after she'd dumped him, and he'd gotten over feeling sorry for himself. But none of them, not even Linda, had touched him the way Brianna Reagan did. She had the voice of a siren and a smile that made his heart skip a beat. But beyond that, he was at a loss. Introspection wasn't his thing. Doing was.

If he found something he liked, he went after it. And he definitely liked Brianna Reagan.

There had to be a lot of her in the boy sitting behind him still jabbering happily about something Will had completely zoned out on. Maybe that was what attracted him. He'd only known Sam for a few months, but everything he'd learned he liked. If he ever had a son someday, he'd want him to be like Sam Reagan.

"Aunt Zoe isn't really my aunt, you know." Sam paused, apparently waiting for Will to respond.

Dragged back into the conversation by Sam's question, Will murmured his understanding of the relationship.

"But I call her that 'cause she's Mom's best friend. Anyway, her little baby can't hear very well. That's just not fair."

Again Will murmured agreement. It wasn't fair, but then life wasn't always fair.

His brother Jake had been completely broken up about the hearing issues when they first found out. There had been a sheen of tears in his eyes as he imparted the news to Will and their parents. What a bittersweet night for Jake. The woman he had fallen head over heels in love with had accepted his proposal of marriage. But only minutes before that, Jake learned that the baby he'd delivered in the middle of a hurricane had been born with severe hearing loss. Jake was horrified, thinking it might have been something he had done wrong on that stormy night when it was just him and Zoe laboring to bring her baby into the world. Zoe assured him it was not his fault, but the relief was brief, because Jake already loved the little girl as much as if she'd been his own child, and his heart ached for the difficulties she would face in life.

"So, I want to learn sign language. It's in the Wolf handbook, you know," Sam explained, bringing Will back to the current conversation a second time.

Will had checked out the pages with a chart of the more common illustrations for American Sign Language after he'd talked to Jake. He'd been skimming the book to get up to speed when he took over the den last fall, and because of Molly, those pages had caught his attention. But then he'd forgotten them until now.

"I think that would be an excellent plan. Maybe Rick would like to work on it with you. Molly is his cousin, and he'll need to know how to talk with her, too."

Sam flung himself back in his seat with a grunt of disapproval, then was ominously silent.

Will glanced at him in the rearview mirror. There was a frown on Sam's face.

"That a problem, sport?"

"I'm still going to be her special cousin. Aunt Zoe said so." Sam's lower lip protruded belligerently, and he stared resolutely out the window, not meeting Will's gaze.

Will's former street came up on the left, and he had to wait for a gap in the traffic before he could make the turn. A pang of nostalgia tugged at him. He was going to miss living on this street lined with old homes and older trees. Many of the stately homes, like the one Will had lived in for the last three years, were divided into two-family homes, with an apartment up and another down. The sidewalks were paved with old bricks, uneven in many places where tree roots had grown close to the surface. The elegance of the neighborhood was still impressive in spite of the run-down appearance of some of the dwellings.

"We're here," Will announced as he turned into his old driveway.

Judging by the sulky look on Sam's face, it looked like there was a serious discussion ahead. Will got out of the Jeep, walked around to Sam's door, then opened it, and squatted to Sam's level.

"Want to talk about it?"

"I got to see her first. I'm her special cousin," Sam answered after a lengthy pause. "I wanted to learn the signs so I can teach her, and we can be able to talk to each other. Just her and me."

Will rocked back on his heels. Rick and Sam were the best of friends, but it appeared Sam had a little case of jealousy. He was an only child, and maybe that had something to do with it. Bree and Zoe had been friends since their early teens, so it was natural that Sam would feel like Zoe was someone special in his life, and by extension, Zoe's new baby.

Will's nephew Rick, on the other hand,

had one brother already, and his mother was pregnant with twin girls. Rick had a half-dozen cousins, but maybe Sam had none at all. That might explain this jealously guarded honorary cousin.

"Learning how to sign is a good plan, Sam." Will put a hand on Sam's knee. "You can get a bead for your uniform, and then you can teach everyone else how to sign. Molly will need all the special people she can get, starting with you. And if everyone can talk to her, think how much happier that will be for her."

"I guess." Sam's lip had receded.

"How about if I learn the signs with you? Would that be okay? I'm Molly's uncle, and I might need to learn them, too."

Sam looked up into Will's eyes. The expression of loss and hurt struck Will's heart like a blow. "I wish you were *my* uncle," Sam said in a soft, pained voice.

Will didn't want to promise Sam anything he couldn't deliver, but he wanted to take away that lost look in the bright blue eyes that were so like his own. "I can be your friend."

Sam looked uncertain.

"Sometimes friends are better than relatives. Cousins and brothers are born to you, but a friend is someone you choose."

"I'm just a kid."

"Well, sometimes my family thinks I'm just a *big* kid."

"Little kids can't do lotsa stuff, and I always gotta ask my mom before I can go anywhere."

"I think I can deal with that. As long as you can deal with me having to do grown-up things you can't do a lot of the time, there are other things we could do together besides learning how to sign."

"What kind of other things?" Sam looked willing to be convinced.

"Have you ever been fishing?"

Sam shook his head. "Mom says Daddy used to go fishing, but he never took me. I wasn't big enough. Do you think I'm big enough now?"

"You are definitely big enough." Will stood up and stepped back. "I've got plenty of extra fishing gear. It's one of the things I came back to get today. That and Bruce."

"Who's Bruce?" Sam unbuckled his seat-belt and jumped to the ground, his sunny humor restored.

For a moment, Will had feared that mention of his father would sink Sam further into gloom, but it hadn't. It was a subject Will knew would probably come up at some point, but he was glad it wasn't going to be today.

"Bruce is my cat."

"I didn't know you had a cat." Sam bounded toward the house.

"Well, I didn't have one before this week. He belonged to the man who used to live downstairs from me. But my neighbor went to live with his son, and he couldn't take Bruce with him."

Will caught up and reached around Sam to unlock the door. Bruce was waiting just inside and began winding his way around Will's legs as soon as they stepped into the hall.

Will introduced Sam to the cat and went to collect the cat's litter box and dishes. When he returned, Sam was seated on the floor petting Bruce, and the cat was responding by arching his back with every stroke. Will took the stairs to his old apartment two at a time and took a quick look around to make sure nothing had been left behind. Then he returned to the first floor and found the cat carrier in the sunroom where his former landlord told him it would be. He blew the dust off and carried it back to the kitchen.

Sam clambered to his feet. "I've gotta pee."

Will pointed the way to the bathroom, then gathered the cat into his arms and eased him into the carrier.

Sam appeared at Will's elbow. "There's no water coming down in the toilet."

"What do you mean, there's no water?"

"I pushed the lever, but no water came down."

"Guess we better check it out, then."

Sam scampered back to the bathroom and was pushing the lever repeatedly by the time Will caught up. "See? No water." He pushed it one last time for emphasis.

Will lifted the lid off the tank. The chain linking the stopper to the lever had broken. All his desk stuff had already been moved to the new apartment.

"I could fix this in a jiffy if only I had a paper clip." Will racked his brain trying to think what else might work, but his tools and other odd bits and pieces had been moved over to Ben's garage. Maybe a leader from his tackle box?

"I know where there's a paper clip," Sam offered, his face alight with eagerness.

"You do?"

"Yeah. I saw one in the little pocket on the door in your Jeep. Want me to get it for you?" He was halfway out the door before Will had a chance to agree.

A minute later Sam was back triumphantly bearing the paper clip. It took only seconds longer to reconnect the two ends of the chain. Will put the lid back, then gestured to Sam. "Give it a try."

Sam flushed, then grinned as if Will had performed some miraculous sleight of hand. "You must know how to fix everything."

"A lot of things, but not everything. Especially not computers. I'm betting you're better than me with computers."

"Mom says I'm a whiz with computers," Sam agreed. "If you ever need your computer fixed, just ask me." He led the way out of the bathroom.

Bruce sat hunched in his carrier blinking slowly in the way of wise cats.

"Are you strong enough to carry Bruce out to the Jeep?"

Sam bunched his fist and showed Will his muscle. "You bet I am."

Will gathered up all of Bruce's paraphernalia and held the door open for Sam. It looked awkward with the carrier banging against Sam's knees, but Will decided not to help. He locked up the house and followed Sam to the Jeep. "Now all we need is my fishing gear."

RAP, RAP, RAP. Sam banging a toy on the rail of his crib. I should get up, but I'm so tired.

Ed's due home in just two days, and there's so much to do. He likes everything "squared away." Just a few more minutes.

Rap, rap, rap. Bree dragged her eyelids open. Late afternoon sun slanted across the bed, and for a moment, she couldn't recall where she was. Then it all came back to her.

Ed was gone, and Sam hadn't slept in a crib for years.

Rap, rap, rap.

Someone was at the door.

She pushed the afghan aside and got to her feet. She stopped at the dresser to run a brush through her hair, frowned at the bed wrinkles still visible on her cheek, and tried to rub them away.

Rap, rap, rap.

"I'm coming." She tried to keep the impatience out of her voice.

It couldn't be Sam. He had his own key. But she wasn't expecting anyone else, was she?

She pulled the door open and stared stupidly at Bob. Her mind was still half asleep, and her head felt like she'd been drugged.

"Aren't you going to ask me in?" Bob squinted at her. "Are you all right?"

"I'm — I was asleep." She backed into the living room to allow him entrance. "How did you get into the building?"

"Your downstairs neighbor was headed out just as I was arriving." Bob started to step past her, then stopped. "Did you forget about the meeting?" He reached a hand toward her face, then let it drop without touching her. "Your nose is red. Are you feeling all right?"

She *had* forgotten about the meeting. She'd pretty much slept the day away. A luxury only possible because of Will's generosity in letting Sam tag along with him first to church and then to his old apartment this afternoon.

"It's just a cold. I'm feeling much better now. Better than I was this morning, anyway. But I don't think I'll make the meeting, after all. I'm sorry you had to drive all the way over here for nothing."

Bob hesitated. "Don't worry about it. Do you want me to stay? I can skip the meeting. If you're hungry maybe I can order a pizza or something."

"No need. I've got leftovers to heat up. And it's an important meeting. You should go."

"If you're sure." He hovered between her and the door.

"I'm sure."

"Well, then," he said as he stepped back

into the hall. "I'll call you tomorrow and fill you in." Then he turned and strode down the hall toward the elevator.

Bree shut the door behind him and leaned against it. She'd better call Meg and let her know why Sam wasn't getting dropped off to spend the evening with Rick. Then she was going to make herself a cup of tea and see if she could restore herself to some semblance of a human being before Will returned with her son.

Chapter 6

Bree hadn't been the only one unable to make the historical society meeting, and a makeup meeting had to be called to address two pieces of important new business. Bree could barely contain her enthusiasm for the new project she had just volunteered for. They were finally going to start working on the restoration of the old Jolee Plantation. The Restoration Committee of four — Tony Jenkins, the town tax collector's husband, Bob, Zoe, and herself — was eager to get started, and they'd come to Joel's to discuss it over coffee and dessert.

Their small party sorted itself out, and Zoe led the way, sliding into a booth first. Bree followed her in, ignoring Bob's frown. Bob pressed his lips into a tight line as he joined Tony on the opposite bench. Bob was irritated by her behavior, but she didn't care. His touchy-feely possessiveness had begun with his insistence on picking her up for the historical society meeting she'd been planning to attend with Zoe, and it had continued all evening. If it hadn't been for Tony's suggestion to stop at Joel's, Bree would have been happy to pick her son up and go straight home.

"So, we're the new committee. Anyone care to volunteer to chair it?" Tony was a tireless advocate of the historical society, but he already chaired two other committees and was probably hoping not to add a third.

Bree kept silent. She and Zoe were the newcomers in the group. Bob enjoyed being on committees and getting involved, but Bree knew he didn't feel comfortable taking on the job of making things run smoothly.

"I will," Zoe offered tentatively.

"Excellent." Tony applauded her. "So, Madam Chairwoman. Want to bring this meeting of the Restore the Jolee Plantation Committee to order?"

"Hi, folks. What can I get you?" Margie Barnes leaned over the table, then air-kissed Bree and Zoe. She nodded at Bob and Tony. "We've still got a few slices of Joel's best pecan pie. Coffee all around?" She made a circle with her forefinger.

"No coffee for me," Zoe demurred. "Got any decaf tea? No pie either, thanks."

Margie took their order — pie and coffee for the men, tea for the ladies — then turned away to check on the next table over.

"I call the meeting to order," Zoe said, then grinned. "What's the first order of business?"

"Money!" Tony rolled his eyes. "It's always money."

"As in fund-raising?" Zoe asked.

Tony pulled a sheaf of folded papers from his pocket and laid it on the table. "The whole society will get involved, but we need to come up with ideas to present first."

Bob turned the papers his way and studied Tony's notes. Then scribbled a few of his own in the margins.

"We have no idea what this project is going to cost, to start with," Bob said.

"I'm sure I can get Jake to help with that," Zoe offered. "He's mostly into new construction, but he's done a couple restorations over in Wilmington. He won't mind pulling together a ballpark figure. Something to aim for."

Bree finally had an idea to offer. "The Spring Festival is in just a couple months. Can we get something going before then?"

By the time the pie and drinks were delivered, Tony had added another whole page to his original notes, and they'd moved on to rumors of ghosts on the property in question.

"If it's ghosts at the old Jolee place you're discussing," Margie said as she set the pie in front of the men, "I know just who you need to talk to."

"Who?" Zoe and Bree asked in unison.

"Emmy Lou Davis knows everything there is to know about the old plantation. She was second cousin to the last Jolee who actually lived there. I think she used to play there. Back when they were kids, that is. Stop by her antique shop some afternoon and ask. Once she gets going, you won't be able to shut her up. Why are you interested, anyway?"

Bob jumped in to explain that the historical society had decided to take on the project of restoring the old plantation. Some years earlier, the last owner had given the property to the town as a gift, but nothing had been done. Until now.

Margie shivered theatrically. "I've heard some of the ghosts that haunt that place aren't really ghosts, if you know what I mean, and the state troopers have been called in to investigate. Maybe you should check with them before you start traipsing around over there. Will Cameron might be able to fill you in. He's —" she broke off when a gentleman at the counter called to her.

Hearing Will's name unexpectedly did funny things to Bree's breathing. She tried to ignore it, and before she could ask why Will would know anything about intruders at the plantation, Tony jumped back into the conversation.

"I'll ask Sheriff Nicholson," he said as he tossed a few bills on the table and slid out of the booth. "He'll know if there's been any hanky-panky going on up there. But right now I've gotta get home, or my wife will think I'm hanging out at the bar instead of coming straight home from the meeting, and she'll be sending Nicholson to fetch me."

Bree gathered up her purse and slipped out of the booth. "I need to get home too. It's a school night, and Sam needs to be in bed." Sam had been left in Jake's care to play with Molly and finish his homework while Bree and Zoe attended the specially scheduled meeting of the historical society.

Bob studied the bills Tony left, frowned, then added a couple more.

"Thanks, Margie," Zoe called as they filed past the register and out the door.

Margie blew them all a kiss and turned back to her customer at the counter.

After Bob and Bree dropped Zoe off and picked Sam up, her son chattered all the way home about Molly and how he was learning sign language so he could talk to her. Bree was relieved for the reprieve Sam's presence provided. Sooner or later, Bob was going to want an explanation for her reluctance to move their relationship forward. Trouble was, she didn't understand it herself.

Less than two weeks ago she'd viewed Bob as a safe date. A man who wouldn't break her heart even if she let him into her life. But something had changed. She wasn't sure if the change was in Bob or in herself. She should never have asked him to help with the Pinewood Derby racer because her asking had apparently given him the wrong idea about where their relationship was going. Until their dinner at the country club he'd always been a perfect gentleman, never asking for or even hinting that he was impatient for more.

But all that had changed with the handing over of Sam's derby kit.

Instead of dating casually now and then, Bob seemed to assume she was ready to take their relationship to the next level. He came on to her more aggressively when they were alone. He touched her way too intimately and kissed her when she didn't want to be kissed. She didn't think she'd led him on, but maybe she was wrong. Maybe his misunderstanding was all her fault.

Bob pulled into an empty spot in front of the apartment building and killed the engine. Sam sprang from the back seat like he was in a race to beat everyone to the door. Bree grabbed her purse and reached for the door handle, but Bob stopped her. Sam disappeared into the building, and Bob pulled Bree back toward the console.

"Nice kid, but he sure puts a kink in an evening that has already been pretty frustrating." Bob laced his fingers into the hair cascading down Bree's back and drew her face toward his.

Bree gave up fighting the inevitable and let Bob's mouth descend on hers. She tried to muster up some level of passion, but when his tongue began probing her lips, she drew back.

"What's wrong, Bree?" Bob let the back of his fingers skim over her jaw and down her neck to her collarbone.

"It's late, Bob, and I have to get Sam into bed." She clutched her purse between them like a shield.

"I get the feeling you're not as excited about me as I am about you. I thought we were —"

"It's too soon," Bree freed herself from his embrace. "And I'm not ready."

"You've been widowed for more than three years. How much longer do you need?" Bob sighed in frustration.

"I don't know."

"Is there someone else?"

Bree's head jerked up. "No!"

Bob's eyes narrowed. Then without warning, he put a hand on either side of her face and kissed her hard. When he let her go this time, her lips felt bruised. "Good. Patience I can do, but jealousy brings out the worst in me." He reached past her and opened her door.

Bree slid out of the car and bent so she could see Bob's face. "Are you still going with me Saturday?" Maybe it would be better if Bob said no.

"Do you still want me to?" There was a hard edge to his voice. Bob closed his eyes, and his jaw tensed. Then he relaxed and opened his eyes again. "I'm sorry. Of course I am. What time should I pick you up for this affair?"

The "affair" was an open house at Kett's. Bree had asked Bob to be her escort because there really hadn't been anyone else to ask. She should have opted to attend solo.

"Six thirty," she told him as she backed away from the car.

"See you then." He blew her a kiss.

She hurried up the steps and let herself into the building knowing he would not pull away from the curb until he knew she was safely inside. But then, as the taillights of his car faded into the night, she pressed her forehead to the glass, and his shattering question tumbled through her head.

Of course there was no one else.

So why did an overgrown Boy Scout spring to mind?

Chapter 7

Bree finished putting a pair of dangly silver earrings on just as the door buzzer sounded. That would be Bob. She hurried out to the living room to the intercom and pressed the button giving him access to the building.

"You ready to head upstairs?" she called to her son, who was still in his bedroom doing who knew what. Will had offered to let Sam join him for pizza and movie night upstairs while Bree headed to Kett's for the open house. Bree had a suspicion that it might have been Sam who had done the asking, but it was too convenient to pass up. Besides, it was to be a sleepover, so Bree wouldn't have to worry about how late the event went.

She took one last look in the mirror by the door. Then Bob's knock came.

"Hi," she said a bit shyly as she swept the door open. After the way they'd parted three days ago, she wasn't sure how tonight would play out. She liked Bob and didn't want to hurt his feelings, but the friendship they'd started out with had begun to feel like something else. Something she didn't think was right for her. That wasn't really Bob's fault. It was hers. And she was beginning to feel she had not been fair to him.

"Wow!" Bob stepped into the apartment and shut the door behind him. His gaze took in Bree's low-cut evening gown, lingering over her breasts on the way back up. "Nice dress." He held out a small box.

"What's this?" She opened the box. Sam's Pinewood Derby car sat inside, painted bright green and looking very glossy and speedy. "Wow! You did a nice job." She lifted the little race car out and inspected it.

Sam came around the corner with his backpack over one shoulder.

"Look, Sam." Bree held out the car. "Look what Mr. Cahill did for you."

Sam glanced at the car, then at Bob, and finally back at Bree. "So, he made a car. What's that to me?"

"Sam!" Bree was appalled at her son's rudeness. "This is your Pinewood Derby racer. Tell Mr. Cahill thank you for helping with it."

"That's not my racer." Sam's mouth hardened into a flat line.

"But it is. I asked Mr. Cahill if he could help you with it."

"He didn't help me with it," Sam said. "He did it all by himself. I didn't get to do any of it."

Bree looked helplessly from Sam to Bob, her heart plunging at her mistake. Sam was right. Bob hadn't worked on it with Sam. But what was done, was done and couldn't be undone. She bent close and spoke firmly in Sam's ear. "Mr. Cahill thought he was helping, and you need to say thank you, Sam."

Sam glared at her, his jaw set.

"Sam."

"Thank you," Sam muttered in a barely audible voice.

"I didn't hear you," Bree prompted.

"Thank you for helping with my racer." Sam turned back to Bree. "Now can I go?"

She nodded, feeling like a coward.

Sam dropped the racer back into the box and shoved the lid on. Then he dashed for the door and disappeared into the hall.

"I'm sorry," Bree started to apologize.

Bob shrugged. "Don't be. He's just a kid."

"But after all the time you spent. I —"

"If it earned me a night in your company, then it was worth it." Bob slipped his arm around Bree's waist and drew her close for a kiss. "You look fabulous."

Bree kissed him back, trying to make up for Sam's ungratefulness, but when things began to get a little too hot, she backed away. "We should be going."

"We've got all night," Bob said agreeably as he draped her wrap about her shoulders.

"He didn't even let me pick out the color," Sam pouted as he tossed a small box on Will's kitchen counter.

Will lifted the cover off Sam's box and peeked inside. "You don't like green?"

"Green's okay, but —"

"But what?"

"But it's not my race car."

"Then suppose you explain." Will held the racer on the palm of his hand. The color was the least of Sam's problems. This car would be lucky to make it to the end of the racetrack without the wheels falling off, never mind have a chance to win.

"It was supposed to be *my* car, and Mr. Cahill was just supposed to help me make it."

Will couldn't refute that. "Maybe he didn't understand."

"He never even asked." Sam folded his arms and plopped his chin on top of them.

"I hope you said *thank you.*"

"I said it, but I didn't mean it."

"We can't always feel the things we should, but at least you said the right thing."

Will had no idea what he should be telling Sam. If it had been his project, he'd have been just as upset and probably just as reluctant to give any credit for good intentions. But he doubted Bree would want him to share that information with her son.

He was saved from getting any deeper into the quagmire by the door buzzer. He hit the intercom.

"Domino's," the disembodied voice announced.

Will pushed some bills across the counter. "Want to go answer the door and pay the man for our pizza?"

After will had tucked Sam into the guest bed, it had taken only moments for the boy's eyelids to drift shut. They'd watched two movies. Sam had barely made it through the second one, in spite of the edge-of-your-seat car chase at the end.

Will gathered up the remnants of their boys' night of pizza and movies and carried the dirty dishes to the kitchen. He rinsed them and stacked them in the dishwasher, then grabbed a beer from the fridge and settled at the counter to study Sam's racer and decide what he could do about it.

He couldn't change the color without anyone being the wiser, but he could definitely tweak the axles, which were crooked and wobbled dangerously. Thankfully, Cahill hadn't thought to paint the wheels, so they could be sanded smooth and maybe soaked in some furniture polish before he reattached them.

It needed weights, too. No telling how closely either Bree or Sam had studied the car, but if he drilled a hole in the underside of the car and dropped pennies in, chances were he could get away with it without getting found out.

Will hunted down his tools and got to work.

St. Theresa's fellowship hall hummed with activity. Pinewood Derby Day had arrived, and dozens of excited Cub Scouts chattered and made bets with each other as their fathers and den parents called each group of scouts forward and helped them place their racers behind the starting blocks. Three cars in each heat, the winners moving on to the second round and then semifinals.

Meg and Bree were manning the lunch counter, but Rick and Sam had assured them they would come get them when it was time for their races to begin.

"Man, this is crazy," Meg said as she replenished the tray that had once been piled with jam and cream cheese sandwiches. Two of the scouts were allergic to peanuts, so peanuts in all forms had been banished from the menu. "Ever tasted one of these?" She held one out to Bree.

"I doubt I'd ever want to give up peanut butter, but these are surprisingly good." She took the proffered sandwich and bit into it.

"Where's Bob? I thought he was helping Sam with his car. I'd have thought he'd want to see how it raced," Meg said before popping a sandwich bite into her own mouth.

"He's coming later." Bree tore into a new case of bottled water and started lining the bottles up on the counter. "He has a new client. A big shot. The guy insisted he needed to go over some stuff this morning. Bob doesn't dare say no."

"Ben would tell the entire police department to take a flying leap off the Cape Fear Memorial Bridge before he missed something as important to Rick as the Pinewood Derby."

"Of course, he would. But then, Bob isn't Sam's dad."

"True," Meg agreed with a smile. "My boys are pretty lucky."

Bree tried to picture Ed milling about in this crowd, eager to cheer Sam on. He would have, so long as there had been no deployment to take him away from home. "Ben is pretty special."

Meg's eyes searched the room until they found her husband. She smiled. "Yeah, he is. But Will is pretty special, too." Meg looked pointedly at Bree.

Bree felt herself growing hot. "Sam certainly thinks so."

"How serious are things between you and Bob?"

"I don't . . . know," Bree answered hesitantly. The change of subject caught her by surprise.

Meg turned to look directly at Bree. "What don't you know? Whether things are serious or whether you want them to be?"

"If I want them to be. No. That's not entirely honest. Bob wants to get serious. I don't. But I'm not sure how to go about ending it. Lately, he's been giving me the feeling I haven't been fair with him."

"Did you give him any reason to think you felt the same as he did?"

Bree shook her head. "We were friends. I thought."

Meg snorted. "Most men don't believe in friendship. Not unless it comes with benefits." She went back to watching the crowd.

"Wisdom gained in the Marines?" Bree bit her lip and wondered how many *friendships* Meg had been offered over the years.

Meg was silent for a long while. Long enough for Bree to feel like she might have stepped over the boundaries of their relatively new relationship. But then she turned back to Bree. "Did you know I first met Ben when I was only fourteen? He was nineteen and all grown up. I was in love with him, and I couldn't wait to grow up so I could be his girlfriend instead of just his friend. And he waited for me all those years. He was the best friend I had back then. Or now. But he's not your average kind of guy."

"Are you talking about me?" Ben appeared behind Meg and slipped an arm about her waist.

"Your ears must be burning." Meg laughed and turned her head to look up at her husband.

Ben grinned, hugged her tighter, then looked over at Bree. "Sam sent me to tell you his race is next."

"Thanks." Bree turned and hurried out of the kitchen.

She worked her way to the front of the

cheering crowd and found herself standing shoulder to shoulder with Will Cameron. Instantly, her pulse started racing. He was taller than she recalled. Or was it just because he was closer? He was big. Too big and too — too masculine. Too — damned attractive. She eased away to leave some breathing space and tried to get a grip.

Was he like his twin? Or more like Bob? Did Will believe in friendship between a man and a woman? Simple friendship she could be comfortable with. Especially if he became any more important in Sam's life than he already was.

"Watch, Mom!" Sam caught her attention. He reached up and placed his bright green racer on the track, then hopped from foot to foot waiting for the start. As soon as the gate lifted, Sam ran along the side shouting encouragement to his car. For the first several yards, the three cars were neck and neck, but as the flat straightaway began, Sam's car edged into the lead. Slowly over the remaining feet, it pulled ahead and crossed the finish line in first place. Sam scooped it up with a shout of delight.

"I won. Mom. Did you see? I won. It went faster than Flash." Sam held his car aloft and swooped it around in a triumphant circle. Then he noticed Will. "I won, Mr.

Cameron. Did you see?"

"I did indeed, sport. But don't get too cocky. That was just the first round."

Sam crowed with glee and disappeared into the crowd.

"Somehow I didn't think his racer was going to do all that well," Bree said, still doing her best to ignore her runaway pulse. She took another step away from Will's suddenly overpowering presence. Was friendship even possible for her with a man like Will?

"Guess you can't judge a book by its cover." Will's gaze traveled down over her pink breast cancer T-shirt and skinny jeans and the frilly flowered apron that someone had insisted on tying about her waist when she arrived to work at the lunch counter. "Somehow, I never would have guessed you for the apron type either."

His soft, southern voice sent a shiver rippling through her. Years before when her family had first moved to Wilmington, North Carolina, from Virginia Beach, Virginia, she'd thought that smooth drawl was terribly sexy, but she'd gotten used to it and barely noticed anymore. Until now.

Another man with a scout in tow claimed Will's attention, and he turned away before she could explain the apron. But really. She didn't have to explain herself. To Will. Or any man. Right? Just because his proximity did strange things to her insides didn't mean she had to justify anything. He was just a guy. A guy she was determined was never going to be more than a friend.

An hour later, Sam shouted with triumph a second time. Once again his racer had beaten both opponents and would now race in the semifinals against his best friend Rick and one other boy. "I guess green is a lucky color after all," Sam announced, holding his racer up for her inspection. "I'm going to call it Flash after my favorite superhero."

"Sounds like a perfect name," Bree agreed, studying the racer more closely. Something looked different about it, but she couldn't put her finger on it. Not that she had inspected it all that closely the night Bob brought it over. At the time, she had been more concerned with Sam's bad manners.

"I gotta go find Rick." Sam dashed off again, a whirlwind of energy and excitement.

Bree turned and caught Will leaning against the wall watching her. Her heart jumped when their eyes met. Will pushed away from the wall and headed her way.

She squared her shoulders and waited for Will to reach her. "Did you do something to that car?" she demanded as soon as he was close enough to hear without shouting her question over the hubbub.

Will lifted his eyebrows and tried to look innocent.

"You did, didn't you?"

"I might have," he finally admitted.

"Does Sam know?"

Will shook his head slightly. "He was asleep."

"But nothing illegal, I hope?"

Will's eyes widened. He held two fingers up. "Scout's honor."

Bree couldn't stop the bubble of laughter that burst out of her.

"I just didn't want Sam to be disappointed. Not to badmouth Bob's efforts, but the wheels would have fallen off before it got to the end of the track. All I did was install new axles and add a few pennies for weight. Nothing illegal, I assure you. I read the rules carefully."

"Thanks." Bree put a hand on Will's forearm. "His biggest problem at the time was that he didn't get to help build it. Not that your tweaking it included him either, but I appreciate it. It's sure made his day today."

"My pleasure," Will drawled, placing his hand over hers.

"Did I miss Sam's race?" Bob Cahill appeared without warning.

Bree yanked her hand back and turned to Bob. "He's got one more race left. So far, he's been winning." She didn't dare look at Will for fear that their collaboration would show in her expression.

"Excellent." Bob's chest seemed to expand a little. He put his arm about her shoulders, but she shrugged him off.

Since the night he'd accompanied her to the open house at Kett's, she'd been avoiding him. On discovering that Sam would not be in the apartment when they returned, Bob had cranked up the pressure to be allowed to come in with her, but she'd stood firm in her denial. He'd been pretty transparent about the direction of his thoughts the whole evening, ogling her suggestively whenever he caught her eye, and he'd even come right out and told her how much her evening attire turned him on.

In spite of knowing she did not want to make love with him, Bree hadn't known how to get their relationship back onto friendship territory or end it all together. Letting him come up to her apartment would definitely have given him the wrong idea and led to a confrontation when she spurned his amorous advances. She should have let the showdown happen. Easy to see after the fact.

"So?" Bob scowled. "What's between you and the scouting guy?"

"Nothing's between me and Will." Bree didn't pretend not to know whom he was referring to.

"You two looked pretty cozy just now when I got here."

"He — Sam just won his second heat. We were — we were just happy for Sam."

"And where is the triumphant Sam?" Bob scanned the room. "He seems to be elsewhere."

"He went to find his friend." *Please, God. Not now. Not here.*

Bob grabbed her elbow and steered her toward the exit. "We need to talk."

His fingers dug in painfully, but Bree didn't want to make a scene, so she allowed him to guide her toward the door. Out of the corner of her eye, she saw Will start toward them, but she shook her head slightly to warn him off. He stopped but continued to watch, concern etched on his face.

Bob hit the release bar on the fellowship hall door and ushered Bree out onto the paved walkway.

"Let go of me."

"Not until we have this out." He continued to drag her around the corner and away from prying eyes.

"What is *this* that we need to have out?"

"Are we an item, or are you just a tease?"

Bree finally refused to go another step. She pulled her elbow free and straightened her spine. "Neither."

Bob's brows rose. He was breathing hard, and he looked angry. She'd never seen him angry before, and it scared her a little. Maybe she shouldn't have warned Will off.

"I don't like sharing. I told you that before."

"We are not a couple, Bob. I've enjoyed your friendship, but we have never been a couple."

"Could have fooled me." He snorted in derision. "I thought we were. I thought you were just being cautious after losing your husband, and I didn't want to push. But maybe I should have. Now this scouting guy has shown up, and it seems like I missed my chance."

"His name is Will, but there's nothing going on between us."

"That's not how it looked to me."

"We're just friends."

The tension left Bob's shoulders, and regret replaced anger in his expression. "Maybe you're fooling yourself, Bree, but you're not fooling me. I'm sorry it had to end like this. I'd like to say it's been nice, but that would be a lie. I was hoping for so much more." He reached out and cupped her cheek in one hand. He kissed her on the forehead, then let his hand drop back to his side. "I wish you well with your — with Will."

Bob turned on his heel and strode down the walkway and around the corner.

Bree slumped against the warm bricks, feeling like she'd just weathered a hurricane.

There was nothing going on between her and Will. Nothing at all.

If you didn't count the way her pulse raced when he was nearby. Or if she ignored the breathless feeling in her chest when he touched her. Both were things she didn't want to feel at all. No way was she putting her heart out there to be crushed again. Ever.

CHAPTER 8

"Don't Cry." Ed brushed away her tears with his thumb. "I can't bear it when you cry."

"I wish you didn't have to go. I wish you weren't always going away to war and putting your life on the line all the time."

"I'm a soldier, Bree. That's what soldiers do." He pulled her to him, pressing her face into the camouflage pattern of his utility uniform.

"I wish you had an ordinary job. One that wasn't likely to get you killed."

"I'm not going to get killed. I've come home every other time, haven't I?"

Bree lifted her head and squared her shoulders. "But one of these days you might not be so lucky, and where will that leave me?"

"It'll leave you knowing you were once well loved by the best man you ever knew." Ed grinned. Then the smile left his face as quickly as it had come. "But if the worst should happen, know I'll be watching over you, always. Just don't mourn forever. Fall in love again.

Make a new life for yourself. You've got too much love inside you to let it go to waste."

There was no stopping the tears this time. Ed took the possibility of his own death far too easily. It was never easy for her.

"I gotta go." Ed bent and kissed her cheeks, salty tears and all. Then he kissed his fingertips and pressed them to her lips. "I'll be back before you know it." He turned and strode down the jet way, his boots echoing with eerie finality in the air-conditioned tunnel. He turned once to wave. Then he was gone. She could barely see through her tears. They just kept coming and coming. Rivers of them. Her hankie was soaked and useless.

Bree woke from the troubling dream. Her face wet. Her pillow soaked. The cool blue numbers on her alarm clock read 3:13 a.m.

The echo of that last conversation with Ed haunted her. *Don't mourn forever. Fall in love again.*

She had stopped mourning Ed. Mostly. She'd dated Bob with the idea it might lead to more than friendship. But it hadn't felt right. Would it ever feel right? With anyone? Would she ever be able to trust her heart to a man again?

Will's concerned blue eyes following her as Bob escorted her from the church hall appeared in her mind's eye. Bob seemed to think Will might be that man. But she barely knew Will. And she was more than a little afraid of the way he made her feel when he was close. It would be so much easier and safer to keep him as a friend.

She rolled onto her back, and stared up at the dark ceiling, then began cataloging what she did know about Will Cameron.

He made her heart leap when their eyes met.

When he stood too close, her breathing felt odd.

Sam thought he was the best thing that had ever happened in his short life.

Will had an identical twin brother and a nephew who was Sam's best friend.

The man drove a Jeep, and he was Sam's den father.

He lived upstairs with a fat orange cat named Bruce, and he knew how to bake really great scones. He could fix defective race cars, and according to Sam, leaky toilets. Considering what his younger brother did for a living, Will probably knew how to fix a lot of things.

And he was very good with eight-year-old boys.

But that was about the sum of it.

Bree let her eyelids drift shut and pictured Will's bright blue gaze, laughing one minute, concerned the next. The way his face lit up when he smiled, and his eyes crinkled at the corners when he laughed.

Bree stood beside her car with her cell phone to her ear, surveying a very flat tire.

Come on, Sam. Answer the phone. Where are you? Her son should have been in the apartment by now. The bus would have dropped him off ten minutes ago.

If she hadn't tried to squeeze in a trip to the grocery store before heading home to meet Sam's bus, she wouldn't be where she was now. And just maybe she wouldn't have had a flat tire at all. *Sam. Where are you?*

"Hello?"

Relief washed through Bree. "Sam. It's Mom. I got a flat tire, and that's why I didn't get there in time for your bus. I just wanted to make sure you got home okay."

"I came straight home, just like you told me to if you weren't at the bus stop."

"And you're alone?"

"Yes, Mom. I'm alone." Condescension and sarcasm dripped from his young voice.

"And you locked the door behind you?"

Sam sighed loudly.

"Okay, I'm sorry. I just want to make sure you're safe. I'll be home as soon as someone comes to change my tire."

"How come you can't change your own tire?" Eight years old, and already Sam sounded like his father.

"I know how to change a tire, but I've got my work clothes on." Why was she defending herself? "Never mind. Just stay inside until I get there, and don't let anyone in. Got it?"

Sam groaned "Got it."

"There are fudge pops in the freezer. Why don't you have one and get started on your homework?"

"Can I go upstairs and see if Mr. Cameron is home? I want to show him the new signs I learned."

"Mr. Cameron is probably at work. But," Bree added hastily to ward off another round of dramatic sighing, "you can go up and see if he's there as soon as I get home. Okay?"

" 'Kay! Bye." Sam disconnected leaving Bree feeling oddly alone on the only deserted stretch of roadway between the grocery store and home.

She began hunting through her contacts for C.J.'s Auto Shop. Her road club would take forever to get here, but C.J.'s was just down the road, and he or his brother could be there in minutes. The sound of a motorcycle pierced the late afternoon quiet. The rumbling grew, still out of sight around the corner, but loud enough to be either a big machine or more than one.

A nervous fluttering began in her stomach. Not all bikers were a threat. But still.

Then the motorcycle rounded the bend and began to slow. She relaxed. It was a North Carolina State Trooper. She shoved her phone back into her pocket and waited for him to reach her.

The big silver-gray bike pulled up behind her car and rumbled to a stop. The trooper swung his high-booted leg over the back of the bike, and flicked the kickstand down. Then he unsnapped his chinstrap and removed his helmet.

Will Cameron!

Bree swallowed hard.

That was something that had been glaringly missing from the list of things she knew about him.

He grinned as he approached. "Not your lucky day, I guess. Or maybe it is your lucky day considering I'm standing here." Everything about him was overpoweringly masculine. Even the slightly overgrown hair that had been mussed by the helmet.

"I was just about to call C.J.," Bree said, trying to ignore the effect Will had on her libido.

"Pop the trunk. I assume you've got a spare?" This manifestation of Will Cameron was definitely larger-than-life. He seemed taller than usual. And broader. Maybe it was the uniform. Or the bike. Or the fact that he was a trooper, and he was in rescuer mode.

"Of course, I've got a spare." She pressed the trunk button on her key fob and the lid clicked open.

"Then I'll have you back on the road in no time."

He reached into the trunk, spun the big nut that kept the spare in place, then hoisted it out as if it weighed nothing. Which it didn't. A fact she knew because she almost hadn't been able to lift it enough to retrieve an important slip of paper that had managed to slide down underneath a week earlier.

The play of muscles rippling beneath the crisp fabric of his uniform shirt evoked the same breathless fascination she'd felt while watching him disassemble cardboard boxes wearing no shirt at all on the day he'd moved into her building. She wanted to look away but couldn't bring herself to do so. She wanted not to be impressed but couldn't manage that either.

This was not a man it was safe to fall for.

He was a cop. And cops led lives almost as dangerous as soldiers. He might be an easygoing Cub Scout den father, but there was no denying the pure animal magnetism he exuded. That confident grin of his with a deep dimple in one cheek and an extra lift to one corner of his sensuous, kissable-looking lips would charm any woman with a pulse. But she didn't want to be charmed. Not now that she knew who he really was.

"There you go." Will was back on his feet, dusting off his impeccably creased trousers. He tossed the wounded tire into her trunk. "I'd offer to drop it off at C.J.'s for you, but it's a little hard to haul a tire around on a motorcycle."

"Thanks for changing it. Sam says I should have been able to do it myself." *Why am I telling him this?*

"Sam doesn't know what pavement can do to a pair of pantyhose." Will glanced down at her legs and back up with leisurely deliberation. Then he winked.

The rush of color made her cheeks feel like they were on fire. She began backing toward the driver's door. "Thanks again." She felt behind her for the door latch.

Will put two fingers to his brow and saluted. "My pleasure," he responded with that sexy drawl that made her insides melt like a toasted marshmallow. Then he returned to his motorcycle and tugged his helmet down over the disheveled blond locks that made him look both boyishly innocent and wolfishly handsome at the same time.

He started his motorcycle but stayed where he was, straddling the bike with, until now unnoticed, blue lights blinking. With a gulp of understanding, Bree pulled herself together and jerked the door open and dropped into the driver's seat. She yanked her seatbelt into place and started her car. He was waiting for her to pull back onto the road, and the blue lights were to provide a zone of safety while she did so.

As soon as she was back on the road and up to speed, his lights went off, but he continued to follow her. She hadn't done anything wrong, so why were her hands trembling on the wheel? *Please, God, he's not going to follow me all the way home, is he?*

He was still behind her when the entrance to Carlisle Place finally appeared on her right. She turned in, still nervous. Still wishing her savior had been anyone but Will.

He waved and continued on down Jolee Road toward the ocean.

Bree sighed with relief. Maybe it was a

good thing he had been the trooper on the bike. At least now she knew things about him that were important to know. Things that eliminated him from her list of men it was safe to get involved with. If only she could dismiss him from her mind as easily.

Will waved as Bree pulled into Carlisle Place. He'd have liked to follow her all the way home and perhaps find an excuse to spend a little more time with her. Maybe offer to carry the grocery bags he'd seen in the back seat of her car and just maybe get himself invited into her apartment. Even for just a few minutes.

But he had to get his bike back to the garage at Ben's place and locked up for the night.

Neither Ben's truck nor Meg's minivan were in the driveway when he got there, so he stowed his bike and climbed into his Jeep.

As he drove back to Carlisle Place, thoughts of Bree flickered through his head like bright bits of color in a kaleidoscope. He thought about her a lot these days. To the exclusion of many things that had seemed supremely important before he'd picked Sam up for scouts a month ago. His grand plan to cut into Bob Cahill's action had so far not been put into motion. While he'd seen plenty of Sam, moments with Bree had been few and short. Time to step up his game.

He'd caught her watching him while he sliced through boxes the day he'd moved in but had gone on working without letting her know he knew she was watching. He'd also seen the fiery blush when Sam came bounding in. That had to be a point in his favor.

Even before that, he'd sensed her interest when he brought her that ice cream sundae, and then there was the supper invitation the Sunday she'd spent napping to beat back a bad cold. He'd turned her down, thinking the last thing she needed was an extra mouth to feed, but now he wished he'd accepted. He could have helped with supper so she wasn't doing all the work.

At the Pinewood Derby, when she'd caught on to the doctored race car and challenged him on it, there had been amusement in her eyes. Then she'd reached out to touch him, and the amusement fell away as their gaze grew more intense and his heart began to race. He'd been about to ask her for a date.

Then Bob showed up.

He had no idea how the little scene with Bob Cahill had ended. Bree hadn't seemed too happy to be leaving the building with him. In fact, the trooper in him had sensed anger in the other man, and Will didn't know Cahill well enough to know if he'd act on it. He'd wanted to intervene, but Bree had warned him with a glance to back off.

Less than ten minutes later she had returned with an expression that might have been sadness but certainly not distress. Apparently, nothing bad had gone down, but the moment to put his own interest to the test had been lost. Then the final race of the day had been announced.

Sam had not won, and he'd not been happy about it. Reminding Sam that being a gracious loser was more important than winning had ended up becoming a den powwow about good sportsmanship. Sam and another of Will's scouts were in that final heat and would go on to race in the regional derby in Raleigh, but neither had taken first place. Even so, placing second and third should have been a source of pride. The other scout's father had been haranguing the referees and giving the boys a shocking example of what good sportsmanship was *not* about. Will took the boys into one of the classrooms where they sat in a circle and discussed the subject.

By the time they emerged from the room, Sam, at least, was clutching his racer and wearing a satisfied smile. Will wasn't so sure about Gareth but suspected any good their powwow might have achieved would be undone as soon as the boy was back in his father's orbit.

Will hadn't seen Bree since that day until he'd come around the corner and found her standing beside the road with a flat tire.

Home at last, he pulled his Jeep into the empty space next to Bree's Honda and debated stopping on the second floor. Then his cell phone rang.

He looked at the caller ID and groaned. His sergeant. Whatever he wanted, it wouldn't be good. And it definitely meant he was not going to have a chance to see Bree again tonight. He hit the accept button and put the phone to his ear.

CHAPTER 9

Filled with a mixture of hope and nostalgia, Bree left the wedding reception early. Months ago, when the bride's mother had come into the hotel to book the reception, Bree had recognized her eighth-grade math teacher and was surprised when the woman remembered her as well. The wedding invitation was another surprise, and Bree had decided to accept. Tide's Way was a small town, and now that she lived here, she wanted to connect with people, especially people she'd known years ago and remembered with fondness.

As she drove down Jolee Road to pick Sam up at his friend's house, she reflected on the newly married couple. Sally Ann was beautiful, in the way of brides suffused with love and happiness. She reminded Bree of herself on her wedding day. The handsome young husband, obviously smitten, couldn't keep his eyes off his new wife, but like Ed, he was a soldier. With a catch in her heart, Bree prayed that the newlyweds would live a long, happy life together.

She crossed Stewart and turned into Meg and Ben's driveway. Meg appeared on the porch before Bree got out of the car.

"They're out in the woods behind the house. You want to come in for a bit, or do you have to get going?"

Bree glanced at Will's Jeep. Part of her wanted to avoid the man. His charm was too dangerous. Part of her yearned to see him again. "I'd love to, but I've got things I need to get done. I'll just go get Sam. Thanks for watching him."

"Oh, I didn't do much watching. The boys have been out there all afternoon with Ben and Will. I'm not sure what they're up to, but anything that keeps them out from under foot while I get the house clean is a good thing." A phone rang inside. "Gotta go. Good to see you again." Then Meg ducked back into the house.

Bree followed the little bricked path that led around the side of the house to Meg's vegetable garden. Beyond the garden the bricks ended, and the path forked. To the right through deeper grass you ended up at the water. Left headed toward the woods. She paused at the junction to look in the direction of the marsh where the Stewart River flowed into the inland waterway. What a magnificent view. And so close to the ocean that the sound and scent filled the air. Bree lifted her face and sniffed, then turned and headed toward the woods.

Just as she ducked into the line of trees, excited shrieks came from somewhere overhead. Then Sam flew past, eight feet in the air with one foot in a loop of rope that hung from an overhead cable, one hand on the rope, and the other waving wildly in the air like a rodeo cowboy.

Her breath caught in her throat, and her heart squeezed painfully.

A moment later, Evan sailed by; only half Sam's size, he clung to his rope with both hands but grinned just as broadly. Bree's heart about stopped completely as the little boy disappeared into the trees again. Then the deep tones of careless laughter hit her like an assault. Did none of them have a thought to the safety of those boys?

Finally, Sam's buddy Rick whizzed by, as oblivious to the danger as Sam.

Bree marched toward the sound of the laughter.

When the group came into sight, Rick was just stepping out of the loop while his father held the rope. Will and Evan were high-fiving. "Way to go, buddy. I knew you could do it."

"Sam. It's time to go." Bree interrupted Will's congratulations to the five-year-old boy.

"Mom!" Sam came running toward her. "You gotta see me. I went the fastest of anyone." He started to run back to the hill where Bree guessed the high end of the zip line began.

Bree grabbed for him, but he was already running full tilt and out of reach. She turned to Will, anger coursing through her.

"What are you thinking? Sam could get hurt." She glanced at Ben's two boys. "They all could get hurt."

"Not while we're watching them," Will protested. He frowned, looking surprised by her attack.

"But you're just standing around while they go up there and come zooming down all by themselves."

"Not just standing around." Ben stepped up to his brother's side, but Bree barely registered the astonishing likeness.

Outrage boiled up in her like an untended pot of pasta. She'd left her son in Ben's charge and assumed he'd be safe.

"It's our job to make sure they don't run into the tree at the end of the run." Ben pointed to the terminus of the zip line.

Bree glanced at the tree in question and saw right off what he was referring to. But what about the rest of the run?

"We just —" Ben began.

"Geronimo!" Sam's excited voice rang out from the top of the hill.

Will moved so fast, Bree didn't have time to wonder why her son was shouting like a paratrooper. Will stepped under the zip line about twelve feet in front of the tree. As Sam came hurtling down the line, crowing with delight, Will caught him easily, slowed his flight, and stopped him well before he reached the tree.

"It's completely safe," Ben explained as Will held the rope while Sam hopped down. "We took down everything in their path, and the boys promised never to come out here without us to guard the end of the ride."

Rick grabbed one of the ropes and took off toward the top of the hill. "Watch me, Mrs. Reagan."

Still trying to calm her racing pulse and ragged breathing, Bree reached for her son and pulled him against her. A minute later, the same exuberant *Geronimo* sounded, and moments after that Rick shot down the hill toward his father. Ben fielded the flying boy as easily as Will had.

"Can I have one more ride, too?" Evan piped up, his hand already gripping one of the ropes.

"Sure thing," Ben said. "Rick, go help him get started." The two boys trotted back up the hill. "I sure wish I had as much energy. They've worn us out." This he directed at Bree, who still stood there, clutching her son against her chest.

"They've been at it for a while," Will added. "We're ready for a break. I think Meg was baking cookies. You coming back to the house?"

She shook her head hesitantly. She'd already told Meg she had to get going.

"Please can we, Mom?" Sam pried himself out of her embrace and faced her, his best look of supplication on his face. "Just for a little bit. I'll clean my room as soon as we get home. I promise. Mrs. Cameron makes the best cookies. Three kinds all at once."

Bree watched Ben catch his youngest son while she tried to come up with an excuse Sam would buy.

Will winked at her. "He's right. Can't beat Meg's cookies."

Again Bree's heart jerked into overdrive, only this time it had nothing to do with the zip line and her son's safety. It was the safety of her traitorous heart she questioned now.

"Well . . ." Bree delayed.

Rick swooped into the clearing, was brought to a stop by his father, and jumped down. Ben began unhooking the ropes the boys had been riding down on and gathered them up in one hand. "Just to be sure there are no unauthorized rides," he said, holding them up for her to see. "Last one to the house has to put this stuff away."

All three boys took off for the house, but it was clear Evan was going to lose. Will caught up to him, scooped him up under one arm, and chased after the older two boys.

"It's really not that dangerous," Ben told Bree as they turned to follow. "We not only cut down anything they could get caught on or run into, but we lined the run with hay in case they lost their grip and dropped off."

"But Evan's only five. He's too little," Bree protested. "They're all too little."

"Doesn't matter how young they are. Boys think they're indestructible, and you can't stop them from trying things out. Probably things girls would never think of." Ben laughed. "But if we help them learn how to make smarter decisions about what's possible and what's not and teach them about safety, then we can at least avoid some of the trips to the emergency room."

Ben sounded so reasonable. His argument made too much sense.

"I'm sorry if we scared you." Ben reached out to touch her arm. "You okay, now?"

Bree nodded reluctantly.

They arrived at the start of the brick path and turned the corner. Will and all three boys were sitting on the top step as they approached the porch.

Rick pointed at the gear Ben was carrying. "You're last one here, Dad. You get to put the stuff away."

Will winked at Bree. Her insides jumped again. Sam might be safe around Will, but she definitely was not.

Somewhere over cookies and coffee, Meg had talked Bree into joining the fishing expedition at the beach. She had insisted on driving her own car and told herself this was a family outing, but still, the anticipation of an afternoon with Will had her heart hammering with pleasure.

When she and Sam pulled into the little beach lot, Ben's truck and Will's Jeep were already there, and Rick was hopping up and down and waving furiously. Before she could say anything, Sam was out the door and hurrying over to his friend. All three boys took off for the anchor and began climbing on it.

"Off the anchor," Will called as he grabbed a couple fishing poles from the back of his Jeep and hurried after them.

Bree grabbed the tote with her and Sam's towels and jackets, but in her hurry to lock the car and keep up with the boys, she dropped the keys in the sand and had to dig for them. By the time she looked up again, the boys and Will were out of sight, and Ben was just disappearing through the dunes. Meg was still collecting old blankets and a picnic hamper from the rear of the truck.

"Here." Bree reached for the hamper. "I'll carry that."

"Thanks." Meg sighed with relief. "Normally, the twins would have hauled all this stuff, but Ben hasn't been fishing in forever, and Will was just trying to keep up with the boys."

"Probably because I lit into him yesterday about the zip line."

"You lit into Will? Why?" Meg stopped walking and looked over at Bree.

"I about had a heart attack when I saw Sam flying through the air like a kamikaze pilot headed for destruction. I didn't know Will was going to catch him, and I yelled at Will before I had a chance to calm down."

"That must have been a first." Meg chuckled as she passed the old anchor marking the path to the beach. "Will's used to women throwing themselves at him. Considering he's unattached and a hunk besides. And then there's the uniform thing."

"It's the uniform that *worries* me," Bree retorted without thinking.

"Which one? The scout leader or the trooper?"

Bree hesitated. She should have kept her mouth shut. She didn't know Meg all that well, and voicing her fears out loud made her sound a little paranoid. But Meg had been through her own sort of hell. If anyone understood fear, it would have to be a Marine who'd served in a war zone. "The trooper."

As they emerged out of the dunes onto the beach, the sound of the surf grew louder. The twins were already setting up the surf casting gear, and the boys were exploring farther down the beach. Instinct urged Bree to call out to Sam, to encourage him to stay closer and not wander, but for once, she didn't. Meg dumped her armload on the sand and began spreading out an old quilt to sit on. Bree spread a second blanket out and pinned it down with the hamper and her tote. Then she joined Meg on the quilt.

"The North Carolina State Troopers are known for immaculately pressed uniforms," Meg said, picking up the conversation. "Makes them pretty impressive. And then there's always something appealing about a man in uniform, anyway."

"No denying that." It was the man inside the uniform that worried Bree. Will was way too appealing for her peace of mind.

"And that worries you?" Meg persisted.

"Sam is in love with Will," Bree began, ignoring her own growing attraction. "At least he's in love with everything Will stands for. All I hear these days is Will this and Will that. Last night it was all about the zip line, which I take it was Will's idea."

"Well, Ben bought into it pretty fast. They went off first thing yesterday and came home with a truckload of hay, but I didn't ask what they were up to. Like I said yesterday, I was trying to clean, and so long as they kept the boys busy and out of the house, I wasn't asking any questions. Do you know how hard it is to get anything done with two boys running around undoing everything?"

Sam wasn't like that. At least he never had been before. "Maybe it's because there are two of them," Bree suggested. "Sam's always been pretty quiet." Ben's comment about boys thinking they were invincible had haunted Bree's dreams. Sam was growing up, and she couldn't guard his environment forever, but did it have to be so soon?

The boys were out of sight now, heightening Bree's alarm. She got to her feet to peer down the beach.

"Don't worry. They can't go far," Meg said with unconcerned calm. "The inlet's just around the corner, and when they get to the end of the dunes, they'll turn around and come back."

That was the sort of thing Bree worried about. Water with a swift current. What if Sam or one of the other boys decided to go wading and got caught in the rip? "Maybe I should go check on them."

"They'll be fine."

Reluctantly Bree dropped back onto the quilt. "How do you do it? Let them go off and not worry?"

Meg didn't answer right off. She gazed out at the ocean with one hand curved protectively about her belly. "I was gone a lot when they were smaller, even before I got sent overseas. Ben was in charge. Nothing bad ever happened, so I guess I just trusted that Ben knew what he was doing."

She looked back at Bree. "But maybe I'd be a worrier too, if I'd lost my husband the way you did, and my boys were all I had."

"If anything ever happened to Sam —" Bree broke off and shook her head to dispel the image.

"Boys are different from girls," Meg said. "I've got a friend who's got one of each. She says they're just wired different right from the start."

"That explains Sam's fascination with his toy soldiers. And the fact that when he plays with his little cars they are always crashing." As a child Bree had inherited a whole case of little cars from her male cousin, and she'd loved playing with them, but her games had always included little neighborhoods and sedate drives between one place and another. Sam preferred to create mayhem and orchestrate crashes.

"Tell me about it." Meg laughed, then rubbed her belly again. "I'm so looking forward to having girls this time. Even two at once."

"When are you due?"

"Six weeks, but I'm ready now. I feel like the Goodyear blimp."

Bree breathed a sigh of relief when Sam appeared, dragging a stick in the sand. The relief was short-lived when he dropped the stick and began running directly toward Will, who was by now thigh-deep in the water. Waves broke around him, ignored, as he reeled in the line, his rod bent hard under the weight of whatever he'd caught.

Bree jumped to her feet, but before she could call out to her son, Will had turned, noticed Sam, and barked a warning. Sam skidded to an immediate halt and watched while Will finished reeling in his catch.

By now Rick and Evan had joined Sam. All three boys plopped down on the damp sand to remove their sneakers and socks. Ben returned to shore and spoke to the boys. They scrambled to their feet and followed Ben up the hard-packed stretch of sand to the pile of fishing gear and a cooler filled with ice just waiting for their catch. Will joined them, a good sized fish wriggling on the end of his line.

Even without being able to hear the conversation, Bree could see the admiration in Sam's stance. Will removed the hook and dropped his fish into the cooler. While Ben assisted his boys, Will showed Sam how to bait a rod of his own. He pointed at Sam's feet, and Sam bent to roll up his trousers.

"Stay out of the water," Bree called out.

"Don't worry." Meg reached over to pat Bree's arm. "Will wouldn't let anything bad happen."

"He'll get his pants wet," Bree protested.

Meg shrugged. "Boys are always wet. I think it's a requirement."

Everything in Bree wanted to argue. The only thing that stopped her was the knowledge that Sam would be upset if she intervened. Wasn't this exactly the sort of thing she'd been thinking about when she'd had the idea of dating again so there might be a male influence in her son's life? Maybe it would have been different if Ed had been around to induct Sam into the world of men, but letting Sam be the kind of boy he was meant to be was harder than she'd ever imagined.

She kept her mouth shut when Sam waded out into the waves, first just ankle-deep, then up to his knees. But there was no stopping her heart from racing as the waves began to buffet his thighs. The only thing that allowed her to remain on the quilt with Meg was Will standing directly behind Sam. Will's long legs and sure footing provided a bulwark between Sam and the danger of being overrun by breaking waves as he guided Sam's hands on the rod, teaching him how to cast.

Sam's first efforts only made it about six feet into the surf. Bree could see her son getting frustrated, but Will was patient, and his patience rubbed off. Sam tried again and caught his hook in the fabric of Will's shirt. Will calmly removed the hook, and they started over. Finally the line sailed out beyond the first line of breaking waves.

By now, Ben and his boys had joined them. Rick had obviously done this before. He had his own rod and was expertly casting the bait well out into the sea. Evan was learning just like Sam, but with less success. It had to be hard being almost three years younger and trying to keep up, but Evan didn't seem bothered by it. He just seemed happy to be one of the boys.

"This is what Sam's been missing." Bree sighed, then realized she'd verbalized the thought.

Meg looked like she was going to say something but didn't.

"I hope Will doesn't mind."

This time Meg did respond. "He's loving it."

Suddenly Sam was jumping around. Hopping on first one foot and then the other, excitement in every movement.

Will grabbed for the pole, closing his hands over Sam's. Then he showed Sam how to reel the line in. The bend in Sam's pole was small by comparison, but Sam still had to work at it. His effort was rewarded when a slender silvery fish emerged from the water. He whipped around, looking to Will for approval, then turned to hurry toward the quilt where Bree waited.

"Look what I caught, Mom!" He dipped the pole toward her, and the little fish wriggled in front of her nose.

Carefully, Bree took the line between her thumb and forefinger and held the fish away from her face. "Good job, Sam. Your first try, and you got a fish. I'm proud of you."

"Mr. Cameron helped." Sam glanced back to where Will stood watching them. "Mr. Cameron's the best. Right, Mom?" Without waiting for an answer, Sam turned and trotted back to Will.

"Right," Bree agreed under her breath. *But best for whom?*

CHAPTER 10

"Sam asked Will to sit with us at the Blue and Gold Banquet," Bree told Zoe as they sat talking in Zoe's living room while the baby nursed.

"You make that sound like a bad thing." Zoe removed Molly from her breast and laid her against her shoulder, then started patting her back.

"I just feel a little uncomfortable about it. Will is Sam's den father, but he's also den father to seven other boys. He shouldn't be playing favorites."

"He has to sit somewhere," Zoe argued reasonably. "And it's not like he has his own kids. Besides, won't it be a lot nicer to have someone else at your table that you already know? Relax and enjoy the company."

"Will gave Sam a ring, too. A silver Cub Scout ring that Sam says was Will's when he was a Cub Scout. I don't know what to do about it."

"What do you mean, what to do about it?" Zoe frowned.

"It's like an heirloom or something. Shouldn't he keep it for his own son some day?"

"I'd say that's up to Will. If he didn't want Sam to have it, he wouldn't have given it to him."

"But —" Bree broke off, remembering the look of pride and happiness in her son's face when he'd shown her Will's gift. Sam was learning to care about the man too much. "I'm afraid Sam's getting too attached."

"I think it's a good thing for Sam to have a man take an interest in him. Ed's been gone a long time, Bree. Almost half Sam's life. Maybe it's time he got attached to a strong male role model," Zoe suggested. "Even if *you* aren't ready to get serious with anyone yet."

"But why Will?"

"Why not Will? He's a good man. Good with kids. And he's willing."

Molly produced the burp her mother was looking for. Meg offered the infant her other breast, then looked up and asked the question again. "Why not Will?"

"Because the more Sam gets attached the more it's going to hurt when Will marries and starts his own family or just moves on up the food chain with the Highway Patrol and gets stationed somewhere else."

"Why are you so certain Will's interest in Sam will end?"

"Why shouldn't it? There's no connection between them other than scouts."

"You've lived in Tide's Way longer than I have, so maybe you've already heard this from somewhere, but if you haven't, let me fill you in. Did you know that Meg never knew who her daddy was?"

Bree shrugged. "I guess I just figured her father was the same as C.J. and Stu's."

"Nope. C.J. and Stu's father was killed shortly after Stu was born. Mary Ellen started drinking and hanging out at that dump of a bar on seventeen. She brought so many men home, I don't think even Mary Ellen was ever sure who Meg's biological daddy was. But when Meg was around five or so, Mary Ellen hooked up with a really decent man, a cop from Wilmington. They lived together for three or four years, and Meg totally loved the guy. He was the daddy she never had, and he treated her just as if she was his daughter."

"What happened to him?" Bree had no idea where Zoe was going with this story, but she couldn't help being curious.

"Mary Ellen wouldn't stop drinking, and

eventually that killed the relationship, and Bobby moved out. But he didn't abandon Meg. He visited her and took her places every week. When he quit the police force and joined the Marines, even then, he stayed in touch. He called her, sent her cards, and never forgot her birthday. He was there for her graduation, and he gave her away at her wedding, too. So, just because things didn't work out with Meg's mother, he was still Meg's daddy in every way he could be.

"So, even if you and Will are never more than just friends, that doesn't mean Will would just move on and forget all about Sam. He's not that kind of guy."

"I still think Sam should give the ring back."

"Why, Bree? So Will can get his feelings hurt? And what about Sam? How is he going to feel if you make him give back a ring that obviously means something special to him? Part of the reason it means that much is because he likes and admires the man who gave it to him. Maybe to you it seems like something Will should save for his own son, if he ever has one, but apparently Will felt like it was more important to give it to Sam."

"I never thought about it like that."

"Besides, the way I hear it, Will is pretty taken with you, too." Zoe wagged her finely arched red brows.

"He's no such thing."

Zoe grinned. "Why do you think he moved into your apartment building?"

"Because he needed somewhere to move into until he figures out where he's going next, and there just happened to be a vacant unit for rent upstairs."

"*Beep!* Wrong answer. There are lots of better places he could have chosen. Places a lot more convenient for a trooper with a motorcycle and a trailer, not to mention all his toys."

"His toys?" Bree asked, refusing to think too deeply about the implications of her friend's suggestion that the only reason Will moved into her building was because he was interested in her.

"His surfboards, his fishing gear, his kite-boarding stuff, his parachutes. Those kinds of toys. He's big into all that kind of thing."

The list took Bree's breath away. All that many more reasons not to get involved with Will. Anyone who jumped out of airplanes was crazy. Will was just as wrong for her as Bob had turned out to be but for totally different reasons.

"Will told Ben about the new apartment

right after getting reacquainted with you. Ben kidded him about moving there just because you lived there, and Will didn't deny it."

"Because of me?" Bree echoed faintly. A tumult of emotions raced through her. Excitement and dismay were neck and neck, followed closely by alarm. "Surely Will must have a girlfriend. Any guy that sexy can't be unattached."

Zoe snickered. "I'm glad to see your senses aren't completely dead. I have to admit, I was beginning to worry about Bob. About you getting involved with him seriously, I mean."

"Bob and I are over."

"Good. He was all wrong for you."

"He was safe."

"Safe is overrated," Zoe retorted.

"You wouldn't think so if you were me."

"Molly's father would have been safe. Safe and rich. But I'm glad I sent him packing. What if I'd taken safe and missed the chance of being married to Jake?"

"That's different."

"How different? Are you saying this just because Will is a trooper and carries a gun?"

"He lives a dangerous lifestyle. He's — he's —" Bree searched for words to explain her distress. "He's like this bigger-than-life hero. Just like Ed. I don't think I could bear that all over again."

"Life doesn't come with guarantees, Bree." Molly let go of Zoe's nipple with a soft pop, and her head lolled. "You want to hold her?" Zoe asked, offering the sleeping baby to Bree.

Bree took the infant and cradled the bundle of warm baby and blankets in her arms. Molly smiled in her sleep, trusting and adorable.

"Jake could fall off the scaffolding at work," Zoe said, interrupting Bree's happy baby thoughts. "He could get trapped fighting a fire. For that matter, he could get run off the road coming home from work. I'd be heartbroken, but I wouldn't give up loving him or being loved by him just to avoid the possibility of being hurt."

"But I've already been there. I don't want to go there again. I don't think I could live through it a second time."

"Will is not Ed, Bree. For one thing, Will wouldn't be deployed more than he's home. He may seem like an overgrown kid some of the time, but deep down, he's a good man. He's been hurt before, too. You're not the only one who's lived through a broken heart."

"Oh?" Bree's curiosity overcame her

reluctance to know anything personal about the man she was trying not to care about.

"Will was engaged before. For a couple years, according to Jake, but Linda would never set a date."

"What happened?"

Zoe shook her head. "Will got home from work one day, and Linda was gone. No note. No explanation. Just his ring sitting in the middle of his dresser. A couple months later Will got an email from a mutual friend who thought Will would want to know that Linda had married an airline pilot and moved to London. If you want to know what I think, I think she must have been cheating on Will even before she left him, and he's better off without her, except he's never gotten serious about a woman since."

"He's not serious about me, either. He can't be," Bree argued. "We barely know each other, and we haven't even been out on a date."

The memory of Will leaving scones and a get-well note beside her bed came back to tease her. Followed by the memory of a highly charged moment on the day of the Pinewood Derby races. A moment filled with emotions Bree hadn't dared to think about too closely. But even Bob had noticed and commented on it, and that had precipitated the end of her involvement with him. Clearly, she'd been leading Will on somehow, but it had to stop. Maybe Bob was right when he called her a tease.

Before they parted an hour later on Zoe's front porch, Zoe grabbed Bree's arm. "Don't rule Will out, Bree. At least give him a chance."

I've taken all the chances I want to take in life. The argument hovered on the tip of Bree's tongue, but she didn't say it. "I'll think about it."

"Good." Zoe kissed her on the cheek and added, "At least don't spoil things for Sam just because you're afraid to get hurt. He needs a man in his life, and for now at least, that man seems to be Will."

Because Will was a den leader, they arrived early for the Blue and Gold Banquet. Bree hung back, feeling out of place as Will joined the other leaders and began setting up tables. Sam and two other Cub Scouts were tasked with unfolding the chairs and setting them around the tables.

"Hi! I'm Katie Mann. You're with Will Cameron, right?" A slender, dark-haired woman held her hand out. "Come on over and meet the crew. You can help put the tablecloths on." Katie didn't wait for Bree's answer as she turned away.

Bree wasn't sure how she would have answered anyway. She and Sam had come with Will, but she wasn't *with* Will. Not like they were an item or anything.

"Hey, ladies, this is —" Katie broke off and turned to Bree. "Brianna Reagan. Right?"

"Just Bree." Bree stuck her hand out and had a pile of tablecloths plopped onto it. Then a teenage girl who looked a lot like Katie Mann placed two rolls of crepe paper on the pile.

In less time than Bree would have guessed, the church hall was transformed into a banquet hall with blue and yellow stripes down the center of each table. While the women lit the Sterno cans under the hot dishes and began setting out rolls, salads, and desserts, the men and boys disappeared behind the curtain on the stage at the end of the hall.

Sam had been gleefully secretive about what would be happening once the banquet was over, but as Bree listened to the low rumble of men's voices and the excited chatter of the scouts, she smiled. Considering she'd been instrumental in pulling together Sam's costume, she was pretty sure what the upcoming skits would be about. It would still be fun to see Sam perform, though.

More scouts began arriving and disappearing behind the curtain while their families began staking out places at the tables. Bree looked for a likely spot for herself, Sam, and Will but didn't know if they wanted her to save seats or if they'd prefer to choose for themselves. Then Meg and Ben breezed in with their boys.

"You're here early," Meg said. She glanced down at her younger son, who was yanking on her jersey. "No, Evan, you can't go with Rick. Go help Daddy find a table with enough seats for all of us." Meg patted his butt, and he scurried off. "Sorry. He so wants to be a scout, and he's feeling left out."

"Well, I was feeling a little left out too, so I can sympathize. I was helping with the tablecloths, but —"

"And no one introduced themselves?"

"Katie Mann did."

"Katie's a busy lady, but she's really nice. She runs the day care here in town. The place Zoe takes Molly to."

Before Bree could comment, Sam appeared. "You are going to be so surprised." Then he made a gesture of zipping his lips. "Where are we sitting?"

"Find Evan, you'll find our table," Meg told him.

A moment later they were all jockeying for seats. Bree had planned on having Sam sit between her and Will. But by the time she figured out which seven seats Ben had claimed, the only chair left was between Will and a man she didn't know.

"Come on. I won't bite," Will said as he pulled out her chair for her.

Bree slipped into the proffered chair and settled her purse on the floor by her feet. Will's arm lingered along the back of the chair as if staking a claim.

"You can save me from" — he leaned close to whisper in Bree's ear — "the man-eating dragon."

"Save you from — ?" The subtly seductive scent of Will's cologne made her forget what she was asking. Cedar and leather and God only knew what else. It flirted with her pulses and made her want to be even closer to the source.

Will lifted his chin in the direction of a woman in a clingy electric blue dress who was clicking noisily between the tables on four-inch heels.

"She eats dragons?" Bree whispered back.

"Only men. She's the dragon. She had a thing for Ben while Meg was away, but Ben managed to stay clear of her. Now she's got her sights set on me. At least some of the time. She's not an exclusive sort of woman."

Bree studied the woman as she prowled through the group. She'd seen her before but couldn't recall where. With that mane of reddish-blond hair paired with emerald green eyes and a figure any woman would die for, Bree would have thought her a nice catch for any bachelor.

"And you're not interested?" How could he not be?

Will shook his head. "I've known her since high school. She's a looker, I won't deny that, but she's a siren, and she destroys men. Even married ones. She's got a nephew in my den. I suspect that's what brought her here tonight, but she'd use any excuse to corner me if she could. So —" He let his arm drop from the back of Bree's chair onto her shoulders and drew her against his side. He swooped in and gave her a brief kiss. "I'm counting on you to protect me."

Bree's lips tingled, and her heart raced. She could barely catch her breath. Then he winked.

And who is going to protect me from you?

CHAPTER 11

When Zoe arrived at Bree's apartment for the historical society committee meeting, she suggested they move it out to the picnic tables behind the building. The unusually warm streak of days lingered, so it would be a shame to waste even one of them inside. Bree's balcony wasn't big enough to accommodate more than a couple people, so Bree agreed. She texted the two men to let them know she and Zoe would be out back.

Bob arrived with Tony and a box of donuts. They came around the corner, Tony kicking through the scattering of magnolia leaves like a kid, Bob with confident strides that said he had no time to waste playing.

Not knowing how Bob was going to behave since their strained conversation the day of the Pinewood Derby, Bree held her breath as the men approached the picnic table under the magnolia tree. To her relief, Bob acted as if there had never been anything between them beyond their commitment to the restoration of the Jolee Plantation.

Zoe poured them both a tall glass of sweet tea while Tony spread out the sketches he'd made up.

"I thought we were all going to go over to the Jolee Plantation and take a lot of photos before we started making plans," Bree said, feeling like the men had deliberately left the women out of it.

Tony looked up abashed. "Oops. Sorry. I thought you two were going to interview Emmy Lou Davis and get all the ghost stories collected while we did the reconnaissance."

"Emmy Lou's been out of town visiting her niece in Colorado, so we haven't been able to talk to her yet," Zoe said.

"Did you take photos?" Bree asked.

"A few." Bob slipped his phone out of his pants pocket, brought up his photo album, and offered it to Bree.

Bree scrolled through the pictures. There were only a dozen photos. None of the derelict slave quarters. Only two of the front of the main house and one each of the other out buildings. *You'd think he was paying for film and processing!* She handed the phone to Zoe.

When Zoe was done, Tony took the phone and scrolled to a photo of the big barn, which he held out for the two women to see. "This building is probably not worth saving." He scrolled again. "Or these, but . . ." This time he reviewed all the photos a couple times before frowning and handing the phone back to Bob. "How come you didn't take any of the slave quarters?"

Bob shrugged. "They all looked like ruins to me. Just partial walls, no roofs, no windows, or anything."

"There were never any windows," Tony said. "And the roofs can be rebuilt once we shore up the walls." He pushed the drawings toward the women and began explaining what he thought could or should be done.

Remembering that she was supposed to be taking notes, Bree got busy with the notebook and pen she'd brought down with her. The more Tony outlined of his plan, the more exciting the project became. Bree scribbled faster to keep up.

Once they all agreed on the proposed renovations, the topic of fund-raising got under way. Thankfully, that was not Bree's job. The last thing she ever wanted to do was go begging for money. It would be hard enough begging for people to do the work. It would probably take at least a year to raise enough capital to even get started.

Zoe reported that Jake was willing to take on some of the actual construction part of the project in his free time, and he thought some of his men would be willing to put in some hours as well. But he was not an expert in old historic buildings, and he wanted to consult someone who was before he did anything. So there would be a consulting fee to raise along with the costs of supplies, permits, and bringing the place up to code with the electric, plumbing, and handicap accessibility.

By the time the meeting adjourned, Bree had several pages of notes and made a promise to visit Emmy Lou and record all the stories she knew about the property. Zoe volunteered to create a Facebook page for the project and start a blog to report progress for those who made donations and wanted to stay in the know. Tony accepted the mantle of chief beggar, and Bob was to assist. Until they had the funds, nothing else was really needed.

After the men left, Zoe gathered her belongings and got ready to leave. "You need help with getting any of that stuff back upstairs?" She nodded at the tea and donuts.

Bree hugged her friend. "I think I'll just stay out here for a while longer. Don't worry about this stuff. I can manage."

With one last hug, Zoe headed toward her car. Bree returned to her notes and began adding comments in the margins. She could type them up on the computer later, but if she didn't jot her ideas down now, she'd forget half of them.

Emmy Lou wasn't due home for another week, but in the meantime, there was no reason she couldn't go over to the Jolee property and take a look around for herself and take *lots* of photos. Zoe could use some for the blog and for posting to Facebook. Besides, the few Bob had taken were just not enough.

"Mom! What are you doing down there?"

Bree looked up to see her son hanging over the railing of their little balcony. Sam was home from scouts sooner than she had expected.

"I'll be right up."

Quickly, she gathered up her notes, the box of donuts, and the pitcher of tea. Then she had to juggle the glasses, which promptly flew out of her hands and scattered across the lawn.

"Let me." Will's deep voice shot a jolt of pleasure through Bree. Where had he come from?

Quickly Will gathered up the rest of the glasses and held his hand out to take the pitcher from her as well.

"You want these?" Bree shoved the box of uneaten donuts toward him instead. "Cops like donuts, right?"

"That's the rumor," Will chuckled as he accepted the box.

She headed for the back entrance to the apartment building, but Will beat her to it and had the code punched in and the door open for her. As she passed by him, that faint but intoxicating combination of cedar, leather, and musk caught her unprepared and stirred her pulses just as it had the night of the banquet. If Anne Royko was a siren, this man was the male equivalent. She crossed the rear lobby to the elevator.

Will was ahead of her again and pushed the button to summon the elevator. Once inside, Bree leaned against the rear wall in the far corner while Will stood, legs spread in the center of the car. The sight of all that alpha male confidence did a number on her senses. It made her want things she hadn't yearned for since Ed died. And the power of that yearning scared her.

It's just lust, and it's just because it's been too long. Get your mind out of the gutter. Bree stared at the red numbers above the elevator door, willing the number two to appear. Seemed like this car moved slower every day.

When they stepped out of the elevator, Sam was grinning broadly from the open door of their apartment. "Mom!" He hurried toward her. "Can I go to the beach with Mr. Cameron tomorrow? Please? I really want to go. Rick's going too. Please, Mom?"

Bree looked from her son's pleading face to Will. "Are you sure?"

Before Will could respond, Sam plopped something made of brown paper on top of the notebook in her hands. "Look, Mom. We made these in scouts today. We tried to fly them in the parking lot, but there wasn't enough wind. That's why we want to go to the beach tomorrow. Mr. Cameron says kites fly really good on the beach 'cause there's always wind."

"Don't you have better things to do with your weekend than spend all of it with kids?" Surely the man had at least a dozen activities he'd rather be doing. According to Zoe he liked kiteboarding. A far cry from flying paper kites.

"I like kids."

Zoe's comment that Will was often accused of being an overgrown kid hovered in Bree's mind. Last weekend it was the zip line. Now kites at the beach? What next?

"Actually, we're killing two birds with one stone. Ben wants to take a couple of his service dog trainees and give them a workout in paying attention to business in spite of distractions. So, the boys get to fly kites while the dogs learn how to do their job even when there are more interesting things going on around them. Mom and Dad invited us to have lunch at their place, so we probably won't get back until just before dinnertime."

"Rick says his grampa built a fort we can play in, too." Sam hopped eagerly from one foot to the other, awaiting her reply.

Bree hesitated. Letting her son go to the beach without her to keep an eye on him was not in her nature. But he'd been safe with Will while fishing, and letting him go would free up her afternoon to go take those photos she wanted. An entire afternoon to poke about the old Jolee ruins, taking all the photos she wanted without Sam fretting to do something more interesting was tempting.

"Are you sure?" she repeated her earlier question.

Will smiled, his dimple creasing his tanned face, making him look absurdly boyish and at the same time devastatingly masculine. It made Bree's insides quiver with the same heady anticipation everything else about him did.

Heaven help me.

"What was that?" Will's eyebrows rose toward his hairline.

Good grief. Had she really said that aloud?

Both Sam and Will watched her with almost identical expressions of entreaty.

"Okay, you can go," she addressed her son. "But you need to listen to Mr. Cameron and do everything he says. When he says it, not when you get around to it."

Sam hugged her hard. "Can I call Rick and tell him?"

Bree nodded, and Sam disappeared into the apartment.

"What time are you planning to go?" Bree asked Will over her shoulder as she followed her son.

"After church. Tomorrow will be Rick's first Sunday serving on the altar, but it's the ten thirty mass so right after that." Will set the stack of glasses and pitcher of sweet tea on the counter.

"By the way. I've been meaning to ask you something." He turned to face her. "Mr.

Cameron seems like a mouthful all the time. Once a week at den meetings it's not so bad but . . ." He trailed off, looking a little uncomfortable.

"Don't they call you Mr. Cameron at work?" Bree had reacted to *Mrs. Reagan* with the thought that people were referring to her mother-in-law for several years before she got comfortable with the formality, but it didn't seem like it would be the same for men. They were Mister whoever all their lives.

One side of Will's expressive mouth drew up in a half-smile. "Not so much. Troop, Trooper, or Cameron mostly. Everywhere else I'm just Will. If it's okay with you, I'd feel comfortable having Sam call me that, too."

Bree shrugged. "I guess. I mean, so long as he doesn't get disrespectful. Or Uncle Will, maybe? I know you're not really an uncle, but some kind of honorific would seem —"

"I think just Will would be better. I had a chat with Sam the day he went to help clean out my old apartment. He wanted to learn sign language so he would be able to talk to Molly when she gets old enough. It's one of the electives in their scout book, so I suggested maybe Rick could learn it too since he was Molly's cousin. Sam got upset with the idea."

"But Rick is his best friend," Bree broke in.

"Sam told me you and Zoe told him that Zoe is his special aunt on account of your friendship, so he's decided that Molly is his special cousin. I didn't know if Sam had any real cousins or not, but he seemed pretty upset that Rick might cut in on something he wanted to have all to himself with Molly."

"I didn't know . . ." The idea that Sam felt left out was new to Bree. Sam had never said anything to her. But he'd felt comfortable enough to tell Will? A niggling jealousy tugged at her heart. Of course Will had been Sam's den father for months now. Maybe it was normal for that level of confidence to develop between guys even separated by a generation in age.

"I don't think even Sam realized how he felt. It was just the way he reacted to my suggestion. Anyway, if he called me Uncle Will, it would be the same as Rick. I think he'd be happier if it was just Will."

And the rapidly growing dependency would be that much stronger, leaving Sam even more unprepared when Will moved on. But Bree couldn't think of a way to say that without insulting Will or hurting his feelings.

"You can think about it if you want," Will offered as he moved toward the door.

"I don't need to think. But if he gets too casual and stops being properly respectful —"

"I don't see that happening. You've done a tremendous job raising him. He's the nicest scout in the den. Don't tell Ben or Meg I said that though. I'll deny it completely." Will grinned.

"I've been meaning to thank you," Bree said, laying a hand on Will's forearm when he would have opened her front door to leave. The warmth of his skin under her fingers made the gesture seem suddenly too forward. Too personal. She took her hand away. "I meant to say something at the banquet, but I got sidetracked."

"For what? I haven't done anything yet."

"For the ring you gave Sam. I'm surprised you didn't save it for — for —" Bree floundered. Will wasn't married. Wasn't even dating anyone or engaged so far as she knew. Maybe he planned to be an unattached bachelor all his life.

The teasing grin slipped off Will's face and was replaced with one far more serious than Bree had seen on him before. "I found it when I was hunting for something else. I was surprised I still had it. But right away I thought of Sam, and I wanted him to have it. My godfather gave it to me. He was a special person in my life, and I treasured the ring because it was his when he was little. I hoped Sam would too."

Bree suddenly felt like crying but wasn't sure why. She stared at the buttons on Will's shirt, then found the courage to look up into Will's kind blue gaze. "Sam thinks you're pretty special, and he treasures the ring. Probably more than you know. Thank you."

"My pleasure," Will mumbled, looking touched. He turned the handle and opened her front door. "See you after church? Or do you want to ride to church with me?"

Sam came bounding back into the living room. "Rick says we're going to help his dad train two of the dogs."

Will squatted down to Sam's height. "I know you know the Cub Scout motto, but do you remember what the Boy Scout motto is?"

"Yeah! It's 'Be Prepared,' " Sam replied eagerly.

"Good. So tomorrow you need to be prepared, so we can get going as soon as we get home from church. You need to remember a warm sweatshirt or a jacket, and don't forget a hat. And maybe an extra pair of sneakers and socks in case you get your feet wet." Will looked up at Bree. "Sometimes there are puddles in the fort when it's been raining like yesterday." He looked back to Sam. "And what else will you need to have ready to go?"

"My kite?"

"Anything else?"

Sam frowned, trying to guess what Will wanted him to remember.

"Water. We always take drinking water with us. Right?"

Sam smiled. "Right."

"List everything again?" Will prompted.

"Water." Sam started holding up fingers. "A jacket, a hat, extra shoes and socks and . . . and my kite," he finished with a big smile.

Will stood.

"See you after church," Bree said before Will could offer a ride to church a second time.

"See you tomorrow, sport." Will saluted Sam and went out.

Sport and Will. Sam was going to be so hurt when Will eventually moved on. Unless Zoe was right about Will hanging in for the long haul.

■ ■ ■ ■

The sun felt hot out of the breeze, so Bree removed the windbreaker she'd put on for her afternoon photography session and tossed it back into the car.

She'd been to the Jolee Plantation before. But not since the historical society had met there shortly after the property had been turned over to the town. This was the first time she'd been here all by herself, feeling free to explore everything at her own speed, and she was eager to get going.

The drive up to the main house was long and straight and lined with huge magnolia trees. They were certainly old but not as old as the plantation itself. Bree snapped several photos of the long tunnel the trees made. In another month they would all be in blossom. She'd have to come back and take more pictures then.

When she reached the end of the magnolia tunnel the drive forked into a loop that surrounded a horribly overgrown mess that must once have been a lush green lawn punctuated by raised gardens. Bree crossed the gravel drive and strode into the tangle of tall grass and wildflowers. In the first raised garden she came to, roses fought for space with the wild growth. They were loaded with buds, and they too would blossom soon.

She took another twenty or so shots of the tumbled fieldstone walls and struggling roses, then moved on toward the house itself, stopping every few feet for another angle of the house. It was a grand place, with a wide veranda that ran around all three sides that she could see. Attached under a rotting breezeway was a summer kitchen to the left. A matching breezeway arced around on the right to another smaller building. There was no chimney, and Bree couldn't guess what it might have been.

The drive widened directly in front of the house, and a spur ran off down the gentle slope toward the ruined barn Bob had taken photos of. Bree took photos of all the buildings in sight, then stepped up onto the veranda and crossed it to peer into the long windows.

All the furnishings had been removed years earlier, leaving only pale patches to mark where carpets had once been. The fireplaces were enormous, tall enough in one of the rooms that Bree thought she could probably stand up inside. The front hall was vast with a curving staircase to the second floor. Bree rubbed a circle in the dirt coating the window with the tail of her shirt. *What a glorious place this must have been.*

She tried the door, but a new lock had been installed, and it held firm. So, she followed the veranda around to the right, then remembered it actually went entirely around the building. At every new window she paused and checked to see what she could see from this new vantage point. A ladies' sitting room, perhaps? Smaller than the main parlor.

The library was obvious by its tall bookshelves that lined two walls. One window opened toward the unidentified outbuilding, and the other overlooked another tangle of overgrown grass and weeds. Stewart Road cut through the expanse, and beyond that the Stewart River flowed, its surface glittering in the afternoon sun.

Taking a moment to enjoy the view, she sat down on the edge of the veranda and dangled her legs over the side. If she squinted, she could see the ocean off to her left. That's where Will would be, helping Sam to fly his kite. Maybe Zoe had been right about Sam needing a man in his life. Her warning not to mess things up for Sam just because his mother wasn't ready for a relationship had irked at the time. But Zoe had been right about that too.

Bree sighed. If only the attraction she felt for the man wasn't so hard to ignore. She didn't want to fall head over heels in love again. She didn't want to be that vulnerable. But there was no pretending the feelings Will's presence aroused didn't affect her. His smile made her heart jump, and his touch did a whole lot more. His thoughtfulness messed with her mind even more than the physical desire.

She scrambled to her feet. Thinking about Will had totally distracted her from her mission. She had things to do.

Bree hurried toward the next long window. This was obviously the dining room considering the massive chandelier that hung over the space a table would have occupied. A doorway led into what appeared to be a pantry where dishes and cutlery might have been stored. A rear staircase led off the hall at the back of the house as well, and another new lock had been installed on the door that opened out to the river side of the mansion.

Next time she'd be sure to ask for the keys so she could tour the inside.

Bree stepped off the veranda and strode toward the presumed kitchen. That building was not locked. She pushed the door open with difficulty. The hinges needed oiling. The only window no longer had any glass in it, and the place was littered with an odd collection of rubbish. In lieu of a flashlight, Bree dug her cell phone out of her pocket and turned on the flash app. A huge pile of two-liter bottles filled one corner. She started to pick one up to inspect the remaining contents, then thought better of it without gloves to protect herself from bacteria. What looked like used coffee filters were scattered around, some on the stone ledge that ran along one side, more on the floor.

Bree had a bad feeling about the refuse but didn't know why. Maybe it was the odd smell. She backed hastily out of the old kitchen and headed back across the veranda and down on the other side. Nothing about that building gave her a clue to its possible use. There were no windows and only a row of shelves across one end. They seemed too far apart and too deep for storage of food. Besides, that would have made no sense with the kitchen all the way on the other side. A totally different stench made this room unpleasant. It smelled as if animals had once lived there. Perhaps wild ones still did?

As she returned to the daylight, long

shadows creeping across the grass caught her attention. How had it gotten so late? She hadn't even checked the slave quarters yet. For a moment, she stood torn by indecision. Will and Sam might return home at any moment, but she really wanted to check out the rest of the outbuildings. She turned toward the area she knew the quarters had been in.

They were pretty much as Bob had described them, just remnants of the wooden walls with no roofs. The bricks did surprise her. Somehow the idea of bare dirt floors was what she'd had in mind, but the crumbling brick foundations made that seem unlikely. There must have been wooden floors. She shot several more photos before the creepy sensation of being watched hit her.

She whipped around, but no one was there. Slowly, she turned in a full circle, squinting into the lengthening shadows. Nothing moved, but the hair on the back of her neck still twitched.

"There's no one here," she told herself sternly. But the feeling didn't go away.

Briskly she hurried back to the gravel drive and retraced her steps down the long drive to where she'd left her car. By the time she reached it, she was running. Embarrassed even though there was no one to see her hasty retreat, she unlocked her car and dropped into the seat. She sat there, trying to catch her breath and assure herself she'd been entirely alone the whole afternoon.

CHAPTER 12

"You went where?" Alarm bells went off in Will's head.

"I went up to the Jolee Plantation to take pictures." Enthusiasm filled Bree's eyes, and he could hear the excitement in her voice. "We're going to restore it and turn it into a showplace that all of Tide's Way can be proud of."

"You have no idea who or what you might run into up there. It's not safe." A chill hitched its way up his spine.

"The place is run down and abandoned with a lot of trash around, but I don't see what's so bad about me going up there. The ghosts can't hurt me, if there really are ghosts there."

"It's not ghosts I'm worried about." Will's anxiety ratcheted up another notch. "What kind of trash?"

"Just some old soda bottles and coffee filters. I thought it was kind of odd, but —"

"Old soda bottles and coffee filters are dangerous."

Bree's eyebrows rose in incredulity. Some of her eagerness faded as if he'd crushed her pet project.

"I'm serious. That kind of trash is typical of shake and bake labs and they are very dangerous. So are the kind of people who create them."

"But, the place is deserted. Why would anyone go there anyway?"

"To cook meth!" His voice took on a warning edge in spite of his efforts to remain cool.

Bree stared at him, clearly not comprehending the danger she could have been in. "Meth?"

"Don't ever go there again." He sounded like an overbearing trooper, but he couldn't stop that either.

"What do you mean, don't go there again? I have to go there again. Probably a lot of times. It will take months to get the place ready to open to the public."

Will struggled to stay calm. This restoration plan was a pet project. And she was clearly very excited about it. But she needed to understand his caution.

"You can't go up there until the place has been checked out. Do you have any idea how hazardous that stuff is?" he snapped. He never snapped. But the lethal mix of his fear and her incomprehension overrode his usual composure.

"I think you're overreacting a little."

"I'm not overreacting, I assure you," he shot back. He loved extreme sports and took his chances in places most people wouldn't, but messing with a shake and bake site was not one of them.

Bree had her hands on her hips. A sure sign a woman was going to dig in her heels and refuse to be reasonable. "I thought you were my friend, Will, but if all you're going to do is growl at me, this conversation is over."

"I'm sorry." Will gritted his teeth and willed his frustration back under control. "But please, on this you gotta trust me. Meth is one thing you do not want to mess with. Let me get the SBI team down there tomorrow. The State Bureau of Investigation has the equipment and expertise to deal with illegal meth labs. They can go over the place inch by inch."

They'd already done so just a few weeks back, but they'd just have to do it again. If Bree had seen telltale signs up there, then the criminals had returned. Or new ones had found the place. Either way . . .

Bree still had her hands on her hips, but the mutinous glare was fading.

"Promise me," he insisted.

She dropped her hands to her sides. "I don't have to promise you anything. You know that, right?"

"I know, but I'm still going to worry until I know if it's safe for you to be poking around the place." He wished he did have the right, but he didn't. Not unless the place was taped off and everyone excluded. Then he could enforce it because of who he was.

"Okay. I promise."

Relief flooded over him like a warm shower. "Thank you." The tension left his shoulders. "I'm sorry I got upset. I was just concerned you didn't take the danger seriously. I can tell this restoration is something you're really into. And it's a good thing. Once we get the place cleaned up." He glanced at his watch. There might still be time to call someone tonight. "I guess I should be going."

Bree opened the door and held it for him. Some of the warmth was back in her eyes again. He wanted to kiss her, but decided that would be a bad idea. "I'll let you know what they find." He stepped into the hall.

"Good night, Will. And thanks. For everything. For taking Sam out to the beach and promising him a bike ride next week." She chewed her lip and offered him a smile. "And for the warning."

"Good night, yourself."

She looked up at him then, her head tipped toward the doorjamb, and he couldn't help himself. He kissed her. It was brief, but the bolt of sensation hit him like a freight train. Rather than see withdrawal in her eyes, he turned and left.

Bree closed the door slowly as the shock of Will's kiss, chaste though it was, coursed through her. It had been fleeting and gentle, but the feelings it generated were neither. Had he lingered, she would have let him. She would have returned the kiss, too. Being around him stirred things in her she didn't want stirred. He was a friend. At least, most of the time. When he wasn't in his bossy cop mode. Or angry.

She had never seen Will angry before. Not even mildly irritated. He always seemed so together and cool, but then, she'd never seen him in a stressful situation either. Tonight had been an eye-opener. His reaction to her afternoon adventure unnerved her.

Almost as much as the feeling of being watched had. She hadn't told Will about that though. Sure that it was a figment of her imagination, she didn't even want to admit to turning tail and dashing to her car as if something had been chasing her. If she *had* told him about it, he would have been even more upset. But would it have been because he was a cop, and it was his job to worry about people? Or because he cared about her?

His signals had been rather mixed. One moment he was warning her to stay away from the Jolee Plantation like she was an errant child, yet a moment later he'd apologized and ended by kissing her before disappearing down the hall.

She didn't want him to care about her in particular. She wasn't going to get involved with him. At least that's what she kept telling herself. It was safer to think he'd reacted in cop mode. His job description included the words *to protect and serve.* So, he knew more about this meth stuff than she did, and it clearly worried him.

Scared him, more like. But until now she hadn't thought anything would scare Will. She went to her desk and woke up her laptop. She typed *meth labs* into the search bar. A long list of articles appeared. She read through several of them. It wasn't as if she didn't know that methamphetamine was a dangerous and illegal drug, but she hadn't realized how dangerous the making of it was.

Next she typed in *shake and bake.* Will had used that term. A list of recipes appeared, mostly involving chicken and a different spelling, but halfway down the list was an article entitled, "New Shake and Bake Meth Method Explodes." Bree clicked on it.

Wow! Apparently Will had not overreacted. Instead, she'd overreacted when she got huffy with him for trying to warn her. It didn't matter why he was worried about her. He'd known what he was talking about, and his exasperation with her had been justified.

She'd have to report this to the committee. Once the police had dealt with it, they could go forward with their plans, but until then, they'd have to be patient. She hadn't read about any of this in the local paper. How many other people knew? Fund-raising would be next to impossible if folks knew the place was overrun with criminals and meth addicts.

She retrieved her camera and connected it to her computer, then began downloading the photos. She scanned through them, remembering bits and pieces of her afternoon and the thoughts that had occurred to her as she explored. Grabbing her notebook, she started taking notes so she wouldn't forget everything. When she was done, she shut her laptop and sat back. Her thoughts returned to Will.

He was right about meth being dangerous, but the memory of him with his blue eyes blazing worried her. That was not the man she'd begun to trust with her son's welfare. Justified or not, he'd been a little out of control.

Perhaps she should rethink the bike ride he'd suggested taking Rick and Sam on the following weekend. Really, she didn't know what to think. Or whom to ask. If she talked to Meg, she might not get a straight answer even though Meg had known Will for years. Zoe had already told her not to mess things up for Sam.

Bree had to admit Sam had blossomed in the months since he'd known Will. Her son was more confident, for one thing. Not that he'd been shy or timid before, but lately he'd shown a lot more maturity. He'd begun volunteering for things, both in scouts and in school. He was more willing to try new things and less worried about failing. Which could all be attributed to growing up, but it seemed unlikely the change would have been so noticeable in so short a time if that were all it was. And the only new thing going on in his life was Will.

Sam had been soaked but exultant the day Will taught him how to surf fish. Even though the fish was too small to keep, Sam insisted Bree take his picture with it before he set it free. He'd loved the zip line, of course. And now that she had gained some sense about it, she could see why he loved it. Suddenly the sheltered life she'd provided for him up to now seemed too guarded.

Letting him grow up was only going to get more difficult and probably a lot scarier the older he got. Bree sighed. If only Sam could be her baby forever. But he couldn't. If Will could help Sam develop confidence in a way she couldn't, did she have the right to deny him that?

Of course she had the right. She was his mother. But should she?

Bree got up and headed down the hall. One thing she most definitely was still in charge of was a reasonable bedtime.

Sam's light was off. That was a surprise. He wasn't asleep though.

"I was waiting for you to say good night to me," he explained as she sat down on the edge of his bed.

"Did you brush your teeth?"

"Yup."

"And your backpack is ready for tomorrow with your homework in it and everything?"

Sam nodded. "And I even remembered the permission slip for little league."

She bent and kissed Sam on the forehead. "You are growing up too fast. Next thing I know, you'll be remembering to take a shower without being reminded."

"Oh! I took that too. When you were arguing with Will."

"I wasn't arguing with Will."

"Don't you like Will?"

"Of course, I like Will." Obviously they'd had a discussion about what Sam could call him. "I just did something he didn't think I should be doing. And it turns out he was right, and I was wrong."

"But you're not still mad at him?"

"No, I'm not still mad at him."

"Is he mad at you?"

"He's not mad at me anymore either." *He kissed me good night.*

"Good." Sam rolled over and snuggled down under his covers. On Sam's finger, where it gripped the quilt, Will's ring glinted in the dim light. "Night, Mom. Love you."

Bree settled the blankets more securely about Sam's shoulders. She tousled his hair and touched the silvery face of the ring.

"Love you, too, Sam."

She stepped out into the hall and leaned against the wall. Suddenly, it seemed like her life had shifted into the fast lane. Sam was growing up by leaps and bounds. The comfortable years she and her son had shared since she'd stopped grieving for Ed were slipping away, and the life she'd built for the two of them wasn't big enough for Sam anymore. Considering her reaction to Will's brief kiss, maybe their secure little world was growing too small for her, too.

Telling herself she was not interested in anything more than friendship with the man wasn't working. But getting involved was risky. Letting herself care might only end up with her getting hurt again. She touched her cheek where Will's lips had left their invisible but undeniable mark.

I'm not going to fall in love with the man. I don't care what Zoe says. Or even Ed.

Will sat on his deck, looking out over the swimming pools and tennis courts, thinking about the way Bree had appeared standing in her doorway looking up at him. All the stubbornness had gone out of her, and that beautiful smile of hers lit up her whole face. All the way to her eyes. She had such expressive eyes. Whiskey-colored eyes that had glimmered with the light from the hallway and set his pulse racing. The provocative floral scent she wore enveloped him as soon as be bent to kiss her cheek, and it had taken all his willpower not to move that extra inch and capture her mouth instead.

It was meant to be a kiss of apology and friendship, and he'd damn near turned it into a declaration of passion and possession. They hadn't even been out on a date yet. Unless you counted the fishing expedition to the beach with his brother's family. And why hadn't he invited her out yet?

He'd never been this hesitant about asking any other woman he'd taken an interest in out on a date. Sure, she frequently referred to their friendship, but so had other women before her. Some of them really were friends and nothing more. Some had been angling for a whole lot more. Bree didn't seem like either type, but he had a hard time reading her.

One minute they'd be laughing together over something that amused them both, then she'd touch him without thinking, only to yank her hand back as if he'd burned her.

He was slipping. They'd known each other for over a month now. A month since he'd moved into this building. Maybe it was time to step up to the plate and take a swing.

Can't get to first base until you get up to bat.

Perhaps he should accept that strange vibe that said *I'm not interested* and move on. Except he was already in too deep. The way his heart had shuddered to a near halt when she'd told him where she'd been this afternoon and what she'd seen there made that pretty clear. She was more than a pretty face and a sexy body. She was interesting and spunky, and he was already halfway in love with her.

When she'd softened tonight, perhaps he should have asked her out instead of kissing her.

Bruce wandered out onto the deck, rubbed himself against Will's leg, and jumped up onto his lap. Will patted him, grinning at the way Bruce arched his back, pressing into Will's hand with each stroke. Like a woman when you make love to her. The thought of Bree arching into his touch flitted into his head, and he gave himself up to imagining how she would look. Her blond hair spilling over the sheets. Those enticing whiskey-colored eyes hot with passion. Her voice husky with desire as she said his name.

It took only that image to arouse every need that had been growing in him for weeks. He was abruptly hard and aching.

"Ouch!" Will jumped to his feet, dumping the cat out of his lap. The cat should be declawed. *Or I need a cold shower.*

Bruce dashed back into the apartment and sat, studiously ignoring Will when he followed the cat inside. "Sorry, Bruce." Will scratched the top of the cat's head, but Bruce continued to ignore him and had begun to groom himself with undivided concentration.

"I'll ask her out the next time I see her," he told the unconcerned cat. "Maybe she'll surprise me."

CHAPTER 13

At the sound of footsteps stopping in her office doorway, Bree looked up. Will stood there immaculately clad in his trooper's uniform but looking a lot less sure of himself than the last time she'd seen him wearing it. Or even the last time she'd seen him period.

Surprise didn't begin to describe the emotions running through her. To start with, he was the last person she expected to show up in her office. She hadn't returned to the Jolee Plantation nor broken any laws that she knew of. There was no official reason for him to be here.

Which left personal. She hadn't forgotten her reaction to his kiss or the thoughts that had run rampant through her head as he'd turned away and headed down the hall.

"Hi. What brings you here?"

"May I come in?"

"Of course." She gestured to the chair in

front of her desk.

He stepped into the office but did not sit down. He seemed to fill the office, and her heart began to thump a little harder.

"I came to ask if you'd like to go out for dinner. And a movie maybe." He fidgeted with the strap of the helmet he carried but didn't take his gaze off hers.

Her heart roared into overdrive. Every effort to avoid giving him the wrong impression had failed. But the worst part was that she wanted to say yes in spite of herself. She swallowed hard, took a deep breath, and smiled. Or at least she tried to smile.

"I don't think —"

"Don't think. Just say yes."

His eyes were bluer than she'd ever seen them and more intense.

"But I'm not interested in dating."

"You were dating Bob when I first met you," he argued reasonably.

"That was different." Bob had not been a threat to her equilibrium or her good sense.

Will's gaze became even more intense, if that was possible. "Is it me you're not interested in dating or just dating in general?"

"You," Bree blurted without meaning to. "I mean —" She swallowed again. "That didn't come out the way I meant it."

Now his hands were completely still as he gripped the strap of his helmet. He took a step closer and lowered himself into the chair she'd offered before. "Then how did you mean it?"

"I meant we're friends. A date seems so . . ." So what? So not something friends did? Or something dangerous to go on with this particular man?

"Then it'll just be a friendly date. Friends go out to eat all the time. They go to movies too."

He smiled, and his dimple appeared. It was his beguiling, boyish look. *Does he do that on purpose, or is he just clueless about what it does to a woman? To me?*

"We can even go dutch if it makes you feel any safer."

"Safer?" Safer than what? Who paid for the meal or the movie was the last of her worries.

"More like friends."

Bree hesitated. Part of her wanted desperately to say yes. The other half was just as desperately afraid that yes was the last thing she should say.

"Is Friday good?" Will got to his feet. "Meg says Sam can stay over." He backed toward the door. He was back to juggling the helmet. "I'll pick you up at six. You can choose the movie."

Before Bree could gather her wits, Will touched his fingers to his lips and blew the imaginary kiss her way. He turned and disappeared toward the hotel lobby, his motorcycle boots clicking confidently across the ceramic tiled floor.

Sam went home from school with Rick, which left Bree a whole hour after work to get ready for her non-date with Will. She showered but then couldn't decide what to wear. The first thing she took off the hanger was too — seductive. Not the sort of dress she would have worn to eat with Zoe, therefore, not the sort of dress she should wear out to eat with Will. She stripped it off over her head and tossed it on the bed.

She tried a pair of slacks and a lacy top with her favorite blazer and flats next. She studied herself in the mirror. She looked like she was going to work. She pulled the slacks off and replaced them with a dressy pair of jeans. Okay. That was better. Now for the jewelry.

A knock sounded at her door, and she glanced at the clock. Two minutes to six. Where had her hour gone? Her heart beat in a crazy staccato rhythm as she hurried to the front door. She paused for a moment, trying to quell the breathless feeling of anticipation, and opened the door.

Her greeting caught in her throat. Will looked incredibly handsome in khaki slacks and a blue pullover sweater. The color of the sweater made his eyes look bluer than ever, and the soft cashmere wool made her want to run her hands over his chest. Pulling herself together, she gestured for him to come in. "You look — you look really nice."

Will's gaze returned the compliment. "You took the words out of my mouth." He stepped into her living room, and the teasing scent of cedar and leather he favored swamped what remained of her senses.

"I'll just be a minute." She dashed back into her bedroom and grabbed the first pair of earrings she came to and the necklace Ed had given her when Sam was born. The one that depicted a mother and child. It was her favorite, even if the chain was a bit long and it hung a little too low. She braced her hands on the edge of her dresser and closed her eyes.

This is just a friendly dinner. Not a date. It's not *a date.*

She had to collect her wits and her purse and go back out there. She hadn't even offered him a seat. In another minute he'd be calling out to see if she was all right.

One last look in the mirror. One last reminder that this was not a date. She turned to go.

Dinner was a lot more easygoing than Bree expected. Except for the dangerous lifestyle Will led, they had more in common than they differed on. They had similar tastes in literature, and they talked about recently read books for most of the meal. Although politics and religion were usually not good choices for friendly conversation, they agreed on both, so those had been touched on too.

Will let her run on about the latest committee meeting for the plantation restoration and even offered a few ideas of his own that she thought were pretty good. Then they talked about Sam.

"I try not to have favorites," Will said as he stabbed the last piece of his steak. "But out of eight kids in the den, Sam is . . ." Will bit his lip as if trying to decide how to finish his comment. "Sam is special."

"Well, I certainly think so, but then, I'm his mom. I'm supposed to think that."

"He's pretty mature for his age, I think. I'm not an expert. I'm not even a parent. But when I compare him to the rest of the group, he's got an edge. Maybe it comes of being the man of the family. I don't know. But he thinks about others a lot more than the rest of the scouts. He takes more responsibility. You've done a remarkable job raising him."

Will's words of praise filled Bree with warmth. "Thank you."

"I mean it. My brother — my brothers are pretty hands-on kinds of dads anyway, but they've both had to do more than most fathers. Ben when Meg was deployed and Jake after his wife walked out on them. So, I have an idea just how hard it must be. And I wanted to tell you what a terrific job I think you're doing."

Bree looked down at her plate to hide the tears that suddenly filled her eyes. She finished the last of her dinner while trying to marshal a reply and banish the tears. It was hard being a single parent. It was especially hard when things didn't go smoothly and extra burdens like money and problems at work cropped up. Those were the times she'd wished for a shoulder to lean on, for someone else to share the worry and the work. But the last place she'd have looked for understanding was a bachelor like Will.

"I hope you don't resent me." Will's soft comment surprised her.

Her gaze flew up to meet his. "Why would I resent you?"

"For sticking my nose into your business. For getting involved with Sam outside of scouts. He's a remarkable kid, but it just seemed like he needed a little extra . . . something."

He needs a man in his life. "I'm glad he has you butting into his life. He's been — he's blossomed. You've given him —" Bree floundered for the right words. She didn't want Will to think she expected the extra attention to be permanent. Just to let him know she'd noticed the changes in her son and appreciated Will's part in making them happen. "You've given him guy things to talk about. Even if I don't always show my appreciation, I do value it. Things like the zip line and the fishing. And especially your Cub Scout ring."

Will winked. "I could teach you to fish, too, if you want."

The waiter arrived to remove their plates, saving Bree from having to respond. Which was a good thing since the first image that popped into her head was of them standing thigh-deep in water with Will's body braced behind hers, his arms about her as he helped her learn how to cast. Given the current crazy ideas that took over her brain when Will was around, such a scene would not have been about fishing for very long. *Please, God, don't let me look as flustered as I feel.*

Will said no to coffee or dessert, and the waiter hurried away to prepare the bill.

"I think he's glad to get rid of us finally. Maybe he still has time to get a turnover on our table."

Bree glanced at her wrist and remembered she wasn't wearing her watch. "What time is it?"

"We've been here over two hours."

Two hours! Where had the time gone?

The waiter returned, but instead of splitting the bill as he'd promised, Will slipped the man several bills and got to his feet. "Ready to go see what's playing?"

"You said we were going dutch," Bree said as she buckled herself into Will's Jeep.

"Next time you can buy me dinner." He started the engine, grinned at her across the dark interior, and backed out of the parking space.

Next time? What next time? She started to voice her protest when a pickup truck swerved around the corner and nearly rammed the passenger side door as it swooped into the newly vacated space. If it hadn't been for Will's skillful driving, her next stop might have been the emergency room instead of the theater.

"Aren't you going to say anything to him?" she pulled herself together to ask.

Will didn't respond until he'd reached the end of the lot and stopped to wait for the light. "Are you okay?"

"I'm shaking a little, but I'm okay. No thanks to that idiot. Can't you do something about drivers like that?"

"It's private property for one thing. He didn't hit us, and I'm off duty. If I got out to give the jackass a piece of my mind, it would just escalate into a nasty confrontation and accomplish nothing."

For the rest of the short drive to the theater, Bree didn't say anything as she contemplated the seeming contradiction that was Will. In nearly everything else he seemed the typical alpha male, competitive, arrogant, and a take-charge kind of guy. Okay, maybe only a little arrogant. But he'd let the other driver get away with his dangerous antics. Will was a lot more complicated than she'd given him credit for.

At the theater, they studied the options. The only Hallmark-type drama was a romance, and the last thing Bree wanted to watch was two people falling in love. But she didn't want to sit through the film that featured soldiers any more than she wanted to see the cop flick, both of which she figured were probably more Will's style. They settled on the only comedy showing.

When Will stepped up to the window to purchase the tickets, Bree was prepared. She shoved a twenty across the counter before he could stop her.

"Can I at least buy the popcorn?" Will tweaked one eyebrow higher than the other.

She patted her stomach and shook her head. "I'm stuffed."

"A soda then?"

She shook her head again and reached for the tickets and her change.

"Then let's go." He put a hand to the small of her back and directed her toward the theater entrances.

She hurried ahead, afraid to let his hand linger too long, seeping warmth and desire into her that she didn't want to feel. The comedy was a popular choice, and it took a while before they spotted two empty seats at the end of a row about halfway down.

"Better than right up front where I'd get a crick in my neck," Will muttered as they inched their way past more than a dozen pairs of knees.

"Or up back where the teenagers are exploring each other's tonsils even before the lights go down." She dropped into the first seat while Will stepped past her and took the seat on the end.

Will chuckled. "Are you telling me you never did that?"

Did I actually say that about teenagers French kissing aloud? "Never did what?" she said, pretending not to understand his question.

"Go to the movies so you could sit in the back row and make out."

The hot flush surging up her neck couldn't have been more embarrassing. The fortunate timing of the lights being dimmed hid her flaming cheeks.

"You're never too old, you know," Will whispered into her ear with a suggestive snort. He was too close, and his proximity was doing odd things to her breathing again.

"Will Cameron!" She tried to sound shocked, but suddenly laughter boiled up inside her and ruined the effect.

Thank God he was only kidding. At least they weren't in the back row, so she didn't have to put that theory to the test.

"I like your laugh. You should do it more often."

The laughter died as quickly as it had come. There was something in Will's voice that touched her.

As the trailers ended and the movie got underway, Will reached over the arm of the chair and took her hand in his. He dragged it back into his own lap as he bent close. "It's okay if we hold hands. I have it on the best authority that friends always hold hands."

Bree had never held hands in a theater with Zoe or any of her other girlfriends. But in spite of that thought, she didn't pull away. She liked the feel of his big warm hand enclosing hers, and except for this one liberty, he'd behaved just as a friend should so far. Mostly.

Just for tonight, she would enjoy this feeling of being pampered and cared for. It had been a long time since anyone had made her feel that way. Maybe friends could hold hands.

Two days later it was Bree's night to have Ben and Meg's boys over while they had a night out. Will had taken the boys on the promised bike hike, brought them back to Bree's apartment, and stayed for dinner.

"You really wore them out today," Bree commented, returning to the kitchen after she saw to it the boys took baths and were tucked in for the night.

She stopped short upon discovering that

the kitchen had been tidied up completely in her absence. The table had been cleared and the dishes done. She peeked in the fridge and found the remains of the pizza Will had ordered wrapped in foil and stacked neatly next to a six-pack of beer that had not been there earlier. She shut the fridge and turned toward the living room.

Will stood with his back to her, studying her collection of CDs. One of the six-pack sat on her coffee table on a coaster normally kept in a drawer in the kitchen, and the Scrabble board had been set up next to it.

"Did we agree to a game of Scrabble?"

Will turned. In addition to cleaning up her kitchen, he'd obviously made time to run up to his own apartment and take a shower. Instead of dirty cargo pants and sweat-stained T-shirt, he now wore jeans and a neatly pressed chambray shirt with the sleeves rolled up. Everything the man wore made him look good. Too good. She had always been drawn to a man in a tailored shirt, especially with the sleeves rolled up to reveal strongly muscled forearms coated with a masculine forest of pale curling hair.

"You said you liked to play Scrabble," Will reminded her. "At the restaurant."

They had talked about so many things over supper. She'd forgotten about his boast that he could beat her.

"So, I'm challenging you. Loser has to pay a forfeit." He grinned at her with a mischievous glimmer in his bright blue eyes. "Winner gets to pick the forfeit."

Bree might be afraid of a lot of things, but losing a game of Scrabble was not one of them. "You're on."

"Any preferences on music?" Will held up a CD. "Or can I assume you like them all since you bought them?"

"Something . . ." Anything that wasn't soft and dreamy. Will made her feel too soft and dreamy without adding music to the mix. She crossed the room to read the label on the CD in his hand. "The Dreamer" by Khay Jhay. Just what she didn't need. The lethal combination of Will and "The Dreamer" would take down her defenses faster than a SWAT team.

Doing her best to ignore the intense attraction of his fresh, clean scent and the crisply pressed shirt, she reached past him and took a musical sound track off the shelf. "After the day I had, that guy would put me to sleep. I need to be on top of my game if I want to pick the forfeit."

"Maybe he'd put me to sleep even quicker. Like the boys."

Will's slow smile tugged at her insides.

She had the most insane urge to reach out and touch that dimple that punctuated his right cheek. She slapped the musical into his hand and backed away.

Rather than sit on the couch and take the chance that Will would join her, she chose the chair opposite and began digging in the Scrabble bag for her tiles.

Will played a tough game. Not what she'd expected from a cop. Even a college educated one. But with less than a dozen tiles left to play, she was leading and beginning to wonder what she could possibly ask for as a penalty that Will wouldn't turn into something provocative.

Will placed his remaining five letters on the board, covering both the triple word and a triple letter squares. *Gripy.* "Sixty points. I think that makes it my game."

"That's not a real word," Bree scoffed. She began to remove his tiles.

"Sure it is. Look it up." Will put his hand on hers. The electric tingle shot from his fingertips to her heart in milliseconds. For a long moment neither of them spoke while their eyes seemed to be eloquent with so much that wasn't being said. Bree slid her hand out from under Will's.

"Why did you do that?"

"Do what?" Bree's breathing made speaking almost impossible. She reached for the dictionary and tried to ignore the way her body betrayed her intentions.

Will took the dictionary and set it aside. "Are you afraid of me?"

Bree shook her head. She was more afraid of herself.

"Then why do you pull back into your shell like a turtle every time I touch you?"

"We're friends. I treasure that. I'd like to stay friends." And his touch made her feel things that were a long way beyond just friendly.

Will hesitated, obviously debating his response. "Friends can be lovers too."

"No. They can't. Someone always gets —" She stood up and moved away from the table.

Will got to his feet as well but didn't try to close the physical gap she'd created between them. "Someone always gets what?" His voice was calm. His blue eyes probed, but they were gentle too.

"Hurt," Bree whispered. "Someone always gets hurt."

"I don't want to hurt you. Don't you know that yet?"

"But something could happen that you have no control over. If I let myself care too much, I could get hurt even if you didn't mean it." Bree fought the rising tide of confusion, alarm, and desire.

"Is that what all this has been about? You're afraid to fall in love again because of what happened to your husband?"

Bree clenched her hands to keep from reaching out to him.

"Is that why you were seeing Bob when we first met? Because you didn't really care about him enough to be hurt by anything he did? Or was it because you thought he would be safe to be with?"

Bree didn't reply. How could she? What could she say that wouldn't offend Will or confirm the disgraceful way she'd treated Bob?

Will did take a step in her direction then. She squared her shoulders and stood her ground.

"And I'm a trooper, so that makes me off limits."

He loomed over her now. All six feet plus of him. His blue eyes were no longer gentle as they bored into hers. He raked his fingers through his blond hair and left it standing on end. Somehow that softened him. Tears abruptly swamped Bree's eyes. She blinked furiously, trying to make them go away.

He cupped her cheek in his palm and ran his thumb across her lips. "Hasn't anyone ever told you to live every day as if there were no tomorrow?"

Having no tomorrow is what I'm afraid of. "Like dance as if no one is watching?" She tried for a lightness she didn't feel. She'd seen that on Facebook the other day. Then she remembered it had been followed by *Love as if you've never been hurt.*

"Has it ever occurred to you, it might be me that gets hurt? I — care about you. About both of you. It would hurt a lot if something happened to you or to Sam."

Bree leaned toward him, stricken by his admission.

"I'm more afraid of what my life will be like if it has to go back to where it was before I met you than you could even guess. We could be so good together, Bree."

He swept her into his arms, pulled her so firmly against him, she couldn't have gotten free if she'd tried. But at the moment, she wasn't trying. This time when he kissed her, there was nothing fleeting about it. Nothing that could be misinterpreted as just friends.

It was not brutal as Bob's kiss had been when he had been angry and upset with her. Will's kiss claimed her just as clearly, but with so much tenderness that it burrowed deep into Bree's heart. He didn't try to force her lips apart, but she felt the yearning desire in him and opened of her own free will.

The kiss became a hot, fiery spiral after that. She clutched at his shoulders for support while his hands pressed her closer. Bree gave up thinking then and let herself be overwhelmed by the sensations of Will's mouth on hers and his body coming to life, touching hers in ways she hadn't experienced in years.

It was Will who pulled back first. His eyes were closed and his jaw taut, his breathing as labored as hers. He dropped his arms and stepped away.

Passion still lurked in his eyes. "Think about it, Bree. Think about how good we could be for each other. If only you can stop being afraid."

He stepped around her and walked to the door. He let himself out and closed it soundlessly behind him.

Bree just folded up until she knelt on the floor. Her heart continued to pound, and her ears rang as if someone had pealed a very large bell right next to her head.

"I care about you, too," she whispered, but Will was no longer there to hear.

Chapter 14

Will planned to claim a kiss if he'd won the Scrabble game, but he hadn't meant it to be anything like what he'd ended up laying on her. He was trying to be patient and earn Bree's trust first. To be the friend she wanted him to be, at least for now. The game of Scrabble had been fun. They'd been arguing over his final word, but it had been in jest. When he'd covered her hand with his, something happened between them. Something that felt good. Something that felt like a step forward, an acknowledgement of shared feelings, maybe.

She'd pulled away from him, spoiling the moment, and the resulting conversation had him nearly declaring himself. But the moment she'd swayed toward him, he'd lost it. Things had gotten a little crazier than he'd intended.

If her dazed expression reflected what she'd felt inside, she had been as stunned as he'd been. But God only knew if her reasons were the same as his. He'd been overwhelmed with desire like nothing he'd ever experienced, and it had taken all the willpower he possessed to step away from her. Perhaps she'd felt the same flaming passion. On the other hand, maybe it had been fear overwhelming her and not desire. But he had to give her a chance to think before things got totally out of hand, otherwise it would not be fair to her.

Right from the beginning, he sensed her reluctance to get involved with him, but he'd chalked that up to Bob and whatever claim he had on her. But Bob was apparently out of the picture, and she still held Will at arm's length, as if trying to protect herself from him.

Logically he understood her reticence. He'd been to too many funerals, seen too many widows devastated by their loss. Both military and police.

But Bree was still a young woman. She had a whole life ahead of her, and he wanted to be a part of it.

That last revelation had ambushed him without warning. At the start, Bree was just a very attractive woman who appeared in his life at a time when he'd been looking for something new. Or someone new. That she had a son Will had already grown fond of just made her that much more appealing.

He'd never dated a woman who already had a child, and if anyone had asked him, he'd have said having a kid would be a downside. It would mean passing up things unencumbered couples could do, like taking impromptu weekend trips together or making love in the middle of the living room floor. But motherhood just added to Bree's allure. Besides being so pretty, she took his breath away each time he saw her, and she was smart, sassy, and enthusiastic about the things that interested her. But there was something different about Bree when he saw her with her son. Softness and unconditional acceptance maybe. Maybe he just didn't have the words to explain it even in his own head. But it was there, and it was very attractive.

Somewhere between that first crazy weekend when he'd moved into her building and now, he'd lost his heart to her. And to Sam. Everything he said last night and a lot more he hadn't said was true. He'd been in lust with Linda. Bree had taken over his whole heart. She occupied his thoughts from the moment he awoke until he fell asleep again.

He'd begun to worry that joining the Rapid Response Team the State Highway

Patrol was forming would take him away from Tide's Way and Bree. Even worse than physical distance, if she thought his current job was dangerous, she'd never accept a man with a job that required SWAT gear and assault rifles.

For sale signs on houses in town had begun to draw his attention, too. The whole idea of giving up his freedom and settling down to the life of a husband and father seemed a lot more appealing now than it would have two months ago. For a man who'd considered skydiving on the weekend the perfect reward for working hard the rest of the days, he'd sure changed. It was a wonder he even recognized himself in the mirror anymore.

Will took the stairs three at a time and strode down the hall toward Bree's apartment, praying he hadn't blown his chances with her completely. At her door, he hesitated, then knocked.

When she opened the door, she smiled as if she was really happy to see him, and some of the tension in him eased.

"I came to report in on the Jolee Plantation like I promised."

She opened the door wider and gestured for him to come in.

"Hey, Will!" Sam jumped up from the

table where he'd apparently been doing homework. "Look what I learned." He hurried over to Will and quickly ran through the American Sign alphabet. "Pretty good, huh?"

"That's excellent, sport." Will ruffled Sam's dark hair. "Pretty soon you'll be so fluent you could pass the whole test."

"Did you finish your homework?" Bree asked.

"Almost." Sam hurried back to the table and sat down.

"Can I get you anything?" Bree headed toward the kitchen. "We just finished supper."

Will followed her. "I ate at Ben's, but coffee would be nice." He leaned his butt against the counter, watching while she poured a cup from a nearly full carafe and stuck it in the microwave. She bustled about with her back to him.

"About last night —"

Bree froze, but since she was facing the other way, he couldn't see her expression. The microwave beeped, and Bree removed the mug of coffee and set it on the counter.

"I owe you an apology."

She whirled around, her eyes wide, her expression troubled.

"Just to be clear. I meant everything I

said. But I'm sorry for taking advantage. I promise it won't happen again. Not unless you start it." *Of course, I've got every intention of making sure you do start things. Sooner rather than later.*

Bree glanced down at her hands. She swallowed hard, then looked back up at him. "It was partly my fault. I should have stopped you, and I didn't. But thanks for saying it anyway."

"There's something you said that I've been thinking about."

"Something I said?" she parroted, looking confused.

"You said you valued our friendship, and you didn't want to mess it up. Maybe those weren't the exact words you used but . . ." Will shoved his fingers through his hair. This apology thing was harder than he'd expected. "And you're right. Friends are important. I hope I didn't ruin it for us."

She shook her head. He felt inordinately relieved.

"So? We're good?" He stuck out his hand.

She hesitated for a moment, then slipped her hand into his. "We're good." She squeezed his fingers and let go.

Will reached past her, careful not to touch her, and retrieved his coffee.

"You want to sit in the living room?"

"Sure," he said and followed her out of the kitchen. He dropped onto the couch and set his mug on the coffee table. "So here's the deal. The SBI has gone over the Jolee place. They located the items you said you found and checked out all the rest of the buildings. They've recommended to the town that locks be installed on all the currently unsecured buildings for starters. The local sheriff's office is going to make regular sweeps of the grounds. And I'm going to add it to my agenda as well. Hopefully, we won't give anyone a chance to set up another meth lab up there. But —"

"How did I know there was going to be a *but*?" Bree frowned.

"Well, there really isn't a *but*. I was hoping I could convince you not to go there alone. I'm willing to go with you any time you need to go up there. Or get that committee you said you were on to go all together. There are guys on it, aren't there?"

Her eyebrows rose toward her hairline. "That's kind of chauvinistic, isn't it?"

She had him there. "You're right. I apologize." He shook his head. "Keep this up, I'll get good at swallowing my own words."

Bree smiled, and Will's heart lifted.

"You really do have the nicest smile, but I guess you already know that."

Bree shrugged as if his compliment didn't matter. It mattered to him, but he'd revealed too much last night. He wasn't about to repeat that mistake. At least not until she got past this out-sized insecurity of hers.

"So, will you ask me to go with you if you can't get the committee to go?"

"I'm done, Mom," Sam announced as he joined Will on the couch. "Can I play on the computer like you promised?"

"Please say excuse me before interrupting," Bree admonished her son.

Sam turned to Will. "I'm sorry. I didn't know you were still talking." Then back to his mother. "But can I, Mom?"

"I wasn't actually speaking when you got here," Will told Sam. "So you're forgiven." Will looked at Bree to see if she was going to relent.

Bree sighed. She closed her eyes for a minute, but Will couldn't decide if she was debating her verdict or frustrated with him for taking the wind out of her sails. "Yes," she said, opening her eyes again.

Sam bolted for his room and his computer.

"So, will you ask? If you need someone to go with you?"

Again, Bree sighed, but this time she didn't close her eyes or look as stern. "Okay.

I guess that's fair."

Relieved to get that mission accomplished, Will moved on to his next request. One he suspected he might run into more resistance on. "I've another favor to ask. Well, not exactly a favor. I just need your permission. And before you jump to conclusions, hear me out?"

Bree folded her hands in her lap and waited. Her expression seemed to be open at least. "What do you need my permission for?"

"Ben gave Rick a knife."

Bree's expression closed up slightly.

"The old man my parents befriended taught us all how to whittle. Ben still does it, like a hobby, and Rick wanted to learn how. So that's why Ben got him the knife. But I got to thinking about it. You remember I told you about Sam and the sign language when we talked about Sam calling me Will instead of Uncle Will?"

"Yeah," she said slowly as if suspicious of where Will was going with this line of discussion.

"Well, I thought that if Rick got a knife, and Ben was teaching him how to use it, Sam might feel left out. So, I wondered if it would be okay if *I* gave *Sam* a knife and taught him how to use it safely. I'd make sure he knows he needs to ask permission before getting it out, and before he even gets it, he'll have to know all the rules in the Boy Scout handbook on the safe use of a jackknife. It's not in the Cub Scout book, but he can borrow my scouting handbook to study." Will said everything fast, thinking she might not give him a chance to get it all out, but she hadn't interrupted or even seemed like she wanted to. "Well?"

Bree looked down at her hands, twisted them together, and flattened her fingers across her knees. Finally, she looked back up at Will. "I guess you already know I'm not eager about this, or you wouldn't have asked for my permission."

"I know, but I assure you —"

"The other night I was thinking about what it's been like for the last three years," she began, seeming to be completely off the subject. "About how Sam is growing up and maybe ready for things I never thought about. Being a girl is different than being a boy."

Will laughed suddenly. "You can say that again."

"I hope my trust won't be misplaced if I say yes. Because . . ." She swallowed and smiled, but there was a hint of sadness in her eyes. "Because I'm just getting around to accepting there are things Sam needs that I can't give him. He likes you. He admires you. So maybe, at least for now, you're someone he needs in his life."

This time when she paused, her eyes seemed suddenly swamped with unshed tears. Will wanted to pull her into his arms and chase away whatever was making her sad, but the logistics, with her on that damned chair and him on the couch separated by the coffee table, didn't allow an easy way to achieve it.

"If his dad were still alive . . ."

So that's what had brought the tears to her eyes.

"He would probably have taught Sam all kinds of things I'd never approve of." She made an effort to smile. "So, I guess" — she sighed — "it's okay. For the jackknife. And the lessons."

Giving will permission to teach her son how to use a jackknife had been a big concession. Ever since she'd done so, all manner of unhappy scenarios played out in her imagination. Sam cutting himself badly when no one was around. Sam deciding to take the knife to school, which would get him suspended. Sam and Rick thinking up things to do with their knives that neither

Ben nor Will taught them. But perhaps Ben and Will were already on top of that. They were boys once, too, and they probably knew better than she ever would the kinds of trouble boys could think up to get into.

In the week since Will had brought the idea up, Sam's excitement and enthusiasm had more or less confirmed Will's guess that Sam might feel a little envious of Rick. The fact that Sam was growing up and his world was expanding beyond her ability to keep pace was now just another thing to worry about.

Sam devoured the chapter on knives and other scouting tools with sharp blades in the book Will lent him. Only two days after he'd started, while Bree prepared dinner, Sam sat on a stool in the kitchen, reciting all the rules he'd learned and a lot more insight he'd figured out on his own. Including the prohibition on taking knives to school. Now it was just a matter of getting the knife and learning how to use it without any mayhem.

Bree was thinking about Will's idea and Sam's eager reaction as she turned into Carlisle Place and drove around the curving drive to her building. When she pulled into her usual parking spot, she noticed Will's motorcycle. At least she assumed it was his.

How many state troopers would be parking in front of her building? Will rarely brought his bike here. Why today?

Wondering about the reasons for Will's bike to be parked out front occupied her mind until she got to the apartment and found Sam's backpack dumped just inside the door. That's when she recalled that Will had met Sam's bus that afternoon instead of Sam getting off with Rick as he usually did on Wednesday afternoons.

"Sam? Will?" Maybe they were up at Will's apartment. She dropped her briefcase on the couch and headed to her bedroom to shuck her heels and slip into something more comfortable. On her way, she stopped at the deck door and slid it open to let in some fresh air.

Sam and Will were at the picnic table out back, heads bent over something she couldn't see. Bree stepped out onto the little deck. Will straddled the picnic table bench, one arm resting on the table and the other elbow on his knee as he watched Sam. With his legs dangling off the bench, Sam hunched low, and it took a moment before Bree realized he was wielding a shiny new pocket knife. One hand clutched a stick as he carefully shaved the bark off it.

As she watched, a wave of sadness flooded

into her. Ed should have been here for Sam. There were so many things Sam had missed that Ed would have provided. Guy things. Guy activities. And more than that — simple father-son companionship.

Sam laid the stick on the table and folded up his new knife, cautiously keeping his fingers clear of the blade. He looked up at Will for approval and must have gotten it because he beamed with pleasure. Then he threw his arms about Will's neck and hugged him.

CHAPTER 15

"Hey! Cameron!"

Will looked up from gassing up his bike to see his friend and fellow trooper Mateo Diaz standing on the curb outside the café attached to the gas station and convenience store. He wore civvies and a huge grin. Will waved as the nozzle clicked off.

"You have time for lunch and a cup of coffee? I've got some news you might want to hear."

"Always have time for coffee, but I just had a sub for lunch," Will answered as he claimed his receipt and climbed back onto his motorcycle. He released the brake and propelled the bike toward a parking space.

"I'll save you a stool." Diaz disappeared into the café.

A few moments later Will sat down at the counter next to Diaz. A steaming cup of coffee already awaited him along with a slice of pecan pie.

"Figured you could still find room for dessert," Diaz said as he gestured with his fork.

"What are you doing down this way?" Diaz normally patrolled north around Jacksonville.

"Came to see my new nephew."

"Well, tell your sister congratulations." Will took a bite of pie and followed it with a swallow of coffee.

"I will. Nick is so totally puffed up with pride it's a wonder he can button his shirt."

Diaz chuckled. "Just wait 'til he's been up floor walking a few nights."

"He'll survive. I'm told there's something kind of special about being up with a newborn in the middle of the night. It's dark and quiet, and it's just you and this miniature human being who trusts you totally. My brothers survived. Nick will too."

Will thought about Sam and the fact that his father had never been around to walk the floor much. Ed Reagan had missed a lot. Why he'd continued to sign up for more tours baffled Will. And in the end, he'd missed out on too much.

"Hey, Tina." Diaz hailed the waitress and signaled for a refill on the coffee.

Will held his cup out to the slender redhead. "Thanks. You didn't have to hustle down here quite that fast. My buddy here, he's always impatient." He turned to his friend. "So, what's the news you're so eager to impart?"

"I got a look at the short list. You're on it."

"The short list?" Will's mind went blank. What list?

"For the Rapid Response Team."

That list! The last time he'd thought about the new teams, he'd been dismayed to realize he wasn't so eager as he'd been when he first applied.

"You don't want to know how I know?"

"I figure you'll tell me."

"You didn't hear this from me, got it?"

Will nodded and took another bite of his pie.

"The captain called me into the office to ask about a case I'm on. He got called out for a few minutes. I wasn't snooping, I promise, but the list was right there in his in-basket. Couldn't miss it."

"You didn't have to read it," Will chided with a chuckle.

"I tell ya, it was right there. How could I *not* read it?"

"By minding your own business."

"What's got into you today? I thought you'd be pleased to know there are still eight slots left, and there were eight names on the list." Diaz turned to frown at him.

Pleased was not the emotion swirling through Will at the moment. Having his name on a list of men headed for SWAT training was probably not helpful while he was doing his best to change Bree's mind about troopers and the dangers they faced. He hadn't asked, but he suspected she wasn't even happy about the motorcycle he rode every day.

"Aren't you even a little excited?" Diaz asked, looking puzzled.

"Of course, I'm excited." Or he would have been a few weeks back.

The frown lifted from Diaz' face. "I'm on it, too. This squad is going to kick ass!" He punched Will in the shoulder.

Will finished the last of his pie and stood up. "I appreciate the heads-up, but I've got to get back to work. Don't forget to tell your sister congrats for me." He turned and strode out of the café.

The moment she heard Will's voice coming from the direction of the café counter, Bree stopped listening to Emmy Lou Davis and her ghost stories about the Jolee Plantation. Sitting in a booth with her back to the row of stools, she couldn't see him, but Bree would recognize Will's deep-pitched drawl anywhere.

He was polite to the waitress and even sounded genuinely interested in his companion's family news. The comment about sleepless nights wormed its way into Bree's core. Will made it sound as though he might even envy the new father. That said something about a man who wasn't even a husband yet.

Bree tried to drag her attention back to Emmy Lou and the story about a slave woman who had died of a broken heart according to legend.

"Of course," Emmy Lou said, "no one really dies of a broken heart. A heart attack, sure, but not because it got broke. But in this case Kezia helped it along."

Now the other man was talking about a list that Will's name was on. It sounded dangerous.

Emmy Lou touched Bree's hand. "Are you all right, Brianna Marie?"

"I'm fine. Why?"

"Well, you seem a little distracted." Emmy Lou leaned across her nearly empty lunch plate and lowered her voice to a whisper. "It's not those handsome young men at the counter that's got your attention, is it?"

Bree felt the color rise in her cheeks. She didn't bother to deny the charge. Emmy

Lou had sharp eyes and a keen sense for local gossip. She wouldn't have believed her anyway. "Tell me the story. I promise to listen." Will was distracting all the time, but at the moment his stated excitement about an opportunity that was, in his companion's words, kick-ass, filled her with unexplained dread. It was hard to pay attention.

"Her husband was sold," Emmy Lou replied. "Sometimes when a slave got sold, he or she just went to another nearby plantation. If that had been the case, the couple would have been able to see each other now and then. He could have come sneaking back in the night, if you know what I mean." This time it was Emmy Lou's turn to blush. "But they took him all the way to Missouri. The poor woman knew she'd never see him again, and her children would grow up never knowing their father."

That got Bree's full attention back. Sam would grow up not knowing his father either. But she hadn't died of a broken heart, even though it had felt like she might at the time.

"A few weeks after Kezia's husband got sold away, she committed suicide."

Shocked, Bree blurted, "What about her children?" That a mother would do something so drastic and leave her children behind was unthinkable.

"She killed them first. She wasn't literate, she couldn't leave a note or anything, and no one could tell for sure, but the other slaves insisted it was because Kezia wanted to take her sons away from the master in revenge for his having sold her husband. There were three of them. Just little boys, not old enough to be trained up for service yet, but they would have been."

"That's awful."

Emmy Lou made a face. "I know. But slavery was pretty awful. I don't know that I blame Kezia for what she did. And she's paid for it. For almost two hundred years."

"How has she paid for it?"

"Those innocent boys went to heaven, but Kezia was doomed to remain here. She looks for them all the time. She roams about the old plantation, looking for them and weeping. That's a long time to pay for a broken heart, don't you think?"

Bree nodded, not sure how to answer since Kezia hadn't really died of a broken heart anyway. She had committed a mortal sin. She'd taken the lives of three innocent boys and then her own. Was Kezia's spirit the eyes Bree had felt watching her the day she'd gone exploring at the plantation?

"Your lunch hour must surely be over by

now." Emmy Lou pushed her plate away and dabbed at her lips with her napkin. "You just drop me back at my place and be on your way before Mr. Kett starts fretting."

"Mr. Kett does not fret. At least not about me taking a long lunch." Bree laughed but gathered up her things and slid out of the booth.

A few minutes later, Emmy Lou waved to Bree from her front door and disappeared inside. Bree pulled away from the curb, thinking about Kezia and her little boys, but by the time she arrived back at work, Will and his new kick-ass job prospect returned to her thoughts.

Ben walked in from the kitchen and handed Will a beer. "Meg's asleep along with the boys. She was reading to them, but she must have been tired and never got to the end of the book." He dropped down on the other end of the couch.

"I'm not surprised. I'd get worn out carrying around two extra people all day. If guys had to do the incubating, there'd probably be a lot less people in the world."

"And that's not even counting childbirth." Ben doubled over and groaned.

Will smiled at his brother's theatrics but turned back to the basketball game on TV.

"So, what's on your mind?"

"What makes you think I've got anything on my mind?" Will glanced at his brother, then back at the TV.

"I'm your twin. Remember? Besides, you've been more than a little distracted all evening."

Will took a swig of his beer and studied the bottle as he dragged his thumbnail down the side of the label, tearing a long, narrow gouge in the damp paper. "I've got a decision to make."

Ben grabbed the remote and turned the game off. "Tell me about it."

"I'm apparently on the list for the response team I applied for."

"Congratulations."

"I haven't been offered the job yet." Mateo's news would have filled Will with eager anticipation just a few short weeks earlier. Now the possibility filled him with questions he didn't have the answers to.

"But just that you're on the list — that's excellent news. Isn't it?"

Will sighed.

"But you're not excited about it. What's changed?" Ben put his beer to his mouth and swallowed.

"Brianna Reagan."

Ben set his bottle down and met Will's

gaze. Ben's blue eyes were so like his own that it felt like looking in a mirror. Sometimes he felt like Ben could see right into his soul.

"I didn't know you two had gotten that serious."

"We haven't. Yet."

"But you're still pursuing her."

"She's afraid of getting involved with me."

"Afraid? Of you? Why?" Those identical blue eyes widened, and Ben's blond brows rose.

"She's afraid of falling in love with a trooper."

"There're plenty of statistics to show that law enforcement has a higher rate of divorce than the general population," Ben said reasonably. "Maybe she's just being cautious."

"It's more than that. It's because Sam's dad died in action. She didn't come right out and say so, but it's as if she's afraid as soon as she lets herself care too much, I'll get shot, and it'll be the same thing all over again."

"Well, you can't guarantee you won't."

"When was the last time a state trooper got shot and killed?"

Ben shrugged. "I don't know."

"Two thousand eight. Most officer deaths

are from automobile accidents, and that could happen to anyone."

"You do ride a motorcycle, though."

"The last trooper who died in a motorcycle crash was in nineteen thirty-six."

"Really?" Ben sat back, apparently mulling this bit of information over.

The silence stretched, and Will's mind continued on the what-if treadmill it had been on since Diaz told him about the list.

"So, now you're rethinking this special team thing?"

Will nodded. "Accepting that post might just about guarantee I'd never get her to take a chance on me."

"You're really in love with her, aren't you?"

"I'm totally cooked."

Ben got up and gave Will's shoulder a squeeze. "So what are you going to do when they call to offer you the chance to go?"

"I don't know."

Chapter 16

The invitation to join the Cameron family at Will's parents' home on the beach came as a surprise. Bree let the phone drift away from her ear as several totally conflicting thoughts ran through her head.

Will's mother Sandy sounded so genuinely friendly and eager for Sam and Bree to come. Zoe would be there with her new husband, Will's younger brother Jake. One big happy family. Except she and Sam weren't family.

Will would be there, too. Bree's pulse quickened at the thought.

"C-can I bring something?" she asked, doing her best to keep the sudden breathlessness out of her voice.

"Anything you'd like, but don't feel you have to bring anything. Just you and Sam," Sandy Cameron replied. "You can ride out with Will. That way I won't have to try giving you directions. I'm awful with directions." Will's mother laughed at her own failing.

"Thanks for inviting us. Sam will be thrilled."

"Cam and I are looking forward to meeting you again. Jake's wedding was beautiful, but I didn't get much chance to mingle and talk. See you on Saturday. Bye."

Bree looked at the phone and set it slowly back in its cradle. Why had Sandy Cameron invited her to join a family gathering? Had Will asked Sandy to include her? Or was it because Sam had already been there, and it was Sam who was being invited, and Sam's mother was just part of the package?

Why had she let the warm feeling filling her at the thought of a day spent in Will's company override caution and wisdom? Because she liked him. A lot more than she ever expected to.

After overhearing the conversation at the café, her resolve to keep Will at arms' length seemed to be the right thing to do. He was way too attractive, and his interest in her was not just flattering. It was reminding her of feelings and needs she'd done her best to bury.

Each new thing she learned about Will confused her and made her resolve harder to hang onto. He was easygoing and generous, but he loved action, especially the kind that scared the crap out of her. He was smart and ambitious, and now he was vying for an even more dangerous job than he already had.

She had done some online sleuthing and found several articles on the Rapid Response Team the state was pulling together. Basically, it was a SWAT team. Once Will was on the team, he could be called out at a moment's notice to put on the gear and walk straight into places where gunfire was almost a given. Her heart squeezed painfully just thinking about it.

If she let herself fall in love with him, and Will was snatched away from her in a heartbeat, where would she be then?

Sam didn't remember much about his dad. Ed had been gone more than he'd been home. Sam had seemed stoic in the face of his father's death, but in reality, he hadn't known Ed very well. If anything happened to Will, Sam would be hurt a lot worse. But how could she explain to Sam why he shouldn't hang out with Will so much? Sam's hero worship had already taken over his imagination if not his heart.

Sam was growing up and becoming more independent. Protecting him from everything life could dish out was no longer possible, no matter how much Bree wished otherwise. Last December, when Sam had gotten into a fistfight at school, Bree had been called into the principal's office, not to fix the problem for Sam, but to be included in deciding what punishment he would face. It hadn't mattered that Sam had been standing up to a known bully to protect a younger boy. Fighting was not allowed, and Sam knew it. Therefore he had to suffer the same penalty as the bully.

Protecting him from getting emotionally hurt was turning out to be just as impossible.

Bree prayed she was not making a huge mistake in letting Sam grow ever closer to Will.

The Cameron home was a perfect blend of everything Bree liked about homes near the beach. Set high in the dunes on the barrier island facing the sea with its back decks overlooking the waterway and the setting sun, the house had been there for over fifty years. Will explained on the drive out that his parents had bought it from an old man they had met on the beach shortly after they were married.

The man had been trying to dig a shutter out of the sand after a storm, and Cam had stopped to help. That chance encounter had turned into a friendship, and when the old man decided to leave the home he and his wife had shared for all their married life, Cam had bought it from him. The friendship hadn't ended though. Still missing his deceased wife and being childless, he'd adopted Sandy and Cam and become an honorary grandfather to their kids.

"Grampa Phil was one of my favorite people," Will said as they climbed out of the Jeep. "He lived to be a hundred. Died on his birthday in fact. He told us he was planning to round out the century, but no one believed he'd be so exact."

"Your grandfather was a hundred years old?" Sam asked, his eyes round with disbelief.

"Yup. He's the one who taught me how to whittle." Will ruffled Sam's dark hair. "So, I'm passing his legacy on to you."

"But he's not my real grandfather."

"He wasn't mine either. Except that he loved me just as much as if I'd really been his grandson. You don't have to be related to love someone."

"My grandfather doesn't know how to whittle. He doesn't even have a jackknife. But he's good at writing and drawing. He wrote me a story when I was little."

"You'll have to read it to me sometime."

"I will." Sam beamed at the request. "It's got pictures too that my grandpa drew. Hey, there's Rick."

Sure enough, Rick was hanging over the railing, gesturing wildly for Sam to hurry up. Sam took off at a run.

"Your dad sounds like an interesting guy," Will said as he lifted the rear door and reached in to grab the totes filled with dry clothes and towels.

"He's an editor for the *Star,* and he's written two non-fiction books about the history of the Navy in World War II."

"Was he in the Navy?"

"He was. He was in communications. Pretty much the same thing he's doing now, but for the Navy. One of his postings, long before I was born, though, was on a ship in the South China Sea."

"Sounds like Sam thinks he's pretty special. How come —"

"How come what?" Bree grabbed the bag with the pumpkin bread and cream cheese she'd brought for the meal and closed the hatch.

"Probably none of my business."

Bree smiled at the man walking beside her. "Since when do you worry if it's your business or not?" One of the things she liked about Will was his honesty and straightforward concern. It might frustrate her, like when he was lecturing her on exploring the Jolee Plantation, but it came from a real consideration for her welfare.

"I was wondering how come Sam doesn't spend more time with your dad. Your parents live in Wilmington, right?"

It was the boy needing a man in his life thing. Even Will saw it. "Dad doesn't get around very well since his arthritis got bad. He taught Sam how to play chess, but they really go at it with Risk. Dad has the Star Wars version. Sam has the standard one. They love it."

"I used to play that game with my brothers when we were kids, but I haven't even thought about it in years. I'd challenge Sam, but I think I should leave that as something he shares with your dad."

Sometimes Will's thoughtfulness surprised her. He could be totally alpha one minute, then he'd show another side to his personality that always caught her by surprise. It shouldn't, since he'd started off bringing her an ice cream sundae and then kept her son busy for an entire day while she recovered from a nasty bug.

"Brianna. Don't you look nice. I'm so glad you could come." Sandy Cameron greeted them at the top of the stairs and relieved Bree of the food tote. “Come inside. Meg and Zoe are already here. Kate’s on the way, but she’s always late.”

Bree glanced at Will. He winked at her and dropped their beach things next to the railing and headed around to the front of the house.

“He won’t go far.” Sandy laughed as if she knew something Bree didn’t. “I promise.”

Bree followed Will’s energetic mother into the house.

The entire first floor was an open arrangement. Surely not the original design given the house’s vintage. An enormous double-sided fireplace dominated the center of the room. Bree could see through it to the kitchen and dining area. Comfortable leather furniture was arranged about the room. One could sit on one end of the right-angled sectional to enjoy a fire in the fireplace or the other end to watch the big flat-screen TV mounted on the far wall. A braided chenille carpet in multicolored beach tones filled the space between the sectional and the fireplace with a big square coffee table planted in the middle. Side tables with lamps made of clear glass and filled with shells flanked the ends.

"What a beautiful room!" Bree exclaimed. What she wouldn't give for a living room just like it.

"Why, thank you. We like it. It's functional, comfortable, and easy to keep up. But come check out the kitchen. That's where you get a view of the ocean that will take your breath away."

And take away her breath it did. Bree could not imagine getting any work done with all that ocean to capture one's attention. But apparently work did get done here. Cooking at least.

The large center island at one end of the space was crowded with dishes, some of which flowed over onto the counters beyond. The fireplace she'd been able to see through from the other side took up a good portion of the center wall, and a table big enough to feed a small army ran along the bank of windows overlooking the beach. As she thought about it, Bree guessed they needed a table that big considering Cam and Sandy Cameron had five kids, three of whom were married, and eight grandchildren. And frequent extras if her and Sam's inclusion today was any example.

"Color me green," Bree said as she ran a hand along the black granite counter.

"We're all green." Meg laughed. "You've

seen my kitchen."

"And mine." Zoe hurried over to envelop Bree in a hug. "I'm so glad you agreed to come today," she whispered in Bree's ear.

Bree turned at a commotion behind her. Will's sister Kate came sailing into the kitchen with two little girls in tow. She stopped when she spotted Bree and glanced at her mother with her elegantly shaped blond brows arched up in a question.

"You remember Zoe's matron of honor?" Sandy introduced her. "Brianna, this is my hoyden of a daughter Kate and her girls Jenny and Becca."

"Oh, please!" Kate drawled. "I'm only a hoyden when I'm trying to fend off my brothers." She pulled Bree into a hug and kissed her on the cheek. "You're brave," she said with a wink so like Will's that the familiarity of it hit Bree in the gut.

"Leave her be," Will said, coming up behind his sister and lifting her off the ground.

Kate wriggled free and kissed her brother on the cheek. "See what I have to contend with?"

"Now that Kate's here, we can eat," Sandy cut into the fun. "Go tell the rest of the crew to come and get it."

Will bussed his mother on the cheek and left.

A few moments later the kitchen was overrun with kids and men grabbing plates and helping themselves to the lavish spread.

When lunch had been consumed and the kids were shrieking and tearing around on the beach, the adults lounged on the deck in a collection of beach chairs, deck furniture, and a woven hammock. Will grabbed Bree's hand and tugged her toward the stairs.

"Go for a walk with me?"

Bree hesitated. She loved walking on the beach, but who was watching Sam?

"He's safe." Cam grinned up at Bree and winked. "He gave up trying to drown his girlfriends when he was twelve. And I've got my eye on the kids."

"Thanks," Bree mumbled as she let Will lead her down the stairs to the beach.

The sun was warm, and Bree was glad she'd chosen to wear a sundress. It had a little matching jacket that was perfect for today's weather. That it made her feel pretty and very feminine was another of those contradictions she was battling lately, because she'd worn it specifically with Will in mind, and his compliment when he'd come to pick her up had warmed her cheeks as well as her insides. They were supposed to be just friends. She wasn't supposed to feel like this. Or be giving anyone the wrong impression. Like Will's father.

"Your father thinks I'm your girlfriend."

"He just wants all his kids to be happy, and he knows I'd be happy if you were my girlfriend."

Bree bit the inside of her cheek. "I'm sorry to disappoint him, then."

"And there's nothing I can do to change your mind?"

Bree let go of Will's hand. She looked out over the unusually placid blue water of the Atlantic Ocean. "You should find a woman who would suit you better than I ever could." The idea of Will with another woman bothered her, but she had no right to feel that way if she continued to rebuff his advances.

"You suit me just fine."

"You hardly know anything about me."

"Sure I do." He reached for her hand again, but she shoved her hands into her armpits to dissuade him. "You're a single mom with a terrific son. You've got a pretty sweet job at Kett's that I know you enjoy. You're damned good at Scrabble, and I like your taste in music."

"That's just surface stuff. You don't know

who I am inside."

"I know you've been hurt. I know you're afraid to fall in love again. I know —"

"You don't know anything!" She stopped walking and turned to face him. "You have no idea what it's like to spend every waking moment of your life worrying that the man you love might never come home again. You don't know how dead I felt inside when it finally happened. Or how scared I was that I might never get over him. I can't do it again. I just can't."

Tears sprang to Bree's eyes, smarting and threatening to spill over. She turned away from Will and started walking again so he wouldn't see them.

Will caught up with her and pulled her into his arms. She fought him, but he was stronger. "I'm sorry, Brianna. I'm so sorry you had to live through all that." He rocked her against him, murmuring against the top of her head as she buried her face in the soft fabric of his sweatshirt and gave in to the feeling of being cared for.

She managed not to cry all over his shirt, but it took longer than it should have before she pulled herself together and stepped away.

"You're too nice."

Will's brows rose. "Me? Nice?"

"You make it awfully hard to dislike you."

"But I don't want you to dislike me. I want . . ." He hesitated. Then reached for her hand yet again. "I want to be your friend."

"Not your girlfriend?"

"Just my friend." He swung their hands between them as he urged her to continue their amble along the water's edge. "Since you're so sure I don't really know you, tell me, as a friend, what *do* you want from life? Beyond what you've already achieved?"

She shrugged. She hadn't really thought about it. Her life right now was about being the best mother she could be. And a decent provider so Sam could have all the things he deserved.

"What would make you happy?" Will persisted.

She sighed. "I am happy. Most of the time. I've got Sam and great friends and a good job. What about you? What would make *you* happy? And don't say *me.*"

Will dropped her hand and sat down in the sand. He began taking his sneakers off. "Take your shoes off." He gestured to the sand beside him.

"Why?"

"So we can splash in the water. That always makes me happy."

"We'll get soaked."

"So?" He peeled his socks off and shoved them into his sneakers.

Bree bent and pushed the heels of her sandals off. As soon as she finished, he jumped to his feet and grabbed her sandals out of her hand. He trotted up the beach a bit, dropped their shoes on dry sand, and trotted back.

"Okay, so this is what makes me happy." He rolled up his jeans and walked into the water. "C'mon."

With his hands jammed into his pockets, Will splashed along in the gently eddying waves. In spite of having rolled his jeans up, they were getting wet anyway, but he didn't seem to care.

"Your mom must have been after you all the time about getting soaked."

"She was." He bent suddenly and picked up a shell. He fingered the pearly inside, then handed it to Bree.

Bree took the shell and ran the pad of her thumb over the shiny wet lining. "Pretty," she murmured and started to hand it back.

"Keep it," he told her.

She tucked it into her pocket, wishing all her time spent with Will could be as easy and carefree as these last few minutes had been. Friendship with him was very pleasant.

"So, what else makes you happy? Besides getting your pants wet and playing in water." Maybe he'd tell her about his latest coup at work and the new team he was excited about being on.

"Where do I begin?" He grinned at her. "I'm a pretty lucky guy. Everything makes me happy. Well, most everything."

"So tell me what's the biggest thing that makes you happy lately."

He looked at her, his face suddenly very serious. "Getting to know you."

CHAPTER 17

Will studied Bree's face, waiting for her expression to close in again as soon as he said their friendship made him happy.

"Oh," she said, her voice soft and breathy.

He loved her. He was *in* love with her. He loved everything about her except the fear that kept her from letting him into her heart. She was always beautiful, but today she was especially appealing. Her wavy hair, moist in the air from the sea, framed her face with a halo of curls that caught the sunlight in sparkling abundance. The brightness of the day glimmered in her dark eyes as she gazed at him, clearly at a loss for words.

"If there was one thing that I could change about myself that might change your mind about me, what would it be?"

Her expression shifted. She almost looked sad, as if his question troubled her. She bit her lip, turned away, and began walking further down the beach. He joined her and waited for her answer. Prayed she would answer at all.

"There's nothing about you I'd want to change," Bree began, glancing sideways at him, then back down toward the water swirling around her feet. "I think you're just who you're supposed to be, and if you changed anything, then you wouldn't be you. And you wouldn't be so happy."

"But if you could," he persisted. She'd change his occupation if she could, but he wanted her to say it. If they were ever going to find a way to make things work between them, she had to be willing to talk about the part of his profession that scared her, just as he would have to be willing to consider another line of work.

"If I changed anything about you, Sam would pout."

"Sam never pouts."

"You've never seen him pout, you mean."

"You're still not answering my question."

"I —"

The pounding of several pairs of feet approaching from behind cut off Bree's answer. If she had been about to answer his question at all.

Rick, Sam, Jenny, and Becca came to a halt in front of Bree and Will.

"Mom says if you want any dessert, you need to come now, or it will all be gone," Jenny announced.

"It's an ice cream smorgasbord," Becca added.

Sam grabbed Bree's hand, then one of Will's, and started dragging them back in the direction of the Cameron home.

"Beatcha back," Rick shouted and took off racing.

Sam dropped both their hands and pelted after Rick. The girls joined in, and in moments they were all out of earshot again.

"Ice cream smorgasbord?" Bree asked. Clearly if she'd had an answer a moment ago, the moment was lost, and he wasn't going to hear what it was. *Another day,* he promised himself. Although when that might be, considering how scarce she'd made herself over the last week and a half, he didn't know. He'd been surprised when she accepted his mother's invitation for today's family gathering.

"Mom knows the kids love it, so she does it often. Every time she tries to think up something new to add to the choices of toppings. But she can't leave off anything from before because someone is bound to ask where it is. So she just keeps ending up with more and more choices."

In silence, they detoured away from the water to retrieve their shoes. After they finished putting them back on, Will helped Bree up again and didn't fight it when she took her hand back.

"Would you and Sam like to go to breakfast with me tomorrow?" A threesome could hardly be considered a girlfriend sort of date.

"I'm not sure . . ." she began.

"I like to eat breakfast out on Sunday mornings before church, but it makes me happy when I can eat out with a friend instead of going alone."

Bree stared straight ahead, apparently pondering her answer.

It's not a hard question, hovered on his tongue, but he kept the words to himself and waited her out.

As they approached the house, there was a lineup of kids on the bottom step with overflowing bowls of ice cream and toppings. "Mom always sends them to sit on the stairs because it's easier to clean up."

Maybe he wasn't going to get any reply to his invitation either. He did like to eat breakfast out, but it wasn't like he did it a lot. Except he very much wanted to do so tomorrow. With Bree.

"Okay. At Joel's?" she asked as they

reached the line of slurping kids.

Will's heart soared.

"Good grief, you weren't kidding about the toppings."

He laughed with her, his heart lighter and happier than it had any right to be.

"Everyone's looking at us," Bree murmured as she walked into Joel's Diner with Sam at her side and Will's hand resting lightly against the small of her back.

Will bent to whisper in her ear. "You afraid the news will spread that you've been seen with the notorious Will Cameron?"

Olive Parker, the town trumpet, and her best friend Frances Lenore sat at the most conspicuous table in the place. As Bree followed the hostess to a booth in the far corner, she saw both women turn to watch.

"Your notoriety is not what I'm worried about." Bree slid into the booth behind Sam. "It's mine."

Will took the bench opposite and lifted one quizzical eyebrow. "You must have known Tide's Way was that sort of town when you moved here."

"I prefer it when they're gossiping about someone else."

By the glimmer in his eye and the way he pursed his lips, Will would have said something totally outrageous if Sam had not been there.

Will opened the lengthy breakfast menu and ran his finger down the left side, then tapped her hand to get her attention. The jolt of pleasure his touch brought was getting far too familiar and harder to hide.

"You're paying. Right?"

"I'm . . ." Hadn't he invited her out to breakfast?

"You said next time was your treat," he reminded her with one of his devastating winks.

She had. "Yeah, right. I forgot." If those tabbies looked over right now, they'd catch her blushing as red as ripe strawberries with Will's hand covering hers. She tugged her hand free.

"In that case, I'm having the Joel's 'Man-sized Everything Special.' "

Sam dropped the paper children's menu he'd been reading. "I want what Will's having."

"You can't eat that much," Bree said.

"Sure I can." He made a face. "Will says I'm the man of the house."

"You still can't eat that much." Bree retrieved the children's menu to see if there was a similar child-sized option.

"How about we share?" Will cut in to offer a compromise. He lifted his brows and looked at Bree for approval.

Sam beamed.

"I'm not so sure I like being ganged up on," Bree said, but she was having a hard time sounding put out when her heart insisted on doing somersaults. The brief look of entreaty had left Will's face, and the one that replaced it took Bree's breath away. She tore her gaze away and studied her menu again.

The waitress showed up and took their order. One Everything Special. One fruit and muffin.

Sam brought up the subject of the regional Pinewood Derby and chattered happily about his chances of winning a trophy. Will added a comment now and then, but he kept looking at Bree with a serious, unreadable expression in his eyes. Bree wanted to look away but found she couldn't. It was as if Will was trying to tell her something with that look.

When the bill came, Bree was ready and dropped three tens on it before Will had a chance. She still hadn't managed to dispel the breathless feeling as she slid from the booth and headed to the door. If only she were headed home where she could collect her thoughts and calm the jittery nervous sensation. She hadn't felt this way during a dinner for two that could have been considered a date if she hadn't balked at calling it one. What had changed between then and now?

They left Will's Jeep in the diner parking lot and walked across the street to St. Theresa's. If she'd felt conspicuous walking into Joel's with Will, walking into church was worse. Bree sat through the entire mass feeling as if at least a hundred pairs of eyes were boring into her back. Will had grown up in this parish, and everyone apparently felt some kind of proprietary interest in his love life. Or at least in the women he chose to escort to church. It was a relief when the mass ended, and they were able to blend into the crowd headed toward the door.

Sam squirmed his way out ahead of them and was talking to Rick when they finally emerged into the sunlight. He skipped back to Bree's side to plead with her to let him go home with Rick for the afternoon. Bree gave her permission, and she and Will headed back to the diner parking lot to reclaim his Jeep.

"They'll be asking about a wedding date next, you know," she said as she climbed back into the passenger seat.

Will grinned as he cranked the engine.

"Let 'em ask. We're just friends, right?"

Just friends hadn't been the vibe she'd been getting from the man all morning, but just what that vibe had been, she wasn't sure.

When Will didn't turn in at Carlisle Place, she shot him a suspicious glance. "Where are we going?"

"There's something I want to show you. You aren't in a hurry to get home, are you?" He smiled, and his dimple showed. At least the intensity that had lurked in his eyes for most of the morning was gone, replaced by one of suppressed excitement.

"Is it something I'm going to want to see?"

He lifted one shoulder, but the grin didn't fade. "You asked me yesterday what would make me happy. This is part of it."

"Okay." Bree settled back in her seat. "You're not even going to give me a hint?"

Will's phone beeped. He held up one finger and put the phone to his ear. The smile lingering about his mouth faded quickly. He pulled the Jeep onto the shoulder and put it into park.

A staccato series of *yesses* and *copy that sirs* followed. Will put his hand to his forehead and dragged it down across his eyes. "Yes, sir. I'll be there in ten, fifteen minutes tops."

"I'm sorry. I've gotta go." He glanced over his shoulder and pulled back onto Stewart Road. "Mind if I leave you the keys to the Jeep so you can take yourself home?"

"Of course not. What's going on?"

Will wheeled into his brother's driveway and skidded to a stop in front of the garage. "There's an officer down, and we've got to find the shooter." He left the keys in the ignition and jumped out of the Jeep.

Bree slid from the passenger seat just as Will yanked the garage door open. He pushed his motorcycle out into the driveway.

"Shouldn't you change out of your suit?" The urgency in him was obvious, but surely he could spare a few minutes to change.

"Yeah. Right." He left her standing in the middle of the driveway while he bolted for his brother's back door.

She was still standing there trying to decide if she should follow him when he reappeared wearing jeans and work boots with his white dress shirt. He thrust his arms into a denim jacket with the logo of Ben's kennel on it as he crossed the driveway toward her.

"I'm really sorry leaving you like this. Maybe there'll still be time when I get back."

"I understand. Just go do what you have to do."

He hesitated, then grabbed his helmet off the back of the bike and crammed it down over his head.

"Be safe, Will." Her heart hammered with fear. Her stomach roiled.

One corner of his mouth turned up, and his dimple flashed briefly. "I promise." He flipped the visor down, and she could no longer see his expressive blue eyes.

A moment later, he was peeling back out of the driveway, the bike leaning deep into the turn. His flashing blue lights came on just before he disappeared around the corner. The rumble of the bike faded quickly.

Bree stood in the sudden silence of Ben's driveway, staring at the place she'd last seen Will and feeling like she might throw up. A dread that was all too familiar returned in a flash and settled into her heart. How many times had she sent Ed off to war, praying for his safe return? Prayers that had not always been answered in spite of Ed's confidence.

Blotting out both the memory of Ed and the flicker of Will's smile, she forced herself to focus on the man who had been shot, offering prayers for him and for his family. Or maybe it had been a woman. Will had only said an officer was down. She offered up pleas on behalf of the whole search team. The man they were chasing was armed, and he'd already shot one officer. No one would be safe until he was caught.

"You're welcome to come in."

Bree turned, jarred out of her silent litany. Ben stood a few feet away. "We're sitting down to dinner, but it's easy enough to set another place."

Her stomach lurched at the thought of eating anything. She couldn't just go in there and act as if nothing was happening. She needed to go home. To be by herself. She needed to sort through her feelings and come to grips with the terror raging in her head.

"He'll be okay, you know," Ben tried to assure her.

"I know." She tried to sound like she believed it. "Thanks for the invite, but I think I'll head home. I've — I've got things I need to do. I'll come back for Sam later. Will told me to take the Jeep."

"We're headed over to Kate's around suppertime to collect Evan. We can drop Sam off. In fact, if we loop around and drop him after we get Evan, I can bring the Jeep back so it'll be here when Will gets home. He doesn't like leaving the bike at the apartment."

"Thank you." Bree turned for one last look at the corner around which Will had disappeared, then started for the Jeep.

"If you change your mind, you're always welcome." Ben waved and headed toward his back porch.

Bree pulled herself into the driver's seat and had to hunt for the lever to bring the seat forward. She was average height. Will was taller by eight inches and all legs. As she drove home, thoughts she did not want to be thinking kept coming at her from all sides.

The seat was still warm from his having been in it. His hands had curved themselves around this wheel in a white-knuckled grip the night they'd almost been run down in a parking lot. A small crucifix clipped to the rearview mirror glimmered with reflected sunlight, attesting to the faith that guided the man's life. The tie he'd removed after they left church sprawled along the dash. His choice of music still played on the radio. He was all around her. Even the faint remnants of his cologne lingered.

She was falling in love with him. She had tried so hard not to, but he'd gotten under her skin.

If she could just have dismissed him as a jock or a cop with attitude, keeping him out of her heart might have worked. Reminding herself that he had streaks of arrogance about him, like when he'd ordered her not to go to the Jolee Plantation alone, couldn't banish the kindness in him that popped up when she was unprepared.

She pulled into Will's assigned parking spot, unable to remember any of the short drive between Ben's place and home. Her head had been so full of Will and the feelings he'd brought to life in her stubborn heart. She turned the Jeep off and sat there. She was reluctant to go up to her apartment and leave this feeling of Will being all around her.

Will was out there somewhere, hunting for a dangerous felon with a gun. Putting his life on the line.

CHAPTER 18

Will roared down Route 17 with his lights flashing and his siren screaming. As focused as he was on getting to the scene, he couldn't banish the sight of Bree standing forlornly in the driveway as he left. When he'd returned from pulling on Ben's borrowed jeans and boots, there had been a frightened look in her eyes. He'd wanted to drag her into his arms and assure her he'd be fine. He'd wanted to kiss her.

Except he'd promised he wouldn't do it again until she asked him to. She hadn't asked. She'd just looked so scared and alone.

Will supposed a woman might feel worried about the safety of a friend, but he hoped that panicky look in her eyes expressed feelings that went much deeper than just friendship. Possible ways that he could get her to admit to those feelings reeled through his mind as he drove in spite of his need to stay focused on the road and other vehicles on it.

The haphazard cluster of official vehicles and flashing lights came into view, and all thoughts of Bree ended. He guided his bike into a slot between the local sheriff's vehicle and a black SUV with government plates on it.

"How is he?" was the first question Will asked of the knot of men standing with their heads bent in conversation.

"He made it to the hospital. He'll be in surgery shortly," Luke Nicholson, the county sheriff, answered. "You got here fast enough."

"The captain said it was urgent. The shooter's still in the wind?"

"Afraid so." The circle stretched to make room for Will to join the discussion. In a few concise sentences, Nicholson outlined what each pair of the gathered deputies was responsible for.

"The Holly Shelter land is a labyrinth of narrow dirt lanes, bike paths, and hiking trails where our cruisers can't go. I've got two SUVs out there on the accessible roads, but as soon as Diaz gets here, I'd like you two searching as much of the place as you can get to."

"I can get started, and you can send him

after me," Will suggested. He was used to patrolling alone. It was how state highway troopers worked.

Nicholson shook his head. "That's what got Schaeffer in trouble. I'm not sending anyone else out there except in pairs."

The name Schaeffer was familiar. Will only knew the guy in passing, but he knew him well enough to know the man had recently been married. His wife must be terrified. This was the kind of thing Bree had tried to explain to Will.

Somehow it just never felt like it was going to happen to you. Will wondered how Schaeffer had been caught with his guard down, so he asked, "What happened?"

"Routine traffic stop," Nicholson answered. He closed his eyes as if wishing to open them and discover this was just a drill. When his brown eyes did open again, there was a look of determination in them. "We'll catch the bastard."

"Any description? Anything caught on the dashcam?"

"The guy was riding a Harley. Metalic blue, matching helmet. You and Diaz are the most likely to catch up to him, I'm thinking. I sent cars around to the far side of the park and set up road blocks on seventeen, but there's a lot of wilderness to cover." Nicholson rattled off the known description. "Five feet ten or eleven, a lot of black leather, except it appears he was wearing sneakers near as we can tell without the equipment to blow the picture up. Had a dark braid down his back with a lot of gray in it. All that was recorded before Schaeffer even stepped out of his cruiser."

As Nicolson finished speaking, Mateo Diaz pulled into the clearing, sending up a spray of small stones and dust. Unlike Will, he was in uniform and had probably been on duty. He hurried over to where Will and Nicholson were standing.

"I'll leave you to fill Diaz in. I want to check with dispatch and the hospital. Stay in touch."

As they headed back to their motorcycles, Will repeated everything he'd just learned. "He's armed and not afraid to kill, even law enforcement," Will warned as they revved their bikes and pulled out, headed west on Lodge Road, deep into Holly Shelter game land, looking for the first turnoff where their search would begin.

Could have been worse. Could have been dusk when this guy melted into the woods. Then we might never catch him. He probably knows there'll be roadblocks at the other end. So, where will he try to elude us?

Will was familiar with most of the preservation land, but there was close to fifty thousand acres to get lost in, though not necessarily on a Harley. He only hoped the man they were after was not as familiar with the preserve as he and Diaz were.

Half an hour later they doubled back and headed off on a new set of trails. Perhaps it would have been better if it had been hunting season, then if the guy tried to hijack anyone's truck at least the owners would be armed. But it wasn't, and Will was sure Nicholson would be breathing a sigh of relief that a shooting war wasn't about to begin. The only hikers they passed scuttled up the embankment as they approached. When questioned, they had neither seen nor heard anyone on a motorcycle before the troopers showed up.

After four hours of searching, Will and Diaz pulled into a small parking area where several hiking trails began. It had started to rain, and Ben's borrowed denim jacket was wet through. Will hunched his shoulders against the chill and called Nicholson to check in. Just as he was about to hang up, Diaz caught Will's attention and pointed to a dense thicket.

"Hang on," Will told the sheriff. He shrugged, asking Diaz without words what he'd seen.

Diaz pointed to the bright blue circle in the state logo painted on the gray panel of his bike, then back toward the thicket. Will followed his pointing finger. Then he saw it. A glimmer of metallic blue hidden in the thick underbrush.

"I think we might have something," he whispered into his phone. He gave Nicholson their location and a description of what they'd found.

"Don't do anything rash. I'll have backup there in minutes," Nicholson said.

Not that Will planned to do anything rash. He was not wearing protective gear. They'd only been sent to find the man and to apprehend him only if they could do so without endangering themselves. But there might be a way to gain an advantage.

Will caught Diaz' attention and jerked his chin imperceptibly in the direction of a wide trail opening that started off flat and open before it turned and climbed up to a small ridge overlooking the rest area. Narrower hiking-only trails branched off from the overlook. Diaz nodded, and they peeled out onto the trail opening. When they reached the point where neither motorcycle could go any further, Will stayed on his and kept the engine running while Diaz scrambled the rest of the way up the hill on foot, eventually inching along on his belly to the edge of the ridge.

"We've got him," Diaz announced, sliding back down in a shower of loose dirt.

"How?" Will let his engine die.

"We didn't see it because of the signboard, but I think he didn't make the turn into the lot, collided with the sign, and went crashing off into the brush. He's lying face down about eight or nine feet from where his bike is tangled in the heavy stuff."

"Well, that's just too easy." Will grinned at their good fortune. "But just to be on the safe side, let's leave the bikes here and sneak back down from the other side."

The going wasn't as easy as Will made it sound, but by the time their backup arrived in the form of a deputy's SUV, an unmarked pickup truck, and five men, they had the fugitive cuffed, cussing and sitting in front of the sign that had been his undoing with a huge knot forming on his forehead. Diaz was applying a bandage to keep blood from trickling into the guy's face.

"Good news on Schaeffer, too," the deputy said as they hauled the cuffed man to the back of the SUV. "He's out of surgery and conscious. He was lucky."

"So's this guy," Will muttered. "If he'd

been a better shot, he'd be up for murder one."

"Scumbag." Diaz snorted. He nodded at Will, his eyes raking over the soaked jacket and jeans. "Hell of a way to spend your Sunday off."

Will shrugged. "Better than not finding the guy after all that effort." *And now I can go home and reassure Bree that I haven't met my maker yet.*

Bree hadn't gotten anything done. She'd paced, prayed, and paced some more. She hadn't eaten anything either. Just friends or not, this waiting and worrying had her tied in knots.

She wasn't hungry, but she had to find something to do. The waiting was killing her. Pulling out pans and mixing bowls, she started assembling the makings of quick bread to use up the overly speckled bananas on the verge of attracting fruit flies. She was so distracted she had to read the ingredient list three times before she was sure she hadn't forgotten anything.

Just as she shoved the pans into the oven and set the timer, Sam came in with Ben following. Bree wiped her hands on a towel and dug into her purse for Will's keys. She handed them to Ben, afraid to ask if Will had called.

"Haven't heard anything," Ben said as if he'd read her mind. "But that's not necessarily bad. He's probably too busy."

Bree opened her mouth to agree, but she couldn't force the words out. She tried to read Ben's expression but couldn't do that either.

"I'll let you know if we hear anything." Ben paused in the doorway, his hand resting on the knob. "Call us if you hear first?"

Bree nodded and did her best to force a smile onto her face. "Thanks for having Sam over."

"Our pleasure. By the way, Sam's had supper. We stopped for pizza. And try not to worry. He'll be fine." Then Ben was gone.

"Is Will going to be okay, Mom?"

Bree spun around and went down on one knee to meet Sam's gaze on his level. "Of course he is. Didn't you hear Mr. Cameron say so?"

"But he's been gone a long time. All afternoon."

"Sometimes police work takes a long time."

"But what if he gets hurt?" Sam's worried face echoed the raging angst building up inside Bree.

"Tell you what. If you get your jammies

on and brush your teeth, I'll let you curl up on the sofa and watch a movie while we wait to hear. Sound like a deal?"

Sam's face brightened, and he took off down the hall to comply.

If only Ben's words and her own could reassure her. Some of the sick feeling in her stomach at this point was probably hunger. Maybe a mug of tea would help. And warm banana bread when it came out of the oven.

Sam returned in record time, dragging his favorite quilt. The quilt had been his go-to for comfort since he was a toddler. It said something that he'd brought it with him now. They were both in too deep not to worry about Will. That troubled her, but without crushing Sam's new friendship, she couldn't see a way to protect him, any more than she was protecting her own heart.

Sam curled up on the sofa and pulled his tattered quilt about himself. Bree popped his favorite new movie into the DVD player and hit play.

"He'll be okay," she said as she adjusted the quilt.

"What if I fall asleep before he comes home?"

"Then I'll wake you up." Not that Will had any reason to come to her apartment. His Jeep was back at his brother's place again. If anything, that's where Will would be most likely to go first. But Ben had promised to call.

She sat next to Sam, her hands curled around her mug of tea as if its warmth could ease her anxiety. The movie had claimed Sam's attention, but hers wandered to the window and the realization that it was dark outside.

Where is he? She wished she had put the television on earlier to possibly catch some mention of the manhunt on the news. But she was afraid to find out that things had gone horribly wrong, so she hadn't.

A buzzer sounded. Bree scrambled to her feet as a flood of relief started to wash through her. But it wasn't the door. It was the oven.

She turned to check on Sam, but he had fallen asleep, clutching a fold of his quilt against his face with his thumb in his mouth. Sam hadn't sucked his thumb since those first months after his father died. How much of Sam's anxiety had he absorbed from her and how much was his own? Her head throbbed.

She went to take the bread out of the oven. The tea had helped calm her stomach some, but the smell of the freshly baked banana bread wasn't nearly as appealing as it should have been. She returned to the living room with a second cup of tea, but instead of settling back onto the sofa, she crossed to the window and stared out at Carlisle Place.

The streetlamps cast pools of yellow light along the street, but nothing moved, and Will's parking spot was still conspicuously empty. She watched until her tea was gone, but still there was no sign of Will. Finally, she returned to the sofa, and, pulling the afghan off the back, she curled up opposite Sam to wait.

A soft rap woke her out of a restless sleep, and for a moment, she couldn't recall why she was on the sofa instead of in her bed. Then the whole afternoon and evening came rushing back, and she bolted for the door. Will's hand was raised as if he was getting ready to knock again when she yanked the door open and nearly fell into his arms.

"Nice welcome home," Will murmured as his arms closed around her. He lifted her off the floor as he stepped inside and shut the door behind him with a soft click. He set her down and kissed her temple.

The warm rush of relief made Bree giddy and thankful for Will's strong arms holding her. Then anger blossomed. She pushed away and glared up at him. "This is exactly what I told you I couldn't cope with. And that!" She pointed at Sam, still cuddled under his quilt, but with his thumb no longer in his mouth.

"What about Sam?" Will looked perplexed.

"He was so worried about you he was sucking his thumb." Her voice trembled between anger and desperation.

Will crossed the room and squatted in front of the sofa. "Hey, sport. I'm back." He brushed the bangs off Sam's face. Slowly Sam opened his eyes.

It took a moment for him to wake up and for the import of what he was seeing to sink in, but then Sam launched himself into Will's arms. "You're home."

Will staggered backward but laughed as he regained his balance and stood up. "Did you think I wouldn't come home?" Sam wrapped his legs about Will's waist, and the quilt fell forgotten to the floor. Will's gaze caught Bree's across Sam's head. "Shall I put him in his bed?"

Without waiting for an answer, Will carried Sam down the hallway. The murmur of their voices faded as Will turned into Sam's room, but they must have continued to talk because Will didn't return right away. Bree tried to gather the anger she'd felt moments ago around herself as armor.

She didn't want to care this much. She didn't want to endure another afternoon like this one. She didn't want to love him at all.

"He was tired," Will said, returning to the living room.

"He was worried," Bree countered.

Will gazed at Bree for a long moment before he spoke. "He didn't have to be. The only thing I told the boys was that I had to go into work for a while. What did you tell him?"

Bree tried to recall exactly what she had said but couldn't. She did remember wondering if Sam was worried only because she was. "Nothing," she huffed defensively.

Will's blond brows rose as if he doubted her word. "Did you turn on the news? Is that how he knew about the manhunt?"

"He didn't find out about that from me. I didn't turn the TV on. Maybe you should be asking your brother what they were watching."

Will's shoulders slumped. "Maybe the boys turned the TV on in Rick's bedroom. Ben wouldn't have let them watch news coverage if he'd known it was on. Look, Bree . . ." He held his hands toward her in entreaty. "I'm sorry Sam was worried. I'm sorry I didn't call sooner. I just got caught up in reports and paperwork, and I didn't think."

"That's the whole problem. You don't think. You just do. It's who you are." Her anger was back, and she gathered it around her like a shield.

"I also stopped by the hospital to see the guy who got shot. He's going to be okay, in case you want to know. So, I guess I'll be going now. Where did you leave the Jeep?" Will looked tired.

Bree glanced at the clock and realized it was after eleven. He must be exhausted. She let go of her anger and crossed the room to him. "Ben came for it. He said you didn't like leaving the bike out front." She put her hand on his shoulder and tiptoed to kiss him on the cheek. "I'm glad everything's okay, and you're home safe."

"Tell Sam I'll see him Tuesday for scouts."

Bree followed him to the door, trying to think what else she should say or should have said.

Will stood in the open doorway, gazing at her as if there was something else he wanted to say, too. The lines of fatigue were etched deep around his eyes and mouth, and there was no glimmer of either his smile or his humor.

"Good night, Bree." Will left and closed the door behind him.

CHAPTER 19

Except for a few brief moments when he stopped in to pick Sam up for scouts, Bree didn't see Will all week. When she let herself think about it, curiosity niggled at her. Where had he been planning to take her on Sunday when the call from his captain came in? Will had been brimming with humor and eagerness, and when their afternoon had been interrupted, he'd said he would show her later. But later had not come, and Will had not mentioned it again.

Bree was ashamed of the way she'd lashed out at him. Her anger had created an uncomfortable distance between them that she didn't know how to breach. It was not Will's fault that she'd let her anxiety get the best of her. It hadn't even been his fault that Sam had been worried. Will had been exhausted, yet he'd taken the time to reassure Sam and tuck him into bed. And look how she had rewarded his thoughtfulness.

Sam had bounced back as if the day hadn't happened at all. He'd returned from scouts full of excitement about the Pinewood Derby races coming up the Saturday after Easter. Several fathers had come down to the church basement to set up the race track again so the three boys who would be headed to the regional competition could run their racers through their paces. Sam was sure he had a chance to win a ribbon at least.

Now it was Saturday, and they were both at loose ends. Sam had gone upstairs that morning with the list of things he had been required to learn for his First Holy Communion. Everything on the list had been checked off, and Sam couldn't wait to show Will because it meant Sam had completed another scouting achievement and would get his religious emblem at the next award ceremony. He had come back a few minutes later, despondent because Will was not at home.

Bree thumbed through Sam's Wolf Handbook, looking for another activity that might interest him. Something a mother and son could do together.

"Why don't we take a bike ride today? You can show me all the signals and safety rules you've learned."

"Where will we go?" Sam asked, brightening quickly.

Bree thought about it. They could ride to the beach. It was a lovely day for the beach. But they could also ride in the other direction and visit the Jolee Plantation. Will said the place had been cleared, and the local sheriff was keeping an eye on it. There seemed no reason why she and Sam should not ride there together.

"How about we pack a picnic lunch and ride to the Jolee Plantation? I can take more photos, and you can learn a little history while we're there."

"History is boring." Sam shrugged.

"Maybe in books at school. But it's a lot more fun when you can actually go to the places you read about. I know you've been studying about Tide's Way in school. About how it got settled and that tobacco was grown here before the Civil War."

"I suppose," Sam agreed. "But can I take my kite in case there's some wind, and I can fly it while you're poking around with your camera?"

A short time later, they set off with her camera and their lunch in her backpack and Sam's kite rolled up in his. He demonstrated all the signals he knew before they set off. He was meticulous about signaling for the turnout of Carlisle Place and again when they turned right at Joel's Diner. Following him, Bree was again assailed by how quickly her son was growing up.

They turned off Stewart Road onto the long tree-lined drive to the plantation and followed it around to the right, all the way to the front veranda, where they parked their bikes and removed their helmets.

Just as Bree had done on her first trip to the plantation house, they stepped up onto the veranda and circled the house while Bree explained about the rooms. They walked down to the ruined slave quarters, then back to the outdoor kitchen. Locks had been installed just as Will had told her they would be, but at least they could peer in the windows of buildings that had them. Bree told Sam the story Emmy Lou had passed along about the ghost.

"I wonder what it was like for them?" Sam asked, frowning.

"For who?" Bree asked.

"For the slaves. I wouldn't like to get whipped, would you?"

"Who said anything about whipping?" Slaves had been whipped, and it was a sad and unpleasant piece of American history, but she didn't think that subject had come up at school.

"Christopher told me that the white people whipped their slaves."

"Who's Christopher?"

"He's a kid in my class. He said his ancestors were slaves."

That would explain Sam's interest. "Well, Christopher is right. Not all slaves were treated so badly, but some were."

"I think it's mean." Sam looked at Bree with a mutinous glare in his eyes.

"That's what the Civil War was about. Stopping slavery."

"And Abraham Lincoln made them free on January 1, 1863."

"How did you know that?"

"We learned it at school." Sam shrugged as if the discussion was over. "Can we have lunch now?"

After lunch, while Sam ran down the slope in front of the mansion, trying to get his kite aloft, Bree walked down to the fieldstone wall that skirted Stewart Road to take panoramic photos of the plantation, the remaining buildings, and the fields around them. She was just hiking back up when she heard Sam cry out.

The hair on the back of her neck rose as she ran in the direction the sound had come from. Had Will been right about evil people being up here? Had they grabbed Sam while her back was turned?

The vast expanse of overgrown lawn and tangled vegetation was empty. Bree stopped and searched with her eyes.

"Momma!" Sam's panicky voice came from the direction of a stand of trees and thorny bushes crowding the far edge of the once elegantly sloping lawn.

Bree dropped her camera and ran for the trees. She pushed her way into the dense growth of live oak that sprawled sideways more than it grew upwards. Low branches and swaths of Spanish moss tore at her hair and clothes as she went.

Then she saw him, sprawled awkwardly atop the remains of what looked like an old well house.

"Sam!" she called, her voice rising with fright.

"Help me," he whimpered.

Bree bolted the last few yards. Her heart nearly stopped when she realized Sam's leg had broken through the rotted wooden cover.

"My ankle hurts," he wailed. He rocked back and forth, his hand holding onto his thigh. Tears rolled down his cheeks.

"Don't move!" Bree shouted, terrified at the possibility Sam could fall all the way through. She had no idea how deep the well was, and if he fell in —

Bree grabbed Sam with one arm about his chest while she worked at freeing his foot. "Hold on to me," she instructed. When he wrapped both arms tight around her neck, she was able to use both hands to pull his leg free. With Sam still clinging to her neck, she forced her way back through the tangled vines and brush to the relatively tamer lawn where she stopped to assess his injuries. The ankle looked a little swollen, and there was a long scrape up the front of Sam's shin.

It didn't look as bad as she'd feared, but her heart still thundered in her ears. She felt almost lightheaded with relief. She forced herself to calm down for Sam's sake. He'd need to see a doctor. He didn't need to be afraid of what might have happened. At least not right now.

She picked him up and strode up the remainder of the slope to the mansion where she set him down on the edge of the veranda and propped his leg on one of their backpacks.

Sam continued to whimper. "It hurts, Momma. I can't move it 'cept it hurts."

"You probably just twisted it, but we'll still have to see the doctor to make sure." She prayed it was not broken.

Already it looked more swollen than before, and the scrape had begun to bleed. She dug into the little soft-sided cooler their lunch had been packed in and took out the bag of ice. It was more than half-melted, but it would be better than nothing. She pressed it to the most swollen part of Sam's ankle.

Sam winced, but he stopped crying. He was doing his best to be brave. She brushed his tears away, kissed his forehead, and pulled her cell phone out of her pocket.

"I left my kite on the hill," Sam told her in a wobbly voice.

"Let me get us a ride to the hospital first. Then I'll go find your kite." *And my camera.*

Bree dialed Zoe's home number, and when that went to the answering machine, she called her cell.

"Hey, Bree, what's up?" Zoe answered on the second ring.

Bree explained the problem. Zoe was immediately concerned, but she was visiting her dad and hadn't planned to be home until supper, unless Bree wanted her to leave right now. Bree told her not to worry; she'd call someone closer.

Ben and Meg were the closest. She tried them but got no answer there either. She tried her assistant who was on this weekend at Kett's, but Owen was right in the middle of fixing a sound system problem for the wedding reception going on.

Bree bit her lip, wondering who to try next.

"Call Will," Sam told her. "He'll come. I know he will."

Of course he would. After casting around in her mind for another possibility, she sighed and pressed connect for Will's cell number.

"Brianna?" Will sounded surprised.

"I —" Bree swallowed. "I need a ride to the hospital. Sam's hurt."

"How bad? Where are you?"

"It's just his ankle. I think maybe just a sprain, but we rode our bicycles here. I don't have my car." *And I don't know who else to call.*

"Where?" Will said again, his voice calm but urgent.

"We — we're at the Jolee Plantation."

Will made a sound that sounded like a growl. "I'll be right there."

He hadn't said where he was or what she had interrupted, but his Jeep bounded up the gravel drive less than ten minutes later with Ben right behind him in his pickup truck.

Rick was the first one out of either vehicle.

He hurried over to Sam's side, his eyes wide with ghoulish excitement.

"How is he?" Will strode toward them with a frown furrowing his brow. He glanced at Bree but squatted next to Sam and gingerly began palpating the now ballooning ankle. He pulled a handkerchief from his pocket and blotted the blood on Sam's shin.

"I fell in," Sam said, his voice calm now that Will was on the scene.

"Fell in where?" Will demanded, looking first at Sam, then at Bree.

Conflicting feelings raced through Bree, making her feel a little faint. Will's immediate and unquestioning response to her call for help eased her anxiety the moment she'd heard his voice on the other end of the line. But that relief was shadowed by the glower on his face now and the scolding she knew would come eventually.

"I think it was an old well."

What had sounded like a good idea just a few hours ago, no longer seemed smart, even to her own thinking. They hadn't met with any bad guys, and she hadn't seen any more of the debris that had worried Will before, but Sam had gotten hurt just the same, and it could have been so much worse.

"Show me where."

Feeling a little like she was headed to the principal's office, Bree led Will back down the hill toward the tree line.

"Are you kidding me?" Will asked as she waded into the brambles again with him right behind her.

She wished she was. When she reached the defunct well, Will whistled.

"Jesus!" he exclaimed as he looked into the hole Sam had broken through. "Mary and Joseph," he added, feeling gingerly around the edges with his fingers.

"I can't believe you brought him here." There was an unnaturally clipped edge to Will's usual warm drawl. He turned and shoved his way out, slapping angrily at dangling moss that dared to grab at his clothing. "He's definitely going to need a tetanus shot. There are rusty nails in that thing. He could have fallen in. What were you thinking?"

Will looked as if he might say something else but turned and trotted back to Sam.

"Time to get you to the doctor, sport."

"Can I go too?" Rick jumped up to ask.

"No, you cannot go too," Ben answered for Will.

"But Sam's my best friend," Rick protested.

"And his mother does not need to be keeping an eye on you while she has other things to worry about." Ben was firm. Rick pouted but didn't argue.

"I came to haul your bikes back to the house, so you won't have to worry about them," Ben told Bree. He bent to give Sam's shoulder a pat. "Just think, if it's broken they'll give you a cast, and everyone can sign it. You'll be a star." He ruffled Sam's hair. "Come on, Rick. Help me with the bikes."

"Call me as soon as you get home," Rick told Sam as he turned to follow his father.

Will scooped Sam off the veranda and headed for his Jeep. Bree scurried back to get her camera and found Sam's kite where he'd abandoned it not far away. She grabbed the backpacks and hurried to catch up to Will.

Will settled Sam sideways on the back seat, adjusting the seat belt and shoving a blanket under his foot to elevate it further. Then he climbed into the driver's seat and started the car.

On the way to the hospital, Will entertained Sam with an amusing story of something that had happened to him when he was Sam's age. Bree stared at her hands, twisting them in her lap, worrying about just how bad Sam's ankle was. And just how angry Will would be when the crisis was over.

"It's a rite of passage," Will said, reaching over to put his hand on top of hers. He squeezed lightly and put his hand back on the steering wheel.

She looked at him, surprised by the sudden concern for her. "What rite of passage?"

"It's a guy thing." Will gave her that half-smile of his. The one that told her he was trying to lift her spirits, whatever else he might be thinking. "It's kind of dull living your whole life being afraid to take risks and explore a little."

"He's just a baby," she protested. She glanced over her shoulder.

Sam scowled. "I'm not a baby."

"You're my baby," Bree insisted. "You'll always be my baby."

Sam's scowl deepened.

"Exploring is a guy thing. Worrying is a mom thing." Will caught Sam's gaze in the rearview mirror. "My mom calls me her baby sometimes too."

The scowl disappeared. "But you're all growed up."

"Doesn't matter. That's just how moms are."

Sam rolled his eyes at this bit of intelligence.

Bree didn't know how to respond to what appeared to be two very conflicting vibes Will was sending her way. One minute he looked angry enough to eat nails, the next he was holding her hand and offering comfort.

A few moments later they pulled into the hospital parking lot. Will drove around to the emergency entrance and parked. "How about I give you a piggyback?" he asked as he released his seat belt and turned to Sam.

As careful as Will was to minimize the jouncing, tears returned to Sam's eyes as they made their way across the parking lot. He smiled in spite of the pain and told Will to giddyapp. If this was how boys lived their lives, Bree's life just got a lot harder to understand. Her son was hurting yet daring Will to do something that was bound to hurt even worse.

Will readjusted Sam's position on his back, doing his best to be gentle. Sam's arms tightened around Will's neck. The trust Sam had in him was humbling. So was Sam's brave front during his long ordeal at the hospital, first with X-rays, then the cast, and then more X-rays to check the fit. He had wanted to get himself to the Jeep unaided, but Bree had worried that the pain medication might make him dizzy.

Will stepped off the elevator in their apartment building, careful not to bump the bright colored cast on the doorframe. At Bree's door she juggled the backpacks and Sam's crutches, fumbled with her keys, and finally got the door unlocked. She pushed it wide for Will to enter.

"On the sofa or into bed?" Will asked while Bree dropped her things on the sofa. As he'd lifted Sam out of the back seat of his Jeep, Will had noticed that Sam's eyes were drooping with the pain medication they had given him at the hospital. He wouldn't be awake for long.

"Bed," she said, reaching to take Sam from him.

"I'll take him the rest of the way," Will told her. He wasn't quite ready to relinquish the feeling of Sam's arms about his neck or the feeling that he was important to this boy.

Bree nodded her acquiescence and led the way, flicking on lights as she went. "I'm glad we stopped for sub sandwiches on the way home. He's looking ready to drop. But he still needs to stop in the bathroom first." She pushed the bathroom door wide and turned on that light before continuing on down the hall toward Sam's bedroom.

Will set Sam down in front of the toilet and helped him balance while he peed.

"Now for the teeth."

Sam sighed but hopped over to the sink and plucked his brush out of the holder. "Mom's mad at me," he said around a mouthful of toothpaste and brush.

"She's not mad, sport. She was just worried. Moms get scared when their kids get hurt."

Sam finished brushing and rinsed his mouth. "But tomorrow she's got something important at work. I was supposed to go home from school with Rick. But now I can't even go to school."

"We'll work something out. Don't worry. Right now you need to get to bed and sleep off that stuff they gave you in the emergency room." He scooped Sam up into his arms. "Tonight you get special treatment, but tomorrow, you get to try walking in that thing."

Bree had turned back the covers and laid out Sam's pajamas. Will set Sam down and wrestled his shorts off over the cast while Bree removed Sam's remaining sneaker.

"Can I still play baseball?" Sam asked as

he lifted his arms so Will could tug his shirt off.

"Probably not happening this year." Will slipped the pajama top over Sam's head, then settled him back on his pillows and sat on the mattress next to him. "Maybe we can think of something else you can do this spring to take the place of baseball."

"Fishing?"

"Not 'til you don't have to wear the cast. I don't think it's supposed to get wet."

"But what will I do all day?"

Will smiled at the exaggeration. "Let's worry about that tomorrow. Right now you need to catch some ZZZs."

"Okaaaay." Sam yawned.

Bree knelt beside the bed. She curled her arm about Sam's head and leaned in to kiss him. "I'll be listening really hard, so if you need anything in the night, just call, and I'll be right here." She gave him a hug. "Love you."

"Love you too, Momma." Sam's voice trailed off, and he shut his eyes.

Will glanced at Bree as an overwhelming feeling of closeness crept over him. She pushed Sam's bangs off his face and caressed his cheek with the backs of her fingers. She looked worried.

"He'll be okay," Will tried to reassure her.

"I know." Bree shoved herself to her feet and backed toward the door. Then she was gone.

An unfamiliar contentment settled into Will as he sat there with one hand resting on Sam's thigh as Sam's breathing slowed, and his body relaxed into sleep. Will offered up the prayers Sam probably would have said if he hadn't been so sleepy. Finally, he fluffed the blankets where they draped over the injured foot, turned out the light beside Sam's bed, and stood up. He paused at the door and looked back at the sleeping boy.

It would never have occurred to Will that putting a kid to bed at night could tug so firmly at his heart. It's not like he'd never done it before. He'd babysat for Ben a number of times, but somehow this felt different. Maybe it was just because Sam had been injured. But what would it be like to tuck Sam in every night? The longing to have the right to do just that caught Will unexpectedly. He sighed and headed for the kitchen.

Bree was leaning against the counter in the kitchen, holding a steaming mug to her lips.

"Want a cup?" she said, holding hers up.

"What I want is to know what you were doing at the Jolee place after you agreed not to go there alone." He hadn't meant to challenge her quite so aggressively, but suddenly the whole afternoon telescoped into this. Sam could have fallen into the well and drowned. He could have broken both legs even if there was no water in the damned thing. And all because Bree chose to ignore his warnings. He might not have any rights where Sam was concerned, and Bree had made it clear she could think and decide for herself. But the frustration bubbled to the surface anyway.

Her shoulders stiffened immediately, her withdrawal obvious. "I thought it would be all right just to go there for a picnic."

"The beach would have been a better choice." *Anywhere else would have been a better choice.*

"But I wanted to take some pictures."

"For a woman who spends so much effort avoiding risks, you seem pretty blind about the Jolee place."

"I didn't take any risks."

"Oh, and Sam got hurt because you were being careful?"

"I didn't know about the well. He was supposed to be flying his kite."

"And where were you while he was flying it? If you'd been doing your job instead of worrying about a rundown old plantation,

Sam wouldn't have gotten bored with the kite and gone exploring."

Bree's shoulders caved, and tears sprang into her eyes.

Will changed his mind and grabbed the extra mug she'd left sitting next to the coffee maker. As he poured, he did his best to curb the exasperation that had been building inside him since moment she'd called him. When he thought he had himself under control, he turned to face her.

"I shouldn't have come at you like that. You're a good mom, and that was unfair. Boys do stupid things and get hurt all the time. I should know."

The mug trembled in her grasp, and she set it down on the counter with a clatter.

"Bree. I'm sorry." Will shoved his own mug back on the counter next to hers and pulled her into his arms. She buried her face against his chest, her hands clutching at his shirt. Her whole body trembled.

It was the aftershock. She'd been frightened and alone, but she'd done what she'd needed to do. She'd even called him knowing he'd probably rip into her. He was venting his own fright on her. He rocked her, murmuring his apology again.

When the trembling stopped, Bree pushed free of his embrace, but he kept his hands cupped about her shoulders. "You going to be okay?"

She nodded and offered him a tremulous smile. "I should probably get used to this sort of thing, huh?"

"Some day I'll tell you some of the things my brothers and I put my mom through."

"Maybe you shouldn't. My imagination comes up with too many possibilities as it is."

Her cheeks were still wet with the tears she'd done her best not to shed. He brushed them off her face with the pads of his thumbs. "I'm sorry Sam got hurt, and I'm sorry I got angry."

She buried her face in her hands. He drew her in again, looping his arms around her waist and resting his cheek against the top of her head. The scent and feel of her so close awoke other feelings in him that didn't belong to this moment. He tamped the desire down and just held her because that's what she seemed to need from him at the moment.

She mumbled something he didn't catch. He lifted his head and glanced down into her now upturned face. "What was that?"

"Thank you for being there."

I could be here for you forever if you'd let me. "I'm glad I was close by."

The whiskey color of her eyes darkened. Then, before he could guess what was going on in her head, she reached up and pulled his mouth down to hers.

As her body molded itself to his, and her hands raked through his hair, he tightened his embrace. Sam, the afternoon, his anger, and her defiance all dissolved into flaming desire. When she parted her lips, he took that too, plunging his tongue in to dance with hers. Will was as aroused as he'd ever been in his life.

"I want you," she whispered against his lips when they parted for a breath of air. "I shouldn't, but I do."

Her admission brought Will back to earth with a jarring thud. She was reeling with the aftereffects of a frightening afternoon and overwhelmed with thanksgiving for his having rescued her. If he accepted her wide-open invitation, he'd be taking advantage. He wanted her, but not like this. Not because her feelings were wrapped up in gratitude and whatever other repercussions were going on in her mind right now.

He put both hands at her waist and held her away. For several breathless moments he rested his forehead against hers and waited for the raging surge of blood and need to subside.

"When you want me for *me,* then ask."

He dropped his hands from her waist and stepped away. She frowned as if she was puzzled by his withdrawal. Hell, he was puzzled by it. He'd wanted to make love to her for weeks, yet the first likely chance it might have happened, he'd turned the opportunity down? What was wrong with him? He was acting like a freaking Boy Scout.

"But I —" Now embarrassment seemed to overtake her as she realized the import of what she'd said and done and might have done had he not stopped her. He hoped she remembered she'd initiated the kiss and the heavy-duty arousal that had come of it.

"You're tired, and you're not thinking straight," he offered to her as a way out.

He reached for his mug, emptied the contents into the sink and put the mug in the dishwasher. "Sam says you have something important at work tomorrow."

"I . . ." She frowned and wrinkled her forehead as recollection came back. "I have a seminar. It's a new client. In the afternoon."

"Well, I'm off tomorrow if you want me to stay with Sam.

Bree bit her lip. "But . . ."

"But — ?"

"I should be here with him. I need to take

care of him. I'm his mother."

"I really don't mind, Bree. Besides . . ." Will touched her cheek with his knuckle. It was all he dared let himself do. "I told him I'd think of something to take the place of baseball. Has he ever made a model?"

Bree shook her head.

"Good. That's what we'll do then." He turned and headed for the front door.

Bree followed him and put a hand on his arm when he turned to face her.

"Thanks, Will. For everything. I —" She blushed again.

"Get some sleep. You look like you could use it." Then, before he could change his mind, he let himself out and closed the door.

Chapter 20

Tired as she was, sleep was a long time coming. Snippets of the afternoon kept replaying over and over in her head. Riding down Stewart Road behind Sam, marveling at how quickly he was growing up. Sam with his leg thrust through the hole in the old well cover and panic in his voice. Will caring for Sam with incredible tenderness. Will glowering at her for her stupidity. Will stepping away from her with regret on his face after she'd thrown herself at him.

That last bothered her more than all the rest. If he hadn't put a stop to things, she'd have thrown caution to the winds. Actually, she had thrown caution out the door when she'd admitted she wanted him. She hadn't meant to say it aloud, but the words had slipped out anyway.

He thought her desire was just gratitude. And maybe she should let him continue to think that. But it was way too late to convince herself.

For weeks she'd been telling herself that the physical attraction she felt for Will was only that. Because she was a healthy young woman with normal appetites. Because it had been too long since any man had touched her with desire. Dismissing the lack of any similar yearning when Bob kissed her as not important, she had been lying to herself because it seemed safer not to get involved with Will.

She'd kept telling herself Will was just a jock, addicted to anything that created an adrenaline rush. A cop who enjoyed the dangerous aspects of his job. An overgrown kid with too many big toys. A man she could not afford to love.

But then she'd begun to see the other side of him. Even when she was being argumentative, and in his opinion, unreasonable, he'd been even-tempered and fair. He'd lost his cool only twice, and both times had been fully justified. Even then he'd exhibited restraint and apologized for any harsh words he'd said.

He was amazingly patient with Sam, taking far more time and interest than could possibly be expected of an unattached bachelor, even if he was Sam's Cub Scout den father.

Their date that Will still smilingly insisted was not a real date had been a turning point. Looking back now, it was easy to see, but at the time she'd still been clinging to the fiction that all she wanted was a friend.

But friends did not feel the way he'd made her feel tonight. He'd kept his promise, so she'd made the first move. He'd offered compassion and comfort. She'd taken both and turned them into a heady roller coaster of passion. She'd pressed her aching, needy body to his and let herself be consumed by his answering arousal. If he hadn't stopped her, she'd have taken him to bed.

Was she really crude enough to take a lover without a permanent relationship? Or was she brave enough to let herself fall in love and give Will her heart as well? Was that even what he really wanted from her?

Answers to those questions were troubling, but even without answers, what she felt for Will was not gratitude, and perhaps it was dishonest to let him go on thinking it was. He deserved better than that.

Sam still slept. Bree had left for work almost an hour ago. Will put his feet up on the coffee table, sipped his third cup of coffee, and contemplated his situation.

He could have taken her to bed last night.

She'd been aroused and willing. But then he'd had an attack of scruples. Even a cold shower had not taken the edge off his need. But he was still glad he'd turned her down. If he hadn't, he'd never know what her real reason for wanting him was.

The litany about why she didn't want to get involved with him was getting threadbare, but she'd continued to cling to it in spite of moments he knew they'd connected on some far deeper level than just friendship.

He remembered Jake telling him that Zoe wanted a Cinderella ending. How ironic to discover he was just as idealistic as his new sister-in-law. If he'd made love to Bree last night, he was sure it would have been amazing. But he hadn't wanted gratitude. He wanted her love.

"Momma?"

Will shot off the sofa, glad to have his fruitless thoughts interrupted. He set his coffee mug down and hurried down the hall.

"Where's Mom?" Sam asked when Will reached his bed.

"She's at work. You get me instead. Gotta go the bathroom?"

Sam nodded and started to get up, then looked at his new cast as if he'd forgotten he had it. "Are you going to carry me again?"

"Depends on how bad you gotta pee."

"Kinda bad," Sam admitted, clutching at himself.

"Just this once, then." Will scooped him up and strode to the bathroom where he set him down in front of the toilet and lifted the seat for him. "Be right back."

He had to hunt for Sam's new crutches. Bree hadn't left them by the bed where he thought they'd be. They turned up leaning in the corner by the front door where she must have propped them when they came in the night before. He carried them back to the bathroom.

"These are going to be your new best friends for the next eight weeks. Might as well get used to them."

Sam fitted them under his arms the way the nurse had shown him the night before, took a couple tentative steps, and grinned up at Will.

"I checked the weather, and it's warm enough for shorts. That will make getting dressed a whole lot easier, but I'll help with the stuff you can't do by yourself."

Sam accomplished the task of dressing himself with a lot less help than Will would have guessed. His underwear was the biggest hurdle, but once Will had stretched them over the bright blue cast, Sam managed the rest.

"Now for breakfast and then we have to go out."

"Out where?" Sam asked, hobbling along in front of Will toward the kitchen.

"Two places. First to your school to pick up your books and homework for the rest of the week."

Sam groaned, made a face, then brightened. "And where else?"

"That's a surprise."

Bree sorted through her keys, then remembered the door would probably be unlocked. She let herself into her apartment, and the first thing to hit her was the delicious aroma of something cooking in the kitchen. Curious, she dropped her briefcase and the book she had bought for Sam and followed her nose.

Sam and Will sat at the table, their heads bent over a project spread across layers of newspaper.

Will looked up first. "Hi. How'd the seminar go?"

"It went fine."

"Look, Mom!" Sam held up a half-constructed model of an old-fashioned biplane.

Will got to his feet and met her in the archway between the kitchen and the dining area. For a minute, Bree thought he was going to kiss her. As if this were the end of a normal day, and he always welcomed her home like this. The thought made her heart race, and she rather wished he would kiss her. But he just passed by and headed for the stove.

"What smells so good?"

"Just spaghetti with a twist."

Will had surprised her again. "I didn't know you were so domestic."

"Would it be to my advantage?" He dumped the pasta into her colander in the sink, set the empty pot on a potholder, and winked at her.

"Mo-om." Sam had lost patience with her delay in checking out his project. "Look at what I'm making."

Bree dragged her gaze away from the appealing image of Will with his hands thrust into her kitchen mitts and a grin on his face. He had a smudge of something red on his cheek that she wanted to wipe off. Or kiss off.

She tried to banish that last thought as she turned to her son. Her face burned.

"You're doing a really good job of it."

"It's the first ever airplane." Sam made the model swoop in a circle and land in the middle of the newspaper-covered table. "I saw the real one last year. Remember?"

"Yes, I remember. How is your ankle?" She hugged him, still struggling with the embarrassingly wayward thoughts that only she knew.

Sam held up the blue cast for her inspection. "It's good." He dropped his foot and went back to his model. "Will says maybe we can build a model airplane that really flies next."

Bree turned to Will. "Really?"

"Sure. Why not?"

"Because they're expensive. And hard to fly. Have you ever flown one?"

"No, but I'd like to try. And I'd pay for it."

The last thing Bree wanted right now with her emotions so tangled and her intentions totally up in the air was to feel indebted to Will. She already owed him a great deal, but so far, she wasn't willing to give anything back. That wasn't fair to him. She started to say so, but Will neatly changed the subject.

"Time to put the model away and set the table for supper, sport."

Sam, who usually lollygagged about picking things up, immediately began scooping up tiny plastic model parts and dropping them into the box they'd come out of. He set the airplane on the sideboard and rolled up the newspapers. "I'm done."

"You are a miracle worker," Bree said in a quiet aside to Will.

"I'm a novelty," he replied, setting a handful of tableware in front of Sam. "Wash your hands first. Then set the table while I serve, and your mother gets to sit down and get waited on for a change."

I could get used to this. The thought rattled around in Bree's head as she took a seat while Sam hobbled off toward the bathroom, and Will set a steaming bowl of spaghetti on the table next to a pitcher of sauce.

"It's nothing fancy," Will said. "Just something I saw on Facebook that my nephews and nieces all think is pretty fun."

Bree peered into the bowl. "Whoa! How did you do that?" Cooked spaghetti protruded from both ends of short sections of hotdogs.

"It's magic." He grinned at her and set a plate at each place.

Sam returned, swinging between his crutches as if he'd been using them for months.

Will used her salad tongs to grab a bundle of spaghetti and hotdogs and placed it on her plate. Sam pushed utensils into place and dropped into his seat. Will plopped a serving of spaghetti and hotdogs on Sam's plate.

"Wow! Mom. Look at that!" Sam stabbed a chunk of hotdog and lifted it up to inspect Will's magic. "How'd you make it do that?" He touched the totally limp pasta and looked to Will for an explanation.

"It's my super-secret recipe." Will laughed and ruffled the top of Sam head. "You going to offer grace first or just be a heathen?"

Sam dutifully set his fork down, crossed himself, and held one hand out toward Bree and the other to Will, before rattling off the grace he'd recently learned.

When Will's hand closed around Bree's, her heart jumped. She closed her eyes and tried to act as if his touch didn't distract her from her son's prayer. Sam finished, let go of her hand, and grabbed his fork. Will's fingers tightened around hers before she could draw her hand back.

His eyes, when she finally looked at him, glimmered with emotions she couldn't read. She returned the pressure of his fingers for a moment before he let her go.

When supper was done, Bree told Sam it was time to get into his pajamas. He informed her he could do it by himself and made his way down the hall, the soft thumps of his crutches fading away to nothing.

"You — you don't have to stay." Bree turned to Will. "I'll clean up."

"I don't mind helping." He got up from the table and moved toward her.

"You've already done so much. I can't begin to thank you."

"You don't have to." His voice dropped to a husky murmur. "I enjoyed my day. Sam's a fun kid. By the way, he did all the homework his teacher sent, too."

When Will grasped her upper arms, the heat from his hands sent waves of desire crashing through her, and she wanted to just walk the rest of the way into his embrace. But after last night and her embarrassing behavior, she turned away and began running the water to rinse the dishes.

"I especially enjoyed having supper together." Will stood directly behind her but didn't touch her.

"Me, too," she agreed, afraid to turn around. Afraid of what she might do if she did.

"Well." He sighed. "I guess I'll go say good night to Sam and get out of your hair."

She didn't even hear him move away, but when she finally turned around, he was gone. She felt oddly bereft. She strained to hear anything from the direction of Sam's room, but the soft murmur of voices didn't carry. The next thing she heard was the quiet click of the front door shutting.

Her shoulders slumped. The feeling of loss was huge. They were still just friends regardless of the obvious and mutual arousal of the night before. He'd dismissed her confession of desire as nothing more than exhaustion and worry. He was a guy. Maybe desire for an attractive woman was normal even if there was nothing in the way of emotional commitment.

She argued with herself the entire time she rinsed and washed and put away leftovers. She didn't want to get hurt, so she was better off not getting any more involved than she already was. But it hurt that he'd spurned her. It hurt that he'd left without saying good night. It hurt that she didn't even know her own heart.

Maybe Will was right, that she didn't want him for the right reasons. How had he put it? *When you want me for* me, *then ask.*

CHAPTER 21

On his way home from work, Will detoured through the center of Tide's Way and passed the assisted living center where Jake's mother-in-law now lived. He turned right onto the recently paved street where new homes were being built by one of his brother's competitors. The sign, erected since his last stop here, said Calhoun Drive. The first two homes were nearly completed, and both had *Sold* signs slapped across the *For Sale* signs still prominently displayed on the as yet unlandscaped lots.

Will slowed the motorcycle and put his foot out as he rounded the turn at the end of the short street and turned into the dirt driveway of the house he coveted. He'd been planning to bring Bree out to see it the afternoon of the big manhunt. He'd wanted to just show it to her without comment and see her reaction.

It would be months before the house was

ready for occupancy, but the spaces inside had begun to take shape, and he liked the way they felt. Like his parents' home on the island, the floor plan was very open, with views of the waterway from the first floor and the ocean from the second. Framing for a wraparound porch had been put in with temporary sheets of old plywood for decking. It would be the kind of porch he wanted to spend time on. A swing on the corner under the overhanging upper deck on one end. A row of comfortable chairs suitable for reading the Sunday paper or just watching the sun rise. Perhaps even a rocking chair for his mother because as soon as there were babies to rock, she'd be visiting often.

He parked his bike and strode up the plank that led to the front entrance. No doors yet either, so he walked right in to check on the progress the builders had made. He pounded on an exposed beam here and there, not sure why he did so, but it seemed like the thing to do.

Since his last visit, the fieldstone fireplace had been completed all the way up to the stringers of the first floor ceiling. The place where the staircase would be ran clear up to the rafters, and a skylight spanned the opening. Will climbed the ladder that was currently the only way to reach the second story. The hall subfloor ran around the stair opening, and four bedrooms opened off it. He walked through them one at a time, imagining the way it might look when he lived here.

This could be Sam's room with a window seat he could curl up to read on. Next came the baby's room. He'd have to wait to paint this room until he knew if it should be pink or blue. An extra room for a growing family. Hopefully there would be more than just one baby.

The last room was the master bedroom: the room with a view all the way to the ocean. He loved it. He crossed to the wide French doors, pushed one side open, and stood with his back to the room, staring out at the sea. He thought about Brianna Reagan.

Something seemed to have changed for Bree. He sensed it whenever they were close but couldn't quite define it. It was as if she was on the verge of telling him something important, but wasn't quite sure where to begin. She no longer kept her distance, and she hadn't used the word *friend* in a while.

Since the night of Sam's accident, she hadn't made any further physical overtures, and he was still waiting for her to make the first move. But things had changed just enough to give him hope. Not just hope, but the certainty that if he could just be patient for once in his life, things would turn out the way he wanted them to.

He'd stopped at the real estate office that afternoon and made a deposit on this house. Although the original plans had not called for a garage, he'd paid to have drawings made up for that as well as a tree fort for Sam. He'd also added an alcove to the downstairs that would have bookshelves on all three walls to hold the piles of books Bree had stashed everywhere in her apartment with room to spare for future additions to her library.

He didn't know what else she might like, but the house was still early enough in construction for her to add things. Or change anything she didn't care for.

Funding the house was not a problem. Other than his many toys, he'd lived pretty frugally most of his adult life. His student loans had been paid off a long time ago, and since then, he'd been investing any income he didn't need for living expenses. The old man in Wilmington hadn't charged the full rental value in return for Will taking care of maintenance, so even his expenses had been small.

Will turned back to the master bedroom. How would Bree decorate this space? He liked her taste. At least he liked the way she'd furnished and decorated her apartment. He'd be happy with anything she chose. So long as they were doing it together.

If she turned him down, he'd still move in when the house was completed, but it would seem awfully empty without her and Sam to bring it to life. Without the prospect of a new baby to occupy that pink or blue nursery.

Maybe Bree wouldn't want more children. That thought hadn't occurred to him before. Will retraced his steps to the small room. It could become a guest room. But he hoped not. He wanted a child of his own. Or two or three. Children he would plant inside her and watch grow, knowing they were his. He wanted to be there when they were born and hear little voices calling, "Daddy."

Maybe it was all a pipe dream, but he was going to do everything in his power to make it a reality.

The captain had called him into the office first thing this morning and offered him the coveted opportunity to join the new Rapid Response Team. Will had turned it down.

The captain tried to talk him out of the decision, but Will had made up his mind.

Bree didn't need a man who was more likely than the average guy to get killed on the job. If they were going to make a life together, have kids together, he needed to make serious changes in his life.

The Highway Patrol was his life. Up to now it had been his whole life. But that, hopefully, was about to change. Another position had opened up in the Wilmington barracks for a negotiator, the man who shows up and, from a safe and protected distance, talks dangerous people out of committing mayhem. He wouldn't be riding a motorcycle anymore after next month. He wouldn't be patrolling highways. When he wasn't called on for the specialty of his position, he'd be working a desk at headquarters, writing reports and doing research for the guys in the field.

A month ago, this decision would have appalled him. How quickly a man could make an entire one-eighty turn in his life. Diaz would never give it a rest. Will laughed at himself and turned to climb back down the ladder to the first floor.

He inspected the stonework. The mason was brilliant. Will loved the raised hearth design and could already imagine chilly winter nights spent with a fire crackling in the grate.

He wanted to bring Brianna here to see what she thought. Maybe then he'd go pick out a ring.

"But, mom. YOU promised," Sam wailed in protest.

"That was before you broke your ankle and ended up on crutches. A houseful of boys running around might be a bad place for you right now. You might get knocked over."

"But it's Rick's birthday. Everyone will be there and I won't. It's not fair."

"Life's not fair sometimes." Life certainly hadn't turned out the way Bree had seen it unfolding back when Sam was born.

"But I have to go," Sam insisted. "Pleeeee-ase."

"We're going over with Will for the cake and ice cream and to watch Rick open his presents. Then we'll come home."

"But I want to sleep over with everyone else," Sam whined. "I packed my bag already," he added as if this clinched his argument.

A soft rap on the door stopped Sam's entreaty, and he hobbled to the door before Bree could get off the sofa.

"Tell Mom I gotta stay for the sleepover," Sam greeted Will without ceremony.

Will glanced over Sam's head to Bree with his eyebrows raised. "Why the change in plans?" He stepped inside and set his gift on the table by the door.

"I just thought it might be better if Sam didn't stay overnight. He could get hurt, and I wouldn't be there."

Will turned to Sam. "Where's your stuff, sport?"

"In my bedroom."

"Then go get it. And don't forget the crutches."

Sam half-hopped, half-walked toward his room. Will turned back to Bree.

"Ben and Meg will be there. Nothing's likely to happen anyway, but if it did, they can handle it. And they'll call if Sam needs you."

"But —"

Will put a hand behind her neck and pulled her forward until his forehead rested against hers. "He'll be fine. Besides, you still have a mystery trip you haven't taken yet."

Bree pulled away and looked up into Will's mischievous blue eyes. "I thought you forgot." *She* had. At first. Wherever Will had planned to take her the day of the shooting and resulting manhunt had fallen off Bree's radar while she'd been blaming him for worrying her and Sam for all those hours he'd failed to call and reassure her. Then she'd been busy chastising herself for caring enough to be upset in the first place.

All that had changed in the aftermath of Sam's escapade, but Will hadn't mentioned it until now, so she'd figured it was no big deal. Maybe just a fun excuse to spend an afternoon with her.

"But we're all going to Rick's party." The protest was a token. Being with Will had taken on a whole new urgency.

"We get to leave early and let Meg and Ben ride herd on the boys." Will tilted his head to the side and swooped in to kiss her on the mouth.

His kiss was brief but startling in its intensity. Even the blue of his eyes was more intense as he drew back, his face suddenly very sober.

"I've packed us a picnic supper, and I've got a very special place I want to show you."

"The beach?" Bree breathed. The beach was a dangerous place to be with Will. Especially alone. At dusk. At a time when emotion and need could so easily overtake common sense.

He shook his head. "Not this time."

The letdown hit her unexpectedly. Deep down, she'd wanted to be in such a place. At a time when Will wouldn't blame gratitude for the other things she felt when he touched her.

I am a total mess. One minute I tell the guy to get lost. Then I can't wait to be alone with him. It's a wonder he even bothers with me. Her heart raced in expectation.

"I can't carry everything at once," Sam announced as he tapped his way back up the hall. His duffle bag bounced against his good leg. "The box is too big."

"I'll get it." Will strode toward Sam's room.

"I'm staying for the sleepover." Sam glowered at Bree.

"That's not how you ask, sport," Will said as he returned to the living room, the birthday gift tucked under one arm.

"But she promised." Sam twisted to face Will.

"That's *not* how you ask," Will repeated.

Sam sighed as if being asked to rake all the leaves in the entire complex. He turned back to Bree. "Please, may I stay for the sleepover?"

"Yes. You may stay." She was inordinately pleased that Will had waited to voice his different point of view until Sam was not present and then backed her up over Sam's manners. For the first time in a very, very, long time, she felt as if she wasn't totally alone bringing up her son. Whatever came of her evolving relationship with Will, for now the feeling was pretty nice.

Sam came and hugged her hard about the waist, dropping one crutch in the process. She bent and handed it back to him. "Just be careful. Okay?"

"I will, Mom. I promise."

Chapter 22

When will held the door for Bree, then closed it behind her and walked around to the driver's side of his Jeep, anxiety abruptly settled into his chest. Suddenly he wasn't sure about showing her the house before he declared himself. It seemed to make perfect sense before. But what if she felt like he was pressuring her into something?

Maybe he wouldn't tell her about wanting to fill the house with babies or even that he wanted her to share it with him. Maybe he should just show her the house and see if she liked it. Then decide what to do about revealing his heart to her later.

Maybe he needed to give her more time now that she'd stopped pushing him away at every turn. Time for the fiery attraction that boiled up whenever he held her to work its magic. If they were lovers first, maybe accepting him as her husband would just feel right. It wasn't too late to reconsider his career options, but he didn't really want to. So, he could give her as much time as she needed.

He climbed in the driver's seat and started the Jeep. "Ready?"

Her smile was tentative. "Am I going to like your surprise?"

"I hope so." God, did he hope so. He didn't recall being this nervous since he'd pinned a corsage on the girl he'd taken to his junior prom and nearly stabbed her in the process.

Bree pulled her feet up onto the seat and hugged her knees against her chest. Her gaze seemed to be anywhere but on him as they drove down Stewart Road, turned right onto Jolee, then veered left onto Shoreline.

"I'm glad we finally managed to tear ourselves away. Any later, and it would have been too dark," Will said as they approached their destination. He slowed to turn into Calhoun Drive. As the Jeep left the pavement and bumped down onto the dirt driveway of number eighteen, Bree did look at him, her brow furrowed.

"You want to show me a half-built house?"

"You'll see. Come on." He got out and hurried around to open her door. He took her hand and led her up the packed dirt path. Fortunately, the plank had been replaced with real stairs. The front door had been hung as well — a beautiful rich mahogany door with a moon-shaped window at the top. He opened the unlocked door and led her inside.

"They don't mind you wandering around a construction site?"

He shook his head. "Apparently not." Considering he was soon to be the owner of the place.

"Does this belong to someone you know?"

"Yeah. I know him. What do you think?"

Bree stood in the center of the living space and turned in a circle. She turned back to look at the main attraction of the currently empty room. "What a beautiful fireplace." She walked over and ran her hand along the mantel, which was another new addition since Will had put the deposit on the place.

"But that's not the best part." He grabbed her hand again and drew her around and into the area that would become the kitchen and dining area. Completely devoid of counters, cabinets, or appliances, it was a matter of imagination. But he had no problem picturing a table big enough for a family at one end and an expanse of glossy granite counters at the other. "I love eat-in kitchens. My mom always had a kitchen big enough to eat in. But when it's nice out, you can eat on the deck instead."

He towed her along toward the big French doors, pushed them wide, and stepped out onto the paint-stained temporary plywood decking. He watched her face carefully. He wanted her to love this house. He wanted it to catch her fancy just as it had caught his.

"You can see the waterway," she said in a wondering tone and pointed in that direction as she turned to look at him.

"It's even better upstairs. Come and see." Eager to show her everything at once, he pulled her back inside and over to the ladder. "You don't have a problem with ladders, do you?"

Bree smiled at him, getting into the spirit of exploration. She shook her head, then looked down at her skirt. "You go first."

He climbed quickly to the top and turned to watch as she started up the ladder. Before she even reached the top, she stopped and let out a sigh of delight as she gazed up at the big skylight. Slowly coming up the last few rungs, she kept looking over her shoulder at the windows that went all the way from the first floor to the ceiling on the second.

The sun was beginning to set, and already the windows were awash with pink and orange. "This is spectacular!" she whispered in awe. Will had to agree. He'd not seen the place when the sun was going down before, and it sure was a glorious sight. The kind that takes your breath away when it catches you unaware.

Her eyes still glittered with excitement and appreciation as he escorted her from room to room, skipping the need to return to the hall since the studs were still bare outlines, and no wallboard had been installed yet.

New framing had been added where he'd sketched in a window seat in the room he thought of as Sam's. Bree headed directly for it and stood gazing out the window toward the east. "You could watch the sun rise from here." She turned to face him. "I always wanted a window seat when I was growing up. But my dad said there wasn't a workable space to put one in our house." She turned and headed toward the last bedroom. "This must be the master bedroom," she said as she stepped between the studs.

"It will be when the place is finished." Will followed her and was rewarded with her gasp of delight as she hurried across to the upper set of French doors.

"This is a room for early risers," she said as she pushed open the doors and stepped out onto the balcony. "Wow! You really can see the ocean from here." Bree turned back, her face alight with pleasure. "Look, Will. Just think of the sunrises whoever lives here will see every morning."

Should I tell her I'm hoping to watch those sunrises with her? "Pretty spectacular. Don't you think?"

"Someone is going to love it." She turned and pointed toward the south wall. "If they put their bed there, they can watch the sun come up without even getting out of bed."

"That's what I was thinking when I made an offer for this place."

Her eyes went completely round. "You're the owner?"

"I am. Or I will be once all the paperwork is done. Me and the bank." She loved it as much as he did. Maybe he should have gotten that ring before he showed her the house. He could have proposed to her right here. Right now.

But he still didn't want to rush his fences. He wanted to be sure she had enough time to accept them being together as a couple. To love him enough that whatever risk she feared would be worth taking.

"You are going to love living here. Just think about it."

"I have been thinking about it. I've been thinking about it a lot." *I've been thinking about you living here with me.*

"I love that the porch goes all the way around the house. You can watch the sunrise in bed, then sit in a lounger out front to see the sun set. In the winter you can have fires in the fireplace. It's a terrific house. You'll even have enough space for all your toys." She turned back to the deck and stepped outside to peer down into the deepening gloom of the yard. "Is there going to be a garage?"

Will followed her out onto the deck and pointed toward the south side of the house. "Somewhere in that direction."

She turned to face him, and suddenly they were very close. Close enough to touch, but he kept his hands to himself. "Did you like my surprise?"

"Yes. Yes, I did. I love your new house. I can't wait to see it when it's finished."

"I brought us a picnic. I thought you might like to share the first meal I ever eat here."

"Can we eat right here?"

"I can't think why not. I'll go get it."

Will hurried back through the empty room, down the ladder, and out to his Jeep.

Bree was sitting, leaning against the side of the house when he returned. He joined her and opened the lunch cooler. He handed her a turkey sandwich and opened a split of champagne.

She grinned at him. "So this is a christening of sorts?"

"It is," he agreed as he produced real wine glasses and poured them each a glass.

"To your new home." Bree held her glass up.

"To good friends," Will said, clinking the rim of his glass against hers. "And new beginnings." *And to this just being the first time we'll sit here like this.*

They ate in a companionable silence as the last of the light from the setting sun played off first the ocean and then the waterway before fading into dusk.

"Look, Will." Bree pointed to the horizon. "The moon is coming up."

Fat and full, seeming bigger than usual as it climbed out of the ocean and into the sky, the moon was a beautiful, bewitching sight. Almost as beautiful and bewitching as the woman who sat beside him. With the picnic finished, Will jammed all the remains back into the cooler and scooted it out of the way. His heart hammered as he reached for her hand. She turned her head and looked up at him.

Her eyes twinkled in the dim light. The tripping of his heart grew louder. *I love you,*

Bree. He cradled her face in his hand and kissed her.

She half-turned and rested a hand against his chest as she leaned in to return his kiss. He looped his arms around her and pulled her close. The feel of her in his arms, responding to his kiss, to his touch, felt so good. So perfect. The faint scent of flowers that always seemed to hover about her enveloped him and made him feel a little dizzy.

How had he had fallen so completely in love with this woman? In spite of her initial resistance, in spite of her sometimes feisty disregard of his best advice, in spite of everything that should have been a turn-off? *How can she not see how great we could be together?*

Almost as if she could read his mind, Bree climbed over to straddle his thighs and wrapped her arms about his neck. It was a total turn-on, and he loved it. She kissed him with her mouth open and her tongue teasing his. She wriggled down into his lap and rocked her hips against his.

"Whoa, Bree," he gasped in response. He was loving it a little too much.

But Bree couldn't seem to get close enough. Her hands were everywhere, first in his hair, on his face, sliding down his chest, then around his torso, anchoring him while she squirmed against him. She kissed him with increasing eagerness. Tangling, teasing, arousing.

He was so hard. She had to feel his erection pressing into her warmth. She had to know what she was doing to him when she teased him like this. If he let this go on much longer, there would be no stopping. He wanted her so badly right now he might even sell his soul to possess her.

He lifted his mouth from hers and trailed kisses along her jaw, then down to the place where her pulse beat wildly in the hollow of her neck.

"Are you sure this is what you want, Bree?"

Bree couldn't recall ever wanting a man this much. With so much throbbing, demanding passion. "Yes," she whispered. "I want you to make love to me. I want you — for you."

"Brianna." Will's voice was husky with desire. He cupped her cheek and stared down at her. Dusk had disappeared, and it was nearly pitch dark, but his eyes glittered in the light of the rising moon. "Brianna."

Flames of desire scorched and tingled, banishing everything else but this man and the way he made her come alive. His fingers combed into her hair, and he held her face as if she was something infinitely precious.

"This isn't where I'd have chosen to make love to you for the first time," he murmured as he covered her face with butterfly kisses.

"You don't like moonlight?" she whispered, her breath catching in her throat.

"I love moonlight." The chuckle vibrated in his chest. "But there's no bed. There's not even a blanket."

She'd probably care later and wonder what had gotten into her, but right at this moment in time nothing mattered except that she wanted Will to make love to her. She wanted to feel him inside her. She wanted this raging need to explode in soul-satisfying release. And it didn't matter where they were. "For a man who likes to live dangerously, it hardly seems possible you've never made love anywhere but in a bed."

"Never quite like this." He touched her hair. "You are so beautiful with moonlight spilling over you and turning your hair to silver." He unbuttoned her blouse, slipped his hands inside, pushed her bra up, and cupped her bare flesh in his palms. Bree reached behind her to release the clasp at her back.

"So incredibly beautiful," he murmured.

He touched one nipple with his tongue.

Oh. My. God! In another minute she was going to come completely apart.

She tugged at his clothing, pulling at his belt and trying to unbutton his shirt at the same time.

He grasped her hands in his. "What's your hurry? You mind if I enjoy this part?" He took his time, undressing her one garment at a time, admiring her with his eyes, then waiting while she removed something of his. It should have seemed awkward, considering how they were sitting, but it didn't. It felt like a forbidden adventure and all that much more exciting.

"You are spectacular." He ran his index fingers down the slope of her breasts and settled his hands at her waist.

"You're pretty spectacular, yourself." She clutched at his broad shoulders and admired the expanse of bare muscled chest and the dusting of pale curls that tapered toward his belly button.

They were so close. So intimately close. The heat and urgency in him vibrated all around her. "I knew you liked to live life on the edge." She was suddenly aware of the cool evening air on her naked flesh and the rough boards beneath her knees, but she didn't care about any of it. Will was so warm and so close and as aroused as she was.

"Only way to experience it," Will murmured, cupping her breasts in his palms, then tipping his head down to kiss her nipples. She threw her head back and savored the sensations ripping through her. His calloused hands, rough against her breasts, the warmth of his mouth, his aroused body throbbing against hers. She moaned as desire and need whipped to a frenzy.

Then a chilling reality struck her, and she froze.

"Will," she whimpered in a panic. "I'm not —" She hadn't been on the pill since Ed was killed.

Will reached for his slacks. A moment later he had his wallet in his hand and fumbled in it. "I'm a boy scout. Remember?" He held up a small foil packet.

A bubble of relief fought its way up her throat. Even though she'd tossed common sense and restraint out the window, she treasured his humor and caution. If he'd engineered this tryst, at least he'd been careful enough to come prepared.

"Take me. I'm yours," she declared as she melted back into his embrace, ready to be consumed by everything he had to offer.

In this most unlikely place, in spite of all

the fighting she'd done to avoid getting involved with this man, when they came together, it felt like coming home.

The jeep hummed along, the only sound in the aftermath of the most mind-blowing sex of his life. Never in a million years would Will have guessed that Bree was the sort of woman who would be so eager to make love outdoors without a stitch of clothing to cover her, where anyone out walking a dog might see them. Even more surprising, she had started it. At the brink of no return, when he offered her an excuse to back off, she'd turned it down. She was an amazing woman. She had him, hook, line, and sinker. Especially after the way she'd taken charge of events on the little deck off their bedroom-to-be.

He glanced at her across the dimly lit Jeep. With her feet tucked under her, Bree sat half-turned in his direction, watching him with a lazy, satisfied smile lurking at the corners of her generous mouth.

"Will you spend the night with me?" *Please, Bree, say yes.*

He'd declared his love. He'd committed himself. As he'd pushed his way inside her, he'd uttered the words he'd always avoided before tonight.

I love you, Brianna.

She hadn't reciprocated, but he knew she heard him. He was sure what she'd felt was just as real and just as intense. Her body language told him so much more than words might have. The way she relaxed against him even after the last shudders of their release had faded away. Instead of scrambling to get dressed, she rested her cheek against his shoulder with her face pressed into his neck. He'd caressed her hair and her back and savored the peaceful togetherness, convinced she was just afraid to admit it. Even to herself.

"Just for tonight." He reached across the space between the seats and caressed her cheek. "Please?"

She turned her face toward her lap so he couldn't see her expression.

He put his hand back on the steering wheel. His heart hammered fiercely in his chest. Almost as much as he'd wanted to make love to her, he wanted to share his bed with her, wake up with her, and make love again. Linger over breakfast. A taste of forever.

Somehow he had to find a way to convince her that loving him would not end in a broken heart. But right at the moment, just keeping her with him seemed desperately important. Even if it was for just tonight and even if she withdrew into her shell again tomorrow. He could leave her with a memory she would never be able to erase and with feelings she might not be able to deny.

"Okay." Her whispered acquiescence could barely be heard over the hum of the Jeep's tires, but his heart soared.

Will wanted to make a fist and pump the air.

Chapter 23

"Morning, love."

Will's sexy drawl cut through the drowsy fog of semi-wakefulness. Her eyes popped open and focused on the unfamiliar bedroom wall. They were both still naked, his body warm and comforting. He curled behind her, his knees up under hers with his arm around her waist. He tugged the tangle of hair off her face and tucked it behind her ear, then kissed her cheek. "It sure would be sweet to wake up with you every morning."

"You know we can't." Not with Sam about. "It was just for last night." Everything Bree had been telling herself about herself and Will had been shattered last night. They weren't just friends. They could never be just friends. They were lovers. But could it last forever?

"I'd rather spend *every* night with you." He splayed his hand flat across her abdomen and pulled her firmly against him. "I can't think of a better way to wake up either." He moved his hips, and his arousal was obvious.

Instinct urged her to let him to slip inside her and take her from behind. She loved the way that felt. Without answering his stated desire, she arched her back instead to welcome his lovemaking.

He rolled from her, and cold air sliced between them. Her heart jerked in response to what felt like abandonment. But then the sound of the drawer in his bedside table hit her ears, followed by the snick of foil being removed from a condom. He drew her in again and slid his fingers between her legs, teasing her, making her ready.

She cried out with surprised pleasure when he thrust into her hard and deep and fast. She curled forward into a ball while he held her waist and thrust again. With each stroke, he found that magic sweet spot she'd almost forgotten she had. When the world exploded, he continued to plunge into her, again and again, moaning softly with each effort. She beat him to her climax, but she was so needy and so wet that in just moments, she was cresting again. This time they came together, and the shudder of their mutual release rocked her whole world.

Will stayed inside her for a long time as their breathing slowed and her heartbeat ceased to thunder in her ears. A drowsy, sated feeling crept over her. This she could get used to: this half-waking, half-sleeping sense of connectedness and utter satisfaction.

When Bree woke the second time, Will was entering the room wearing nothing but his briefs and a knowing smile. She had a hard time tearing her gaze away from the washboard abs and thickly muscled arms to notice the small tray bearing juice and steaming scones.

"Breakfast in bed," he announced as he set the tray down on her side of the bed.

She pushed herself to a sitting position, clutching the sheet around herself for modesty, although after the last twelve hours, there was little left that he'd not seen or touched.

"How did I deserve this?" She broke off a bite of scone and popped it into her mouth.

"I'm pulling out all the stops in my effort to impress on you how good it would be if we could wake up together every morning." He smiled, and his dimple creased his cheek with boyish charm. But there was nothing boyish about the rest of him, perched so close that she could feel the heat of him.

Bree thought about the first words he'd uttered that morning. Last night he'd told her he loved her. Could she take such a leap of faith? Could she lay herself open to heartbreak again?

Could she learn to live without him after last night?

He touched her cheek lightly with the backs of his fingers. "I want us to have a forever kind of relationship."

She swallowed the bite of scone convulsively.

"Will, I —"

He pressed a finger to her lips and shook his head. "If you're thinking about saying no, then don't." He bent and kissed her on the mouth without passion, but with a great deal of feeling.

"Before you answer, take time to think about it first. I've been thinking about it for a while, so I guess you need time, too.

"I know I can be impatient and overbearing. I know I'm not always the easiest guy to get along with. I'm impulsive, and I like to get my own way, but with you it's different. I want *you* to be happy too.

"I want to wake up with you in my arms every morning and go to sleep after making wild passionate love. But there's more to it than that. I love you. I love who you are.

Even when you worry about everything."

He dragged his hand through his hair. "I love Sam. I want to be his dad. Not his real dad. I know he already has one in heaven, but I want to be the dad that's going to be around for him to grow up with. I want to teach him about things. About girls and sports and how to be a man. The stuff boys need to learn from their fathers.

"But mostly, I want to be your husband. I know you think I live a dangerous life, but that's about to change too. I want to be around for a long time. I want us to grow old together. I want to love you for the rest of my life."

He paused in his litany.

"But this is about you, too. Don't tell me *no* until you've had time to think about what you really want. What you want deep down inside of you. Because just maybe I'm the guy who can give it to you. So, please, don't say anything right now. Think about it first. Okay?"

Bree thought about it all week. She had trouble thinking about anything else.

If she was ever going to trust her heart to a man again, Will had to be that man. Trusting Will had become her mantra all week. She made every decision, even little day-today ones, with the thought of trusting Will clutching at her heart.

With Sam back in the apartment, there could be no overnights. No falling asleep, sprawled together in sated contentment. No waking with Will's arm tucked firmly around her waist. They made love quietly in her frilled and flowery bedroom long after Sam had fallen into the dead sleep of an active little boy. There were condoms in her bedside table now, and she'd contemplated calling her doctor for a prescription. But the question of trusting Will with forever still loomed.

She had not even told Will she was in love with him. She'd only just admitted the truth to herself. She still struggled with the ramifications of being married to a cop. A trooper, she corrected herself. Will was a trooper. But it meant the same thing. The same dangerous occupation. The same potential for heartbreak. If there was to be any turning back, it had to come soon before she got in any deeper than she already was. But she couldn't bring herself to tell him that either.

Sam was delighted when Will showed up for supper every night. He didn't question the change. He just chattered through the meal, happy to share everything about his day with Will as much as his mom. More than half the time, Will put him to bed, too. Another thing they both seemed to enjoy and another thing Bree worried about if this arrangement was not going to be permanent. She had to make up her mind before she broke everyone's hearts.

As they cruised north in Will's Jeep, Bree gazed across at him, thinking during the whole ride about the issue of trust. They were headed to the big regional Pinewood Derby. Sam and another competing scout whose mom had to work while his dad was out of town were in the back seat arguing amiably over who had the best chance of winning. So there had been no personal conversation, but just the way Will kept looking at her, she knew he was thinking about the same thing.

As they drove into the city, Bree gave up studying Will and glanced out the window.

"I'm glad you're driving. I'd never have found this place," Bree commented as he navigated a warren of little side streets.

"I used to be stationed up here." He grinned at her and turned into the parking lot of a sprawling elementary school surrounded by pavement and chain link fencing. "I've actually been inside this building before. When I was a rookie, I got assigned to a couple of assemblies to talk about street smarts."

"I bet you were good at it." She could picture him charged up with enthusiasm and an auditorium full of grade school kids hanging on his every word.

"I'm a better lover." He wagged his eyebrows at her and made her blush.

He pulled the Jeep into an empty spot and turned to the boys in the back. "Ready to go show them what Pack 84 is made of?"

The boys tumbled out of the car and joined a stream of uniformed Cub Scouts funneling their way into a side door. As Will reached for Bree's hand, he smiled down at her with so much love in his eyes that it made her catch her breath. She still hadn't told him she loved him. She opened her mouth to speak, but just then a hand clapped down on Will's shoulder, and he turned away.

"When did you turn into a Boy Scout?" A man even taller than Will flicked the neatly rolled blue and gold tie that hung down the front of Will's smartly pressed khaki scout shirt.

"I've always been one. Made it all the way to Eagle Scout." Will laughed and turned to Bree. "This is Ross Coleman, the most irreverent trooper I know. Ross, Brianna Reagan." He hesitated as if he wanted to say more and added, "Her son is one of the racers today."

"We'll be cheering against each other then. Ross Jr. is determined to win, and I think he's got a pretty good chance."

The three of them walked into the building together and into the din of a hundred boys and twice as many adults. A man with a microphone was doing his best to get the crowd's attention, but people continued to talk over him.

Bree had a headache already. If she had her way, she'd head right back out the door and wait in the Jeep, but Sam would be very disappointed in her if she did. So, she did what most of the other parent-spectators were doing. She climbed up into the wooden bleachers and found a seat with a good view of the race tracks. She saved a space for Will if he had a chance to join her and concentrated on locating her son. When she spotted him finally, he was standing at Will's side. She relaxed and thought about where her life should go from here.

She pressed her forehead into the palms of her hands and closed her eyes. Doing her best to block out the noise and confusion around her, she thought about the days since she and Will had first made love and thought about the decision she needed to make.

For each of the thirteen days since she had woken up in Will's arms and heard his declaration of love, she had considered her answer. He'd told her to take her time to think about it, and he hadn't put any pressure on her to make up her mind.

He loved her. Probably more than she deserved. And they were good together. They could probably be even better if she committed herself to the relationship as irrevocably as Will already had. It had only been two weeks, but so far there had been no alarms, no nail-biting nights waiting for him to come home from God only knew what kind of day. In fact, he'd been home ahead of her most nights, and her kitchen smelled like dinner the moment she walked in the door.

Because of his crutches, Bree had been driving Sam to school and picking him up, and when they arrived home, Will greeted them at the door. She'd been shocked the first night, wondering how he'd gotten in. But it turned out Sam had "loaned" him his key. It was as if the two were ganging up on her, trying to convince her to say yes.

There was no maybe in Sam's mind. He took their altered situation in stride and made the most of it. Will, for all his confident, can-do attitude, seemed less sure of himself. She sensed it sometimes in the way he touched her. She saw it in his eyes as he hovered over her, staring into her eyes in the hushed, expectant moments before he made love to her. He hadn't said anything, but he acted as though he were walking a tightrope. She wasn't being fair to him, stringing things out like she had.

A fresh assault of shouting brought her out of her reverie. Scouts were jumping up and down as the first heats began. She spied Sam again. He was like a limpet, staying close to Will wherever the man went. He clutched his bright green racer in one hand while the other reached out now and then to balance himself against Will's side.

Everything Will had said he wanted to be for her son, he was already doing a good job of. With no reason in the world except unselfish love, Will was being the father, the man Sam so desperately needed to have in his life. Tears started in Bree's eyes as the realization of her decision coalesced in her heart. Everything Will had promised to be for her, was hers for the taking. She just had to put aside the fear that had isolated her for far too long and reach out.

Bree thought about the house Will had

taken her to see. A kitchen with space for a table big enough to feed a whole Cub Scout den. And four bedrooms. A man alone had no need for such a large place. A man with a growing family did. Will was not an adrenaline junkie looking for his next high. He was a man putting down roots and planning for his future. A future that included her, she realized now. She wondered if he had held off signing the papers because he wanted her name to be on them.

She thought about the Rapid Response Team he'd made the short list for. He hadn't discussed it with her, and she hadn't dared to ask. It sounded dangerous. But if it was something he believed in doing — if he was convinced it was a better way for him to make a difference, then she shouldn't try to dissuade him. Service to others was a part of who Will was. Part of the man she had fallen in love with.

Her gaze followed him as he moved about, talking to another leader for a moment, bending to congratulate Timmy, the boy who'd ridden up with them, on his third place finish. Chatting with one of the race officials with his hand resting on Sam's shoulder. The official handed Sam a bright red ribbon, and Will gave Sam a high five before squatting down and pulling him into a celebratory hug.

Sam hugged Will back as his crutches clattered to the floor. Timmy picked one of them up and Will the other. A moment later they were all scanning the bleachers. Looking for her, no doubt. She stood so they could see her and made her way down the steps to meet them halfway.

To meet her future halfway. There really wasn't a lot she needed to say. Just four words. *I love you,* and *Yes.*

Chapter 24

None of the boys won first place, but they all seemed pretty upbeat as they left the regional Pinewood Derby. Even Gareth wore his ribbon for participation with a grin of satisfaction. Ross Junior had won the derby just as his father had predicted, but Ross Coleman was generous in his congratulations to Timmy and Sam as they said goodbye in the parking lot before everyone piled into Will's Jeep.

As they got on the road, Bree debated how and when or where she would tell Will her decision. Not here in the Jeep because she felt sure such a momentous occasion should be sealed with a kiss. Maybe tonight. Maybe she would include Sam. Or maybe she would wait until he was asleep and they were alone. Her breathing quickened as she pictured Will's face when she told him.

They hadn't been on the road ten minutes before Timmy spoke up from the back seat.

"I have to pee."

Bree rolled her eyes at Will. He shrugged as if he expected as much.

"Can you wait until we find a gas station?" Will asked, glancing at the boy in the rearview mirror.

Timmy nodded.

A few miles later a GoGas sign loomed up on the left. Will pulled in and parked. He got out to accompany Timmy inside.

"You go too, Sam," Bree told her son. "Then we won't have to stop again."

Will ducked his head back inside to ask, "We'll get some snacks and drinks for the trip home. You want anything?" Bree shook her head, and Will hurried to follow the boys inside. Even with his crutches, Sam got around pretty fast.

With the visit to the men's room taken care of, they each chose a drink from the cooler. Will grabbed two bottles of water, just in case Bree changed her mind.

"Only one thing," Will told Timmy, who already had a sleeve of mini donuts and a bag of chips and was reaching for a package of cupcakes.

Sam balanced on his crutches and chose a bag of Doritos that he handed to Will to carry. They made their way to the cash register.

Two hooded men crowded close against the counter in front of the clerk. Will reacted instinctively. He stopped walking and held out an arm to halt the boys beside him as well. His heart raced, but he kept his breathing even and studied the two men closely.

If this was a holdup, neither of the guys wearing hoodies appeared to be armed, but just in case, Will didn't want Sam or Timmy anywhere near what was going down. If the questionable hoodie-wearing guys hadn't been between Will and the door, he'd have left their snacks behind and ushered the boys outside. Then he'd have come back to check things out. As it was, he could only urge the boys back out of sight behind a display of souvenirs.

The boys scrambled into the nook Will pointed to. Their eyes went wide with surprise. Will held a finger to his lips to silence them before either boy could ask him what was going on.

The clerk's hand shot up holding a gun. Will moved instinctively again, but before he could get to them, one of the would-be robbers grabbed the gun out of the clerk's hand. It went off, and the clerk disappeared behind the counter. Will yanked his phone from his pocket and dialed 911. That's when the robbers turned and saw him.

Neither wore masks. Not good. If they'd managed to either wound or kill the clerk, they'd be desperate to get away without being caught. Even though they had no way of knowing Will was a trooper, he could still identify them.

Will dropped his unanswered phone in his pocket and raised his hands.

"On the floor!" the robber shouted. He waved his gun in Will's direction.

Will sank to his knees, praying Sam and Timmy would stay out of sight. The kid with the gun couldn't be more than eighteen, and his hand shook violently. No guessing what he'd do if he got spooked.

Will assessed his chances of disarming the kid. Or getting to the second perp, who stood about five feet away to one side. Not good if the jumpy kid with the gun reacted without thinking. The second robber looked older. Maybe early twenties. Less frightened-looking. He'd probably done this before.

"Keep your eyes on this guy while I check the aisles," the older robber ordered. Will kept his eyes averted while still checking the guy out. His heart sank when he saw the telltale shape of a second handgun in the guy's pocket. He pushed his hand in on top of the gun, and his fingers closed around the grip, but he didn't remove it from the pocket. He'd probably shoot right through the fabric if he felt he had to shoot at all.

For the first few minutes, Will's heart had raced, and he'd just reacted. Now his training kicked in. He was in control and processing his options logically. Eventually the second guy was going see the boys. Will tried to inch his way in their direction.

"Don't move!" the teenager yelled.

Will froze. Before he could come up with an alternative plan, the older robber appeared at the end of the aisle.

"Get out there with your leader," he ordered as he strode toward the now terrified boys.

Timmy scrambled to Will's side. His eyes were enormous and frightened. Sam was slowed down by his crutches. He looked behind him, then at Will with fear in his eyes.

"Move it," the man in the aisle ground out in an angry voice. His gun was no longer in his pocket. He aimed at Sam's head.

Will lunged for Sam, shielding him with his own body as they crashed into the souvenir display. Something slammed into

Will's back just below his right shoulder blade, and he fell. He'd been shot. Not by the in-control youth smirking down at him as he swaggered closer, but by the nervous teenager.

"That'll teach you to play hero, Boy Scout."

Will gritted his teeth against the pain and forced himself to sit up. "Leave them alone."

"Why should I?" the youth sneered.

"They're just kids." Will kept his voice calm.

"Couple of little Cub Scout turds," the youth spat.

"You're going to be sorry," Sam spoke up. "He's a —"

Will jerked Sam's crutch out from under his arm. Sam fell into Will's lap, sending a lightning bolt of pain through his shoulder.

Sam looked at Will in shock, his mouth round with surprise. "Wha—"

"He's an overgrown Boy Scout who's too dumb to do what he's told," the gun-wielding robber snarled. "Now stay put, and don't do anything else stupid." The robber strode across to the counter and ducked behind it. "Get up, you lying sack of shit."

A moment later the clerk who had not been hit got to his feet and started to run. The robber smashed the butt of his gun down over the clerk's head.

"Put that gun in your pocket before you do something even stupider with it." The older of the two was obviously the ringleader. He hit something on the cash register, and the drawer opened. He began shoveling bills into his pockets.

If they planned to kill us, they'd have done it by now. The ringleader would have at least shot the clerk when he made an attempt to flee. Instead, he just put his lights out for a while. I got shot because the kid overreacted. Will began sorting through a series of disjointed thoughts, trying to put together a plan. Then the sirens began. He'd forgotten his phone with the 911 call placed before he'd jammed it out of sight into his pocket.

A moment later blue lights began flashing across the interior of the convenience store.

"Shit!" The older robber stopped grabbing money and shoved the drawer closed.

"Maybe we can get out the back?" the kid suggested hopefully.

"Are you a complete idiot? They'll have the back covered too."

Two uniforms came in the front door, guns drawn, sweeping the area with both guns and eyes. Immediately the older of the two robbers shoved a gun against Sam's ear.

"Back off, or I shoot the kid."

"Let the kid go. We can talk," one of the cops said in a level voice.

"Get out!" the robber screamed and shoved the gun against Sam's ear harder. Sam cried out as tears began rolling down his cheeks.

The cops backed carefully out of the store. Probably calling in the hostage negotiator, Will thought. Like that would help. By the time the guy got here, it would be all over, and someone would probably be dead.

Will weighed the chances of grabbing the muzzle of the gun and deflecting the shot before the kid could put a bullet into Sam's brain. Zero to none. Next best thing . . .

He jerked Sam off his lap, away from the gun, and leaned forward to shield him with his body. He tensed with every expectation of the slicing pain of another hit. The hit didn't come, but the pain did as the older man jerked Will's arms behind his body. A moment later zip ties tightened around Will's wrists.

Will had never felt so helpless in his life. All his training, and here he was, trussed up and useless. For a while, at least, he could ignore the pain and the fact that he'd been shot. But getting out of the zip ties applied behind his back was almost impossible.

If anything happened to Sam, Bree would

never forgive him. If he lived through it, he'd never forgive himself. He managed to get himself upright again and eased back to lean against the souvenir stand. Timmy huddled on the floor hidden from the direct view of the robbers, but Sam was right out there.

"Get behind me," Will whispered to Sam. Sam scooted himself at least partially out of sight, dragging the blue cast decorated with signatures. "Behind me," Will whispered again. Sam shifted another few inches.

"What are you planning to do now?" Will asked the robber.

"I'm thinking. You shut up." He pointed to his accomplice. "Grab a few of those cans of shaving cream and spray the windows, so they can't see in."

The teenager did as he was told, and a few minutes later the windows were white and somewhat opaque. Even if they'd deployed snipers, the sharpshooters could no longer see clearly. Will and the boys and the unconscious clerk were on their own.

"Get some more and make it thicker." Again the teen began methodically adding to the foamy barrier, the hiss of the shaving cans sealing out the daylight and help.

"Will?" Sam whispered in Will's ear. "You're bleeding."

Will nodded. "I'll be okay."

"But you're bleeding a lot."

If only Will had applied for that hostage negotiating course the state offered. He might have a clue what to say next. Instead, he'd been focused on the Rapid Response Team. A lot of good that would have done him. Those guys were probably already outside, but with a gun held to a kid's head, they were as helpless as he was.

"Will?" Sam poked his arm.

Without turning his head, Will whispered back. "What?"

"Will this help?" Sam glanced down at his side. Will's gaze followed. Sam was holding the little jackknife Will had given him and taught him how to use. It was small and only as sharp as Will had dared to make it, but it might work.

"Can you reach the ties around my wrists?" Will kept his voice almost inaudible.

Sam started to turn.

"No. Don't move any more than you have to. Don't attract their attention."

Sam's hand groped along the small of Will's back until he found the bound wrists. "But I might cut you if I can't look."

"I'll take my chances. Just feel for the tie, then put the blade against it and saw carefully."

The nylon tie tugged, but didn't give. Sam applied more pressure and tried again. Still nothing.

"Go back and forth like a saw," Will hissed.

Sam leaned into Will's side and began to work at it again.

The man with the gun glanced over but apparently decided Sam was huddled against Will's side in fear. He turned away, and Sam began sawing again.

Suddenly the zip tie parted. The tip of Sam's knife did nick Will's wrist, but compared to the pain in his back it was nothing. At least he was no longer cuffed. But there were still two perps, and both had guns. He wasn't superman. There was no way he could disarm them both before someone got shot.

"Why don't you let the boys go? You'll still have me and the clerk as hostages." Will hoped his phone was still connected to the dispatcher. If it was, the police outside would know shortly that there were only two scouts and two adults inside the store. Bree would already have told them about Sam, Will, and Timmy, but she had no way of knowing if there was anyone else inside.

"I'm not leaving," Sam declared bravely.

"I will," Timmy piped up. He was terrified, and Will didn't blame him.

"Shut up. All of you." The ringleader turned his gun in Will's direction.

The teenager finished spraying the last of the cans on the windows and came to stand beside the older guy. "Check the clerk and put these on him."

The ringleader studied Will. Hopefully, he was contemplating the suggestion to let the boys go. He had the gun pointed unwaveringly at Will, apparently having decided he was the main risk at this point. Even wounded. "And what good does that do me?" he finally asked.

"They're just kids. You're already in enough trouble. Hurting or even threatening kids makes cops do crazy things. Things they might not do for adults."

"And you'd know that because . . . ?"

Almost said too much. No reason to let them know they have a trooper at their mercy unless I have to. Will shrugged. "That's how it always works on TV."

"Bah!" the ringleader scoffed. "It never goes down the way you see it on TV. No! I think I'll keep the kids. They make better bargaining chips."

Okay, time to offer it up. "Not better than a state trooper."

The ringleader's brows shot up, and his

eyes widened. "You saying you're a trooper?
Will nodded and gave the guy his full name and badge number. "In another minute or so there'll be a phone call, and it'll be someone outside wanting to talk to you. To negotiate with you. Ask them to verify that I am who I say I am."

Bree could have verified it, but the last thing he wanted to do was drag her into this. The only reason his suit had gone nowhere until now was her aversion to men who lived dangerous lives. She wouldn't thank him for getting her involved. He'd be lucky if she ever spoke to him again after today.

Almost as if his statement had conjured it up, the store phone began to ring, cutting loudly into the hushed standoff.

The robber grabbed the phone off its cradle. "What do you want?" He listened, his eyes flat and hard. "Yeah, well I've got a guy in here who says he's a state trooper." The silence lengthened into a minute. Then several minutes.

Will turned to check on the teenager, and his head spun. *Must be losing more blood than I thought.* He blinked and brought the world back into focus. If he could get Sam to put pressure on the wound, maybe he could slow down the bleeding.

"Psst. Sam. Take off your kerchief."

Sam glanced at him with a frown but removed his scouting kerchief. He started to hold it out, then remembered Will's hands were supposed to be tied behind him. "What should I do with it?" he whispered.

"Fold it up into a square. Then I need you to press it against the place where you see the blood."

Sam reached behind Will again and pressed the folded kerchief against Will's back.

"You have to press harder than that."

"Won't it hurt?"

"Don't worry about hurting me. Just press as hard as you can."

The heel of Sam's hand dug in. Will winced and bit his lips.

The ringleader slammed the phone down. "Okay. This is what we're going to do." He waved his gun at Will and the boys, then settled back to point directly at Will's forehead. "The boys can go. You get to stay. And don't try any heroics."

Timmy scrambled to his feet and bolted for the door.

Sam didn't move. His hand still held the kerchief in place. "I'm not leaving."

"Yes, you are," Will said firmly.

Sam shook his head.

"Sam. Your mom needs you. You have to go."

"But you need me, too."

"Not as much as your mom. Now go."

Sam looked like he was about to start crying again.

"Put the kerchief inside my T-shirt. Then go. And remember. Whatever happens, I love you. You've been really brave, and I'm proud of you."

"Enough of the melodrama. If the kid's going, he'd better go before I change my mind."

Sam's hands trembled as he wriggled the kerchief down inside Will's T-shirt. He was crying when he finished. He hugged Will. "I love you, too."

"Come'on kid." The robber kept his gun trained on Will and dragged Sam to his feet. He shoved him toward the door, but Sam slipped and fell.

"He needs his crutches," Will explained. Praying the guy wouldn't shoot first and ask questions later, Will hooked one toe under Sam's crutches and scooted them across the floor.

Sam struggled to his feet and put the crutches under his arms.

"Sam?" Will called out.

Sam turned to look back.

"Tell your mom I love her too."

Sam nodded and hobbled toward the door. The crutches made squeaking sounds as he went, his cast tapping with every step. When the door finally closed behind Sam, Will let out the breath he'd been holding. At least Sam was safe. And Bree would not have a reason to hate him for the rest of her life.

Chapter 25

Will opened his eyes, blinked, and tried to focus. Everything blurred. His head spun as if he was on something. He shut his eyes, squeezed them tight, and opened them again. Slowly the room came into focus.

Muted yellow light seeped in from somewhere, but the room itself was dark. The world outside the room was dark as well.

I'm in a hospital.

He glanced over his shoulder at the beeping monitor. Bags of saline and antibiotics trickled into a drip chamber and down the tube and into his arm.

He tried to move, and pain sliced through him with shocking intensity. He gritted his teeth against the throbbing ache. *My God, that hurt. Of all the crazy things I've done in my life, nothing ever hurt this much.*

Will shut his eyes, willing oblivion to claim him again. His head swam, and the blackness came to get him.

A pool of blond hair spread in glorious disarray over the wrinkled folds of the white sheet that covered him. Will reached down to touch it. So familiar. He'd run his fingers through these silky strands. They'd tickled his bare chest, too. A smile tugged at the corners of his mouth at the memory.

"Bree?" he whispered, his voice a hoarse croak. When she didn't stir, he settled his hand atop her sleeping head and felt peace steal over him.

Sunlight streamed in the window. Will blinked against the glare. A tall, dark shadow was silhouetted against the brilliance. It moved and came toward the bed.

"You're awake." Ross Coleman put his hand on the bedrail and bent down to speak. "We were beginning to worry about you."

I've been shot. Crap! It suddenly came back to him. *The convenience store hold-up. The kid with the gun. Sam. I've never been so scared in my life. Not even when guns were pointed directly at me.*

Will shut his eyes again. The glare was too much. He wanted to ask how it had it ended but couldn't summon the energy. *I must have lost a lot more blood than I thought.*

What came after I conned those jackass kids with the guns into letting Sam and Timmy go? Must have been some kind of skirmish when the Raleigh police rushed the place. Should remember that at least.

Voices murmured somewhere on the other side of the room, too faint to hear. Someone came to stand beside him. He needed to open his eyes and talk to them. The murmurs ceased. Quite settled in again. If only it didn't hurt so much to move, he might enjoy the floating nothingness. He lifted his lids just enough to check the place where Bree's head had rested the first time he woke. Or was that the second time? He couldn't remember. He wanted her back.

Will shifted his shoulders against the rack of souvenirs, careful to keep his hands behind him where they couldn't see that Sam had cut him free of the zip ties. He gritted his teeth against the pain, closed his eyes for a moment, and opened them again. The kid was coming toward him. Where was the older robber? He was right there on the far side of the counter a minute ago.

The kid turned his back toward Will and called out to his accomplice. The other man's voice came from somewhere behind the counter. Must be looking for a safe. Or maybe he's found it, and he's trying to get in. This is probably the only chance I'm going to get.

Will reached up and grabbed the tail of the oversized hoodie. One swift, unexpected yank, and the kid fell over backward and smacked his head on the cement and tile floor. Will scrambled for the gun, came up on one knee, and pointed it toward the place the other man's voice had come from. Hoodie kid sprawled on his back, not moving. Will concentrated on the man behind the counter.

"Toss the gun out here and come out with your hands on your head, and I might not shoot you." Pain rocketed through Will with almost blinding force. For a moment his head spun so wildly he probably couldn't have hit a dumpster from three feet away, but he wasn't going to let that fact be known if he could help it. If he stayed where he was, half-sitting, half-kneeling, his head didn't spin quite so much.

Will's gun hand trembled. He blinked away encroaching darkness. "The gun," he commanded, forcing himself to ignore the pain and dizziness. "And I want to see you. Right now. Hands on your head."

Slowly the man straightened and came into sight. But his gun was aimed straight at Will, and it wasn't wavering. Will pulled the trigger.

Noise filled his head. Confusion and commotion. Shouting. Running feet.

Uniformed police with their guns aimed at him.

"I'm a trooper," he shouted as he tossed down the gun and raised his hands. "I'm a trooper."

"Will. Wake up. It's okay."

Will dragged his eyes open. "I'm a trooper."

"I know. You were having a nightmare." Bree hovered above him with a worried look on her face and exhaustion in her eyes. Her hair fell in a shiny veil about her face. He reached up to touch it.

"You came back."

"Of course I came back." She bent and kissed him lightly on the lips. "Were you dreaming about the robbery?"

"I don't know." There had been a lot of pain. A lot of shouting. Nothing he could latch onto now. "Maybe."

She pulled up a chair and sank down beside the bed.

"I'm . . . sorry," he told her.

She leaned in and brushed her fingers across his jaw. "What on earth are you sorry about?"

He reached for her hand. "I . . . promised not to get . . . shot."

"You saved my son."

His heart contracted. It was about Sam. Not him. "Line . . . of . . . duty," he muttered. He closed his eyes but kept hold of her hand. Whatever they had him on was dragging him down again. "Bree . . ."

"You weren't on duty," Bree whispered. Will had dozed off again. There was so much she had to tell him. If only he'd stay awake long enough.

Will's friend Ross Coleman had told her Will woke briefly while she was downstairs grabbing a bite to eat. A detective from the Raleigh Police Department had been there to take Will's statement. The officer had filled Will in on the details that were still foggy in his head. The fact that when gunshots were heard, the police stormed in to find one robber out cold and the other clutching his bloody right arm where Will's bullet had ripped through the flesh.

According to Ross Coleman, Will hadn't taken nearly as much credit for his own bravery as he'd given Sam for making it possible. Sam, of course, had told Bree all about how he'd cut the ties off Will's wrists and helped to stop the bleeding. They made a good team.

She'd finally accepted the fact that Will Cameron was meant to be in her life and

Sam's, only to have the unthinkable happen. At a time and in a place where it could have happened to anyone. Will had just been unlucky.

Now all she could think of was that line in the old movie *When Harry Met Sally,* at the very end when Harry told Sally that once he realized what he wanted in life, he wanted that life to begin right away. He'd run across an entire city to tell her as soon as possible.

But Bree hadn't even walked across a crowded room. She'd stayed in those bleachers, knowing that whatever Will was, whatever he did for a living, however hard or dangerously he played, she was ready to take the risk. She loved him, and she wanted their life together to begin that very moment. But rather than tell him the first chance she got, she'd put it off, waiting for some perfect moment.

A moment she had come so close to never having at all.

She released the bedrail and lowered it. Then, pulling the chair as close to the bed as possible, she settled in to wait. He looked so peaceful and defenseless as he slept. She smoothed his mussed hair and ran her fingers over the blond scruff that covered his cheeks. This was a whole new view of Will.

She leaned in closer, kissed his sleeping lips, then laid her head next to his on the pillow.

With the pain meds reduced and the healing begun, Will felt a lot better. A lot more like his old self. He was still napping too much, but he'd been up, used the bathroom on his own with a nurse hovering at the door, and tried to talk his doctor into allowing a shower. He'd had to settle for a sponge bath and a shave. But the improvement had been dramatic. He settled back against the nest of pillows to rest until Bree returned.

He drifted a bit, letting his mind wander through memories of making love with her. Showing off the new house he wanted to share with her. Teasing her about the dumb reality show she liked to watch on TV. And the delight on her face when she walked into her apartment that first night he'd fixed supper for her. What had grown between them wasn't just about Sam, and he'd known it once the drugs had been reduced, and he could think straight again.

Of course Bree would very naturally feel gratitude that he'd managed to get her son out of a dangerous situation without getting him hurt, but that didn't explain her sleeping at his bedside through the night. There had been tears in her eyes that first time he'd spoken to her aloud. He might have been loopy on drugs, but he hadn't missed the tears or the way she'd touched his face.

A jumble of voices interrupted his rambling thoughts. Or maybe he'd nodded off again. He opened his eyes to find his room filled with people. Bree sat on the edge of his bed, holding his hand. Her hair was pinned up with flowers in it, and she was wearing a very pretty dress, one he hadn't seen before. Pale yellow and silky. Very flattering. He reached out to touch it. "Hey, Bree," he greeted her softly.

"Hey, yourself." She bent to kiss him and slid to her feet beside the bed.

He took in the rest of the room.

Sam sat with his blue cast propped up on a stool playing a game on someone's smart phone. Ben leaned against the windowsill with his long legs crossed at the ankles. And there was a priest. A priest? What was that about? And Zoe? Will turned back to Bree in confusion.

"What's going on?"

"A wedding is going on. If you'll still have me."

Epilogue

Will leaned back against the comfortably upholstered chaise that occupied a good portion of the little balcony where he and Bree had first made love. He was waiting for her to get home from a late evening at work and thinking about life. His incredibly satisfying life.

This house that he'd stumbled on only half-built one day while he was driving around with nothing much on his mind had turned out even nicer than he'd imagined. But it was Bree and Sam becoming part of his life that had turned it into a home.

In the aftermath of the shooting, his supervisor had sent him for training in negotiation, and patience, a virtue he'd not had much of before, could be learned. And that had opened up a whole new career path. Just recently promoted, he was also discovering that he loved teaching, and a portion of his time was now spent at the academy passing on some of his hard-won knowledge in the field of law enforcement.

Kett's Hotel had annexed a stunning seaside retreat house, and Bree had been tagged to manage it. The Ketts loved her and so did the people who worked for her, but they didn't love her nearly as much as he did. The day she'd come to his hospital room looking like a ray of sunshine with all the necessary arrangements made so they could be married right there and then, he'd thought he couldn't love her more. And he couldn't have been more wrong.

"Hey, Troop. Miss me?" Bree slipped through to door and bent to kiss his upturned face before climbing into his lap.

"Always. Have you eaten?"

She nodded.

Will settled her against his chest and wrapped his arms about her. "I love you to the moon and back." He nuzzled her neck. He'd just finished reading a book by that title to their two-year-old daughter, and the words seemed just right to tell Bree what he was feeling at this particular moment.

A nearly full moon had risen about an hour earlier, and a river of glistening silver stretched across the ocean toward the little deck off their comfortable bedroom. His heart was even fuller than the moon. Sam was curled up in his favorite spot on the window seat in his room playing a game on his tablet. Anna slept soundly in her crib in her very pink bedroom with her butt in the air and her thumb in her mouth. And his wife was carrying their second child. Third, he corrected. Sam was his son now.

Will molded his hand around the swollen curve of Bree's belly. She covered his hand with hers, and a moment later their new son kicked.

"Maybe even to the sun and back," he murmured.

ACKNOWLEDGEMENTS

From my high school English teacher to my newest critique partner and everyone in between, I owe a huge debt for helping me to become the writer I am today.

There aren't words big enough to properly thank my editor Deborah Smith whose faith in me made this series possible. Thanks also to Bell Bridge Books for designing a wonderful cover for this book, and all the BBB staff who touched this book along the way and made it better. My gratitude also to Danielle Childers for her cheerful, unstinting help with getting the Tide's Way books noticed.

Thank you Lilly Gayle, my authority on anything North Carolina, from diction and idiom to what's on the table or growing in the garden. My critique partners, Nancy Quatrano who helped me keep my conflict true and my characters challenged and cheered me when I got it right. And Betty Johnston who read my work with her heart.

And as always, all my love to my biggest cheerleaders: Alex, Lori, Rebecca, Bobbi, and Noel.

ONE OF WILL CAMERON'S FAVORITE RECIPES — FROM HIS MOM'S KITCHEN

BLUEBERRY & WHITE CHOCOLATE SCONES FROM SANDY CAMERON'S KITCHEN

2 cups flour
4 Tbsp. butter
1 tsp salt
2 eggs
1/3 cup sugar
1/2 cup cream or milk
4 tsp baking powder
1 cup frozen blueberries (or raspberries)
1/2 cup white chocolate chips

Preheat oven to 350 degrees

Stir all dry ingredients together, cut in butter with a fork, then add eggs, cream or milk and mix well.

Fold in berries and chocolate bits.

Spoon onto baking sheet lined with foil and

sprayed with Pam. Sprinkle tops with a little white sugar if desired. Bake for 20 minutes until bottoms of scones are lightly browned and top springs back when pressed with finger. Best while still warm from oven but still yummy cool.

ABOUT THE AUTHOR

I have been a member of Romance Writers of America since 1995 and of the Ancient City chapter in St. Augustine, Florida, for the last six years, where I have served as secretary, conference chair and treasurer. I am also a member of Florida Writers Association and the Women's Fiction Writers Association. My publishing credits to date include several non-fiction essays about life as a Peace Corps Volunteer, one mainstream political intrigue, *Whatever It Takes,* and the Tide's Way series.

The employees of Thorndike Press hope you have enjoyed this Large Print book. All our Thorndike, Wheeler, and Kennebec Large Print titles are designed for easy reading, and all our books are made to last. Other Thorndike Press Large Print books are available at your library, through selected bookstores, or directly from us.

For information about titles, please call:

(800) 223-1244

or visit our Web site at:

http://gale.cengage.com/thorndike

To share your comments, please write:

Publisher
Thorndike Press
10 Water St., Suite 310
Waterville, ME 04901